SWING

D1012831

BOOKS BY
PHILIP BEARD

Dear Zoe

Lost in the Garden

Swing

Beard, Philip, 1963-
Swing : a novel /
2015.
33305234534174
sa   08/26/16

SWING

a novel

PHILIP BEARD

A VAN BUREN BOOK

PHILIP BEARD is the author of two previous novels, *Lost in the Garden* and *Dear Zoe,* which was a *Borders Original Voices* selection, a *Book Sense* pick, and was named by the American Library Association's *Booklist* as one of its "Ten Best First Novels of the Year." It is currently being developed as a feature film. He lives in Pittsburgh with his wife, Traci, and their three daughters.

Email him at philipbeard21@gmail.com
Visit his website: http://www.philipbeard.net/
Find him on Facebook: http://www.facebook.com/philip.beard.129
Follow him on Twitter @philipbeard17
Like and *Follow Swing* on Facebook: http://www.facebook.com/Swingnovel

PUBLISHER'S NOTE: This is a work of fiction. Other than the Pittsburgh Pirate players and 1971 World Series game situations, the characters, places and incidents are either the product of the author's imagination or are used fictitiously, and any resemblance to actual persons, living or dead, business establishments, events, or locales is entirely coincidental.

The scanning, uploading, and distribution of this book via the Internet or via any other means without the permission of the publisher is illegal and punishable by law. Please purchase only authorized electronic editions, and do not participate in or encourage electronic piracy of copyrighted materials. Your support of the author's rights is appreciated.

First Van Buren Books Edition, March 2015
Copyright © 2015 by Philip Beard
All rights reserved under International and Pan American Copyright Conventions. Published in the United States by Van Buren Books
CIP data is available
ISBN 978-0-9862474-1-5

Book design by Amy C. King

For David Blake

*And, as always, for Traci, who knew, long before I did,
that this was the next book to be written.*

Contents

1

He was a man who liked to announce things, so I was saddened but not at all surprised to receive this morning in my department mailbox what could only be described as a formal invitation to his memorial service. It was mailed out, in accordance with his will, by the V.F.W. Local 70 of Riverside, PA, complete with an RSVP card and instructions to bring an appetizer, a dessert or a six-pack (bottles only). We are nearly five hundred miles away from the planned festivities—with our two children, two untenured positions, one old dog and one dying fish—and I expect that all of those things will conspire to keep us at home. But Maggie and I would both have legitimate reasons for wanting to attend: mine would be love; hers, a morbid curiosity to see the size of the casket of the man I have been immortalizing, re-inventing and, to some extent, eulogizing for the full fifteen years of our marriage. Lately, Maggie has found reasons to doubt me on a number of fronts, and I think she has begun to believe that he is a figment of my all-too-active imagination. I suppose that makes it all the more ironic that the same piece of folded, off-white cardstock that tells me he is gone will also convince my wife of his existence.

I met him during a part of my childhood that is hard to revisit, so it has been both easy and convenient to see him mostly through my children's eyes. Allie has outgrown the stories, but Walt knows *The Swinger* the way she once did—as a kind of super-hero, invented to put them both to sleep with thoughts of something right and true, someone just impossible enough that they wanted him to be real. Even I sometimes have difficulty distinguishing the character I have created from the man I knew. But knowing now that he is gone, I see him very clearly. Or, at least, as clearly as we ever see our boyhood heroes.

*

It is early October of 1971 and I am eleven years old, standing at a bus stop at the corner of Fort Duquesne Boulevard and Sixth Street in downtown Pittsburgh. I am there alone on a school day, without permission, which adds a sharpness to everything around me: the sidewalk sparkling blood-orange in the low sun; the light breeze cooling where it had warmed only an hour earlier; the bridges across the Allegheny River at Sixth, Seventh and Ninth streets superimposed over one another in a maze of yellow iron. The Pirates, my Pirates, have just beaten the San Francisco Giants to advance to the World Series, and my father has just left us—two oppositely charged facts that make such a muddle of my thoughts that I don't know whether to continue grinding the souvenir ball into the worn, oily palm of my glove, or throw them both into the river. My father left on a Saturday, carrying a single suitcase. On his way out, he put the Pirate tickets on the kitchen table and I sat on the window seat holding them, watching him walk to his car. My little sister Ruthie wrapped herself around his leg in the driveway and screamed. My older sister Sam pounded on the hood of his car, both hands clasped into one big fist, trying to make a dent. My mother stood unmoving in the doorway, resisting a visible urge to comfort her daughters in favor of letting my father's departure become as ugly as possible for him.

Thinking of my mother in that same doorway again, expecting me to get off the school activities bus, is the first time all afternoon that I have given any thought to how I am going to explain my absence. I had hung on the third base railing for more than an hour after the final out to get my souvenir, so the crowd from the game is mostly gone. The few people approaching the bus stop are heading home from work or shopping: a slender, young black woman in a tailored white pantsuit holding her child's hand; two businessmen carrying briefcases, laughing and talking about the upcoming Series with the heavily favored Baltimore Orioles; a fidgety, greasy-haired white man in an ill-fitting shirt and short, wide tie. All of them have come up Sixth Street from town, and that is the direction I am looking. It isn't until I hear the sound of a bus approaching, with the whining downward shift of its gears, that I notice that someone has appeared next to me.

When I say "appeared," I mean that quite literally. And I am momentarily bewildered by the fact that he doesn't look as if he has *finished* appearing. Instead, the man next to me seems to have grown out of the sidewalk, with only his torso having emerged so far. He is hip-deep in the concrete and looks as though he has been there forever, waiting for a young King Arthur, me perhaps, to pull him free. He is a man; there is no doubting that, even though I am looking down at him. His hair is black and gray and mussed, wiry as a pot-scrubber, his nose wide and crooked, and there is a three- or four-day growth of salt and pepper beard on his face. Still, it isn't until the bus comes to a stop in front of us and opens its doors that I understand what I am seeing—staring at, more precisely, in violation of every childhood admonition from my parents to do otherwise. The adults around me do no better, though. They all take an involuntary step backward, the young black woman pulling her child, and I am left standing alone with him.

"Thank you kindly," the man says, as if everyone behind us has, in fact, remembered their manners. Then he winks at me. "You here all by yourself?"

"Yessir," I reply, thinking I must be under some kind of spell to talk to a stranger *and* tell him I'm alone, a double-play of cardinal rules violations in the Graham household.

"You comin from the game?" He nods at my glove still clutching the ball.

"Yessir."

"Lucky kid. What's your name?"

"Henry."

"Good baseball name. Like Hammerin Hank Aaron." He cocks his head toward the bus. "Mind if I go first?"

"Nosir."

"Thanks."

He has no legs, barely even a hint of a thigh. Strapped over broad, powerful shoulders, he wears leather suspenders attached to a thick leather harness that protects the base of his perfectly flat torso. Even concealed inside a flannel shirt it is clear that his arms are massive, and he wears heavy work gloves on huge hands which he now places on the sidewalk in front of him. He presses, his shoulders shrugging downward, and in one smooth motion lifts his torso, swings it forward as if on a set of parallel bars, and sets it down again gently on the sidewalk. He does this two or three more times, all of us watching unabashedly, until he reaches the base of the bus steps. I feel the group around me tense, sure that the man has gone as far as he can go on his own, but equally unsure of how we are to help. He stops and looks up at the driver, who appears neither concerned nor surprised.

"Hey Russ," the half-man says.

"How you been, John?"

"Fine thanks. Hey, what did the bus driver say to the legless man at the bus stop?"

"I don't know. What?"

"*Hey there. How you gettin on?*"

The driver shakes his head. "Come on now. I got other customers."

"I'm comin," he says. Then he places his hands firmly on the bottom step and lifts himself up as easily as I might have lifted myself out of a swimming pool. He takes the second step, then the third, then turns and swings himself down the aisle, out of sight.

"Come on folks," the bus driver beckons, because none of us has moved, and I am the first to break the dazed tableau and follow John Kostka, *The Swinger*, up and into the bus for home.

HENRY

Professor Henry Graham is a good man, and, in a strange way, he has his own absent father to thank. By the time he was eleven, Henry had made a practice—when faced with an important choice—of considering what his father might do, and then doing the exact opposite. It wasn't that good decisions didn't come naturally to him. The exercise was more for his own benefit—a way of assuring himself that he was nothing like his father. Objectively, then, his wife Maggie has no basis for her recent misgivings, but only a vague sense that her husband has become too comfortable with his basic goodness in a way that compromises his attentiveness to anything that might test it.

The decision seven years ago to leave his law practice in D.C. to come here and teach had required no such deliberation. He'd been a reluctant big-firm lawyer from the beginning—having gotten the job based solely on the strength of his academic record and not on any real aptitude for that kind of practice—and D.C. had none of the hold on him that Pittsburgh had as a young boy. So when the hours he'd been stealing to write resulted not only in a mildly successful novel, but in teaching offers for both himself (English and Writing) and Maggie (Drawing and Painting), there was a For Sale sign in their tiny front yard the next day.

Henry does have one secret, however: he is a writer who isn't writing—not a word in the two years since Maggie's surgery—and his constant awareness of this fact, especially when he is here, walking the halls of the English Department, lends a furtiveness to his movements that would be more noticeable were he not such a gangly, awkward type anyway. Now, coming out of the faculty mailroom, Henry tucks the invitation he has just received into his jacket and, still distracted by the news it has brought, runs directly into Atlee Sproul. The only thing that keeps the two from knocking foreheads is Atlee's barrel-chest, which acts like an airbag between them.

"Whoa there."

"Sorry."

Atlee takes both of Henry's shoulders into his large hands. He has a pelt of white hair combed back so precisely that it seems to pull his unruly gray eyebrows up with it.

"Let me guess: your goddess of a wife is home and naked and waiting for a reprise of today's lecture."

"Half right. She's home, but likely in her studio and covered in charcoal."

"Stop. I'm jealous enough as it is."

Atlee is an alcoholic, a self-described (though mostly unconfirmed) womanizer and, judging by his large and loyal student following, the finest teacher in the department by a wide margin. He is also Henry's best friend. Atlee is tall and broad and Heathcliff-British, and Maggie has proclaimed him to be the only man she would be tempted to leave Henry for: "*Assuming I wasn't already twenty years too old for him.*"

Atlee squints at Henry. "You all right?"

"Yeah. Fine."

"Don't let what I said yesterday bother you. They're a bunch of gaping arse-holes, but they usually get these things right in the end.

Even if it's only because they can't agree long enough to get them wrong."

Henry's fellow faculty members (the ones who hold his chances for tenure in their reluctant hands) don't know that he hasn't been writing. One of the advantages of being a novelist is that long periods between publications don't raise suspicion. Still, some of his colleagues rate him "soft" because of his stubborn avoidance of references in class to what is "good" or "bad." His sole function, Henry maintains, is to help his students to frame their stories in ways that are not merely cleansing, but resonant. It's the difference, he tells them, between catharsis and art; the difference between simply yelling at your mother and actually succeeding in making her see you in a different way. He also openly loves teaching, another fact that makes him unpopular with some of the more jaded members of his department.

Henry waves off Atlee's pep talk. "No, it's not that. I just got word that an old friend passed away."

"Sorry. Anyone I know?"

"No. I haven't seen him in close to thirty years myself."

"So it's got nothing to do with either your review or with that lovely young thing waiting by your car?"

"Hm?"

"Because if there is to be more than one predatory academic in our relationship, I'm afraid I'll have to break it off."

"What are you talking about?"

"Didn't get a good look. She was turned round, pretending not to be hovering. Spectacular posterior, though."

"She's probably waiting for you."

"Not next to that car, she isn't." Atlee has been after Henry for years to get rid of his decomposing Honda Civic. Atlee drives an old but pristine Mercedes that Henry would swear he details every morning before pulling it out of the garage. "I'd push a woman home in a wheelbarrow before I'd put her in that car."

"It gets me where I need to go."

"But does it get you where you *want* to go?"

"We've established that I don't want to go to the same places you go."

"No, we've established that you don't want to go with *whom* I want to go. And I'm trying to tell you that if I had a wife like yours, I wouldn't drive her round in a lawnmower with seats."

"Duly noted."

"Good."

"Not that I can fathom how you won that woman with *any* car, let alone that one."

"That makes two of us."

Henry is, by any objective standard, an ordinary looking man. His hair (thinning) and his eyes (farsighted) are both the same nondescript shade of brown, and the thick glasses he wears make him appear constantly surprised. He is slender but not muscular, slightly stooped at forty-five from years of sitting and squinting at a computer monitor. His skin has an olive tint but doesn't take the sun well, so that he is sallow in all seasons. If it weren't for his height (six foot two when standing up straight), he would have nothing to recommend him visually. Even Maggie would admit that she didn't marry for looks. Whatever minor attraction certain of his female students might feel for him results, he is certain, solely from the way he talks to them about their writing.

Atlee ducks past Henry then turns back.

"Lunch next week?"

"Of course."

"Good luck out there."

"What? Oh, thanks."

"If there's anything I can help her with..."

"I'll be sure to let you know."

When Henry reaches the heavy, mullioned back door of Frederick Hall that leads out into the parking lot, he spots Natalie Currant standing by his car. It's not unusual to find a student waiting for him—his car being nothing if not recognizable—but Henry can't remember ever seeing Natalie there. All of his students have his home phone number and the more confident writers (Natalie among them) call him there. It's usually the nervous ones—especially female students unwilling to brave Maggie to get to him—who seek him out here. Maggie has a way of discouraging callers she thinks might be "groupies" with ulterior motives: "How about we chat until he's done on the toilet?" or "I'm sorry, he's at the urologist *again*."

"But I'm not Atlee," Henry argued once. "I don't have that reputation, so why would they bother?"

"Because they *do* know your reputation," Maggie had replied. "And they're all vying to be the first to change it. Trust me. I was one of them once."

Henry smiles at the memory and pushes out into the unseasonably warm March air.

It's strange how little I have in common with the boy who boarded the bus that afternoon. The thick glasses I wear now are the result of too much close work, not faulty genetics, so the boy saw everything with perfect clarity. His small stature gave no hint of the volcanic growth spurt I went through late in high school, when my muscles couldn't keep up with my bones and hunched my shoulders in toward my chest. The boy I remember loved baseball and his father, and I haven't cared much for either in a very long time.

My father had gone *to start a new life with one of his students* — a phrase my mother spit out like a bad grape. He taught American Literature at the University of Pittsburgh, and the day he left us turned out to be merely the first of three times he would trade a former student (this time my mother) for a current one. My father was a handsome, charismatic man with deep-set blue eyes and hands like a pianist, but I have been forced to admit, as I approach the age at which he left us, that he was more stereotype than substance: the elbow-patched tweed jacket and jeans, the thick wavy hair he kept long well into his fifties, even the pipe he almost never smoked jutting from his jacket pocket and enveloping him with an aroma that still makes me turn and look for him. When he died of prostate cancer three years ago, my mother was the only one of his wives to attend the funeral.

It would be easy, even convenient, to say that I was looking for a man to take his place when I followed John onto that PAT bus more than thirty years ago. If it were one of my students writing the story I might even try to convince him to tell it that way. It's a tempting first line: *"I was in search of a father figure and found one in an oddly shaped package."* But what I really wanted more than anything that day was to be alone. That's what passed for therapy for children of failed marriages in those days: we were left alone long enough to work things out for ourselves. It was a different time. All of my friends had two parents. I didn't even know what divorce was until my mother explained it to me, sitting on the edge of my bed the night before. So I'd taken the bus downtown, isolated among strangers in a way I couldn't be on the bus home from school, and then I went to the game and sat next to the empty seat where my father should have been, his untorn ticket still in my pocket. We had good seats in the brand new stadium, my absent father and I, so that at least once every inning someone came down from somewhere further back to ask if anyone was sitting there. "Yes," I told each one of them in turn, my eyes fixed on the field, "my dad's sitting here."

And in a way he was. That empty seat—that small void—was the first real evidence of his absence. He was gone from that space in a different, more precise way than he was gone from our house. When the crowd rose to cheer Al Oliver's two-out three-run home run in the sixth that broke open a tie game, I stayed seated, keeping careful score in my program with the symbols my father had taught me, and needing, I think, to maintain not only my presence there but my solitude. And despite being surrounded by 50,000 others, nothing disturbed my sense of isolation until I climbed the third stair of the bus and turned up the aisle and paused to watch a half-man pull himself into his seat.

I watched only because it was impossible not to, never thinking that I might be violating the same kind of privacy I myself had sought all that day. I had been taught to be polite, not to ogle, but without either of my parents there to remind me, I found myself frozen to the spot next to the driver's glass fare box, watching as the man hoisted himself easily onto one of the long bench seats near the front that faced one another across the aisle and then, with a little more difficulty, turned himself by rocking from side to side. He made short grunting sounds with the effort, the base of his leather harness squeaking as it rubbed against the vinyl seat, but he rotated quickly and settled himself facing the aisle.

"Sorry for the wait, son," he said. "Come on through."

I didn't learn his name until a week later, but John Kostka's face is fixed for me in that instant as if in a photograph I carry with me and take out all the time: the four-day beard hiding small scars all over his face that I only noticed later, in memory; the broken-toothed smile beneath a second-rate boxer's nose; the shaggy brows shading lapis blue eyes that seemed to emit their own light. Of all that was strange to me about him that first day, the strangest was his smile. The mere fact of it. The sadness I was carrying with me felt trivial in the presence of that smile, and when I looked away it was more out of shame than any remembered courtesy. I examined my white, new-school-year sneakers and walked through his gaze to a seat a few rows back.

If any of the others felt the way I did, no one showed it. Those who were already seated looked up absently, then went back to their newspapers or paperbacks or stared blankly, sideways, out the long, tinted windows. The only exception was the young black boy. He was five or six, and his mother was behind him, her hands on the small shoulders of his Pirate jersey. As they passed the half-man sitting on the bench (appearing, now that he was still again, as if he had been dropped in from a great height, his legs piercing the seat), the boy considered him intently and pressed back, dead-weight, into his mother.

"Come on, R.J.," she said. "Everyone's waiting on us."

She shuffled her feet forward and carried him on her shins, his shoulders shimmying left and right with her knees, but his head kept turning further and further to keep John in view, until I could see the stitched "Clemente" on the back of his jersey. They had almost reached the rows of regular seats, which would have blocked the boy's line of sight, when he executed a perfect drop-and-roll out of his mother's grasp and around her legs. She spun and grabbed for his arm, but he was too quick for her and pushed past the legs of the two men in suits to stand in front of the bench seat, staring.

"R.J.! Excuse me, excuse me," the woman said as she squeezed past the two men to get to her son. "R.J., you come back here this *minute*."

The men in suits blocked my view for a few seconds on their way to the back, but, when I could see again, the three participants in this drama were frozen in a comic stand-off. The boy had leaned his chest into the bench, almost touching the base of John's torso as he looked up at him. The mother now had a tight-fisted grip on the back of her son's shirt, and although there was nothing to prevent her from bending down closer and getting both hands under his armpits to lift him free, she seemed intent on keeping her own distance from John and was leaning back as if reeling in a heavy fish. John Kostka, for his part, was smiling and had placed a thick, gloved hand on the boy's head. When the boy spoke, it was as if his voice released them all.

"You ain't got no legs," he said.

"R.J.!"

"Well, he ain't."

"Reginald James McKenzie, you apologize this *minute* and then you come with me."

"He's all right, ma'am. No harm."

"I'm sorry, sir. A boy needs to learn to mind his manners."

"But he ain't, mama."

"R.J., I'm only gonna tell you—"

"What's that you say, young man?"

"You ain't got no legs."

"R.J., you say that one more time and I'm gonna—"

"No legs?" John had an exaggerated, almost theatrical look of dismay on his face.

"Huh-uh."

"You're pullin my... You're foolin with me, right?"

"No."

"R.J.!"

"I mean, No *sir*."

"Please find a seat, folks." The driver's head had tipped up into view in the wide mirror above him.

"Come on, R.J. The bus driver wants us to sit down."

"I wanna sit *here*, mama."

"Well, you can't. Come on."

"Why not?"

"Because I said so, that's why."

"But why not?"

"Folks."

"*R.J.*"

"He's welcome to sit here, ma'am. There's plenty of room. I don't exactly attract a crowd."

"See, mama. He even said. Can I sit here?"

"Folks."

The woman looked at her son, then at the half-man, then at the reflection of the driver's face.

"Oh, all right. Just hurry up about it."

R.J. scrambled into the seat next to John who started to shift over, rocking side to side. "Here, let me move over so you both can fit," he said.

"No need for that," said the boy's mother, trying unsuccessfully not to watch.

"No trouble. Just takes me a bit."

He inched sideways toward the front of the bus, and R.J. scooted with him, leaving the space on the other side of him for his mother. Once they were settled, the bus lurched away from the curb and swung up onto the ramp to the Fort Duquesne Bridge. Three Rivers Stadium passed below, now shaded and desolate and cold in the gloaming, as if the throbbing victory I had witnessed had taken place in another time entirely. No one on the bus as much as glanced toward it, all of us sitting silent, alone together in the rocking space filled with the smells of exhaust and chewing gum and aftershave. Everyone looked straight ahead, the boy's mother staring across the aisle and smoothing the sharp creases in the thighs of her white pantsuit. The only exception, of course, was the boy, who hadn't taken his eyes from John since getting on.

"I know what you're lookin at, son," John finally said.

"Huh?"

"R.J.," the boy's mother said.

"Sorry. I mean scuse me, sir?"

"I know you see what's in my ear."

"Huh?"

"*R.J.*"

"Only kids can see it, so I have to be real careful about where I sit, only sometimes I forget."

"I don't see nothin. Anything."

"Hey, who do you think you're dealin with here anyway? You think I just fell off the turnip truck? Don't answer that. You think I can't spot the eye of a young pirate when I see one? Well you can beg all you want, but I'm only gonna show it to you this one time, and that's it. You got it?"

"Yessir."

"Well okay then. That's better. Here, just a quick look." In one swift motion, John put a gnarled hand to his own ear, and a shiny gold coin appeared between two thick fingers.

"Whoa!"

"You betcha 'whoa.' Now take a look, and then I'm stickin it in my pocket where you won't be starin at it all the time."

"But I didn't even—"

"Hup. I caughtcha in the act, and now I'm showin it to you like I promised. Here."

The boy turned the coin over in his hand again and again, touching the faces, then the edges.

"Don't get too attached now. Give it here."

The boy handed over the coin and it disappeared into a leather pocket in the chest of John's suspendered harness. He made a show of tucking it in, pushing the corner of a dirty handkerchief that protruded from the opening to one side. I had tried all summer to learn simple sleight of hand tricks from a book my father had bought for me. The back cover assured that the *easy to follow photographs* could turn anyone into a *master of illusion.* But watching myself in the mirror revealed otherwise. Still, I had studied those diagrams for hours and I knew the secrets. I knew that the coin had been palmed before it emerged from the man's ear and again as it disappeared into his front pocket. But even watching for it I couldn't spot it.

"There," he said, patting his chest. "Now we can start fresh."

"Yessir," said the boy.

"Now before you noticed my treasure, you were askin me something else. Do you remember what it was?"

"Yeah. What happened to them?" The boy nodded down at the seat. This time his mother said nothing, rolling her eyes toward the line of advertisements curving from the top of the window bank to the ceiling. The man had brought this inquiry on himself, she seemed to say, despite her efforts to make sure he was left in peace.

"What happened to what?"

"Your legs."

"I don't know. Left em in my other pants, I guess."

The boy thought about this and then laughed.

"You think I'm kiddin? Yesterday I left my head at the barber's."

The boy laughed again, and his mother smiled in spite of herself but continued to act as if she was reading the signs above the windows.

"No, really!" the boy said.

"Hey, what do you call a no-legged man trying to water ski?"

"I dunno."

"Skipper."

The boy puzzled over this and said nothing, but his mother's hand went to her mouth.

"Too young, huh? How about this one. Our driver loves this one." He said this loud enough to get a face in the front mirror in reply. "What do you call a man with no arms and no legs in a pile of crisp autumn leaves?"

"I dunno."

"Russell."

"But you got arms."

"I know, but there's hardly any jokes for guys like me. I gotta steal em from those less fortunate. Like Pollacks."

"What's a Pollack?"

"Actually, that's me too. No legs, strike one; Pollack, strike two. If I wasn't so good with the ladies that might be strike three, if you know what I mean."

"No sir."

"Good. Your mama's raisin you right then."

The boy's mother glanced at him quickly and nodded, then fixed her gaze out the opposite window again.

"Yessir."

The boy looked away and was quiet, disappointed, it seemed, because John's acknowledgement of his mother had broken some kind of tacit agreement. It was as if he had been imagining that he and the strange half-man were the only two people on that bus. Now he was diminished by his context: he was someone to be *raised*. But once he saw that his mother had no intention of engaging his new friend, he turned to him again and said, with some urgency this time:

"But where *are* they?"

John shifted from side to side. He placed his hands on the seat, lifted himself clear of it and hung there for a moment, as if the sliver of light between the gray vinyl and the base of his torso was needed as confirmation to himself and everyone else that he was not an illusion. Then he set himself back down.

"I wish I knew. I wish I knew just that much, son. Truth is I could make the story as long as you want. But in the end, they were there, and the next time I woke up, they weren't. Simple as that. Like magic."

"Did you try to find them?"

"No, I didn't."

"How come?"

"Didn't have the energy, I guess. Decided to feel sorry for myself for a long while instead. I don't recommend that."

"No sir. That's what my mama says."

"Well, like I said, she's raisin you right."

They talked off and on for the rest of the ride, two animated figures in a rocking still-life making its way north along the Allegheny, until the boy and his mother stood for their stop. As the boy pushed himself off the bench, John put a hand on his head and rubbed. Then he slid the hand down behind the boy's ear and a quarter appeared between his fingers.

"I been lookin at that thing the whole trip. You gotta hide em better'n that. Here you go." The boy smiled and took the coin and was trying to push it back into his ear as his mother urged him down the aisle.

"See ya," said the boy.

"You betcha."

The bus passed through and rose up out of one river town, then another, then slipped under the Highland Park Bridge and down into Riverside. The stop where the bus would drop me off was less than fifty yards from the Allegheny, our house just three blocks up from there, and yet the river played no part in our daily lives. Train tracks split two thick lines of trees that paralleled the bus route on the main road through town, effectively cutting off both our view of the river and any meaningful access to it. The rivers weren't for leisure; they were for industry. And with the amount and character of waste that was dumped into them for the better part of the twentieth century, they weren't much to look at anyway: brown channels of roiling muck that had killed off all but the most hearty bottom feeders. The running joke at the time was that you didn't have to be Jesus Christ to walk on the waters of Pittsburgh.

At the third stoplight, John reached up and felt above the window behind him until he had a grip on the loose cord that would signal his stop. My stop. The driver looked up at the sound.

"You're not up the hill anymore?" he asked.

"Nope. Busted outa that place. Too many goddamn sick people, scuse my French. Got me a back room over at the VFW."

"Nice. Good for you."

"No more sneakin my girlfriends in through the windows."

The bus slowed. I stood and waited as John rolled to his stomach and eased himself to the floor. When he reached the top of the steps and paused, the bus driver spoke.

"Want some help?"

"No thanks. I'll manage." Then he sensed me behind him. "You go ahead, son. I'm a little slow gettin off these things."

I stepped around him and was conscious of how easily I dropped down the three stairs to the sidewalk, the game program and the mitt with the souvenir ball still in it tucked under my arm. Then I did something I knew I shouldn't have: I turned around to watch.

He couldn't bend down far enough to reach the step below with his hands. Instead, he reached up and grasped the steeply slanting handrails on either side. He swung out and came down too far forward on the first landing, his gloved hands having slipped down the rails. He wavered but caught himself, steadied, and swung out again. Again, his hands slid, and he dropped hard, but centered this time, on the next step. As he swung out toward the last step, it felt as though everything slowed down and I could see what was going to happen before it did. I noticed that the handrail ended too soon, that his hands would be almost behind him when he went to catch himself; that his base would swing out even farther as he fought to keep the upper part of his body back. And that's what happened. The back half of his torso struck the last step and he toppled like a salt shaker onto the pavement at my feet. That's when I realized where the scars had come from, the punched-in nose and the broken teeth. Down would never be as easy as up.

"Shit. Scuse my French," he said without much concern.

"Hey, you all right?" the driver called.

John dragged himself forward a few feet, then positioned his hands close enough to the base of his body that he could right himself. His nose was bleeding and it looked as if he had split his upper lip. He pulled the old handkerchief from his harness—which I now noticed was stained from what must have been countless previous incidents like this one—and he did his best to wipe the blood away. A group of people coming along the sidewalk had stopped and didn't seem to know whether it was all right to pass.

"I'm fine," he told the driver.

I had been staring at him when he looked up at me and smiled. "Hazard of duty," he said. Then he tucked his handkerchief away and began swinging down the sidewalk, trailing droplets of blood and the eyes of people who had forgotten their manners.

NATALIE

The campus where Henry and Maggie both teach sits up on a hill overlooking the town below. Some of the first shallow oil wells in the world were drilled in this part of upstate New York, and the huge Victorian homes that line the streets closest to campus are the product of riches that started moving elsewhere at just about the same time that the male student population stopped wearing jackets and ties to class. Most of the old homes are now student housing or, worse, fraternities, and the stately exteriors that don't show their age from up here on the hill also help to hide the interior ravages of freely flowing hormones and *Milwaukee's Best*. Only the three sorority houses hint at what Panama, New York must have looked like at the turn of the last century. Saved by an ancient local ordinance that classifies as a "brothel" any structure in which more than eight females are living together, and preserved by decades of giving by loyal Thetas, Kappas and Sigmas, these three houses are occupied only during weekly socials and, even then, everyone is required to be out by eleven o'clock, hours before anyone is drunk enough to do any real damage. As a result, they are museum pieces. No one even sits on the furniture. As Henry comes out the back entrance of

Frederick Hall, the houses below are visible through the tops of the silver March branches, and the acting (though reluctant) president of one of those sororities, Natalie Currant, is waiting next to his rusting Honda Civic. Henry buttons his jacket despite the absence of the usual March chill, pushes his glasses up tight and waves a greeting.

When she sees Henry, Natalie makes no attempt to appear as if she hasn't been waiting. She is no nervous schoolgirl setting up a chance encounter. She is tall and unconventionally pretty, with close-cropped brown hair framing a round, open face and wide-set almond eyes that give the illusion of never blinking. The way she carries herself, chin high and forward, makes her appear much older, and she could easily pass for a young assistant professor waiting for a colleague to give her a ride home. The backpack on the ground next to her seems unrelated and out of context.

She is talking before Henry has gotten close enough to shake her hand, a formality he maintains when greeting any of his students.

"I tried you at home but I got your wife," Natalie begins. "God, she despises me."

Natalie Currant isn't one of Henry's fawning fans, and she's not one of the campus's many Connecticut beauties. Her campus-wide reputation as someone to be reckoned with—like her election as sorority president—is borne mostly out of her disdain for the place. One afternoon in Henry's class, when she was railing against the entire institution of sororities, he asked her why she didn't just quit.

"I don't quit anything," she told him sternly, with a look that Maggie might have dubbed *meaningful*.

"She doesn't hate you," Henry assures Natalie now. They shake hands and Henry sets his shoulder bag on the roof of the car while searching his pockets for keys. "It's just that Tuesday is her day off. She draws and cooks. The telephone is the enemy of both."

"It's okay. She thinks I want to fuck you just because everyone else does. But I don't."

Henry has stopped being shocked at the cavalier way his students talk about sex. Something about the faceless, voiceless cyber-communication they all grew up on has made them fearless.

"I don't think either of the conclusions in that statement would be comforting to her," he says, finding his keys. He opens the door and tosses his bag inside. "Do you need a ride down the hill?"

"No thanks. I'm headed to the library. I was just wondering if you'd take a look at these pages before class on Friday." Henry hadn't noticed the manila envelope on the hood behind her. She holds it out to him now but he doesn't take it right away.

"Are you up this week?"

"No. I don't want it work-shopped. Not by those idiots. It's not finished anyway. Just a start."

"Come on. They're not so bad."

Natalie tilts her head and crosses her eyes at him, and for a split second she looks her age. "Hello?" She knocks gently on his forehead once, bumping his glasses off-kilter, then pulls her fist away quickly with an awkwardness that is at odds with her verbal fearlessness. Henry feels a heat begin to rise from his neck into his face, though he is certain that he is uncomfortable *for* her, and not because of her.

"You're too hard on them," he tells her quickly, setting his glasses straight.

"And you're too easy. You let them all think they're good." She waves a scolding finger for emphasis. "No. It's worse than that. You *make* them all think they're good."

"People are going to discourage them for the rest of their lives. That's not my job."

"There's no one in that class who can write."

"Including you?"

"Yes, including me. Only I *know* I can't write. Yet."

"If you could see some of my early stories you'd know there's hope for the others."

"I'd like that."

"Sorry. I've burned them all."

"Bullshit. No one really does that."

"Okay. But I've banished them to a place where no one will find them until I'm dead. And I've blacked out my name."

"Big mistake telling me that, Professor. When you're dead and famous I can provide the final link between you and your unpublished work."

"Unpublish*able*. There's a big difference. And I'll haunt you if you tell."

"Yeah. Well." Natalie again looks her age for the few seconds it takes for her to hand the envelope to Henry. She seems to reconsider, pulling it back briefly before letting go. Henry almost drops it.

"I'll take a look," he says.

"I want the *truth*."

"The whole and nothing but."

"I want to know what it *tastes* like," she says, quoting Henry's own refrain, "even if you hate it."

"No you don't, but okay."

Henry climbs into his car and puts the window down as the engine coughs then rolls over with a growl.

"See you Friday," he says.

"Call me before if you finish it."

"Do I have your number?"

"I gave it to your wife, but it didn't sound like she was writing it down."

"Put it here." Henry sets the envelope containing Natalie's pages on the window ledge between them, and she quickly scrawls her cell phone number. As he pulls away she looks after him briefly, then shoulders her backpack and turns toward the library.

I could have followed him that first day, a macabre Hansel tracking drops of blood that spread and diffused on the sidewalk like tiny suns. But I knew that my mother was waiting for me, and I knew—or somehow sensed—that in the moments after his fall John's desire for solitude was even greater than my own. So I turned away and started walking toward my street, looking back over my shoulder every few steps, not because I regretted my decision, but because his way of moving was still new enough to me that I found it impossible not to watch him. He was apelike in the way that he lived and moved in the space between his arms: broad-backed and fluid and powerful. It was at least a hundred yards to the end of the block and I expected him to stop and rest, or at least slow his pace, but he kept on with the evenness of a metronome, the steady brushing *shoosh* of leather on concrete gradually diminishing until he disappeared around the corner. An approaching train rumbled and blew its whistle as I stood and watched the spot where he had been. I pushed the baseball deep into the web of my mitt, tucked the game program under my arm, then turned and headed home.

Riverside was a planned sidewalk community that dated to the turn of the century when a few wealthy industrialists realized that there was a market for "country houses" for their upper management who couldn't afford the real thing. After twenty years, when only the large corner properties had been developed, the rest of the grid was split into much smaller lots and sold to people of more modest means. The result, as the years passed, was an odd combination of spacious, elegant Victorian corner houses that book-ended, block after block, long lines of unassuming brick homes, row-houses and duplexes. Not surprisingly, the owners of those corner "estates" hadn't liked the way the neighborhood was progressing and moved on, selling to lower management or to landlords who added efficiency kitchens and as many thin walls as could be accommodated to create *a new kind of upscale apartment living*. We lived in one of the few corner houses that had been spared that kind of division, a beautiful old place that my father bought for next to nothing the year he made full professor. He had lived in its ten echoing rooms by himself, hosting frequent faculty/student gatherings that became legendary at the University, until he met my mother.

My sister Sam was fifteen when my father left—the same number of years my parents had been married, though that fact didn't figure into my understanding of the situation until years later. Ruthie was seven. We each reacted in our own way to his leaving. Sam got angry and has remained that way for most of her life. She stayed single until she was thirty-eight then married a meek, diligent accountant with whom she is conscientiously childless. To her credit, she has channeled her anger into a series of passionate causes, most of which are equal parts worthy and hopeless. But when I came home that day her anger was still haphazard, both unfocused and all-encompassing at the same time. I opened the heavy, leaded glass door and the music—Hendrix, I think—was loud and pulsing and seemed to have a thickness of its own. In the living room, records and album jackets lay strewn around the floor, and the clear plastic turntable lid was up. Our mother refused to allow Sam to have a stereo in her room, certain that we'd never see her again. It was only when my mother was out that Sam could do what she was doing now: lying on the couch reading liner notes and playing music loud enough that it created its own kind of silence around her.

"WHERE'S MOM?" I yelled, standing right next to her.

Although she couldn't have heard me come in, she had a practiced way of never appearing surprised, so that she didn't move or register my appearance for a few seconds. Her feet were tucked up underneath a floral gypsy skirt, and I could see the bottom edge of the braided leather anklet she'd started wearing. She had silver rings on every finger and both thumbs, some with turquoise stones, some without, and I remember being ashamed that I noticed she wasn't wearing a bra under her dark green tank top.

"Date," she said.

"WHAT?" I answered, though I thought I'd heard.

"DATE. MAN. DINNER."

I walked over and turned the stereo down.

"What are you talking about?"

"Mom's on a date. With Mr. Garabedian from her office. And for her sake I hope we don't see her again until tomorrow morning. Earliest." Sam didn't take her eyes off the back of the album cover she was reading until I had stood silent for what must have been a full minute. "Ground Control to Major Henry," she said.

"I don't get it. Dad's been gone like three weeks."

"If that's what you think, you're even dumber than I thought. Dad's been gone for a *long* time, buddy." When I didn't say anything, she got up and went over to the stereo. "Dinner's on the counter. No TV until I see the homework."

"But it's Playoff week."

"Mom's orders."

"They're not giving any homework."

"Cool." She turned the music back up and fell onto the couch with what appeared to be six times her actual body weight.

Ruthie always took refuge in her room upstairs when Sam played music, so I knew that's where I'd find her. There was a sign on her closed door that she had made just after my father left—"Quiet Kid at Work"—which was true even without the proper punctuation. I knocked but went right in because she never minded when it was me.

She was lying on the floor, propped on her elbows, intent on a drawing. To her right was a set of colored markers, all still in their assigned color slots along the rainbow other than the one she was working with. To her left was a line of candy bars in the order she would eat them, and the empty wrappers of those that had gone before. It's strange to remember Ruthie on that day, still small, almost fragile looking, on the cusp of what became a quest to grow out of her own skin. She had always had a sweet tooth, constantly bargaining with our mother about the number of bites of her dinner she had to eat before being entitled to dessert. But the bargaining stopped after Dad left, probably because my mother didn't want to deny Ruthie the one thing that seemed to comfort her. She weighed a hundred pounds by the time she was ten, two hundred when she graduated from high school, close to three hundred when she was diagnosed as a diabetic ten years ago. But in October of 1971, she was just my little sister eating as much candy as she could before Mom got home, like any kid might do.

"Hey," I said, closing the door to blunt the music.

"Hey."

"What're you drawing?"

"Just a design."

"It's nice."

"Thanks."

Ruthie never drew people or animals or flowers like other kids.

Instead, she'd take a black marker and, eyes closed, run it around the page. She'd alternate between sharp and loopy turns, filling the page with random shapes that were cut smaller and smaller as her hand passed, trailing boundaries. Then she'd open her eyes and meticulously fill in every space she'd created with color. Unlike the shapes themselves, the colors were anything but random. She would choose one and spread its appearance evenly around the page before choosing another. When she was finished, the colors had an even, kaleidoscopic symmetry to them that made the shapes themselves, haphazard in creation, appear ordered and balanced. Because she was difficult to distract when she was at work, I sat down next to her, took the ball from my mitt and set it beside her pad, the *Major League Baseball* logo facing up.

"Where did you get *that?*" she asked, her eyes wide.

Since the day my father left, Ruthie had been sleeping in the other twin bed in my room, listening with me every night to the rapid-fire rasp of Bob Prince's voice calling the Pirates' run to the division title. She didn't just listen, though; she asked questions constantly: "What's a balk?" "How come a foul ball isn't strike three?" "What does he mean, '*There's a bug loose on the rug?*'" Prince's pet phrases—this one describing a ball hit to the gap on the new Three Rivers Stadium Astroturf—gave Ruthie more trouble than the actual rules of the game, none of which ever had to be explained more than once. In the Prince vernacular, a double play was a "*Hoover,*" a ball down the line was fair "*by a gnat's eyelash,*" and a Willie Stargell home run was "*chicken on the hill with Will.*" Prince was nearing the end of his twenty-eight years calling Pirate games and was more identified with the team than any of its players. Sometimes the game did nothing more than provide the pacing for his rambling stories, and Ruthie and I were just two of the hundreds of thousands of Pittsburghers who didn't turn off their radios, no matter what the score, until The Gunner signed off with his nightly farewell: "*Goodnight Mary Edgerly, wherever you are."*

"Who's Mary Edgerly?" Ruthie asked one night.

"No one knows."

"Probably a girlfriend who broke up with him."

"Naw. He's married."

"So is Daddy," she said.

When I set the baseball in front of her, she immediately put down her marker and took the ball into her small hands. She squeezed it hard and worked her palms in opposite directions like a pitcher might, then traced a finger along the raised fault line made by the laces.

"Where did you get this?" she asked again.

"The game."

"*You went to the game?*"

"Yep."

"How?"

"Dad got us tickets."

"You went with *Daddy?*"

"No. Just by myself."

I saw her face register the orange box seat that had sat empty next to mine.

"I wanted to take you," I told her quickly. "But Mom would have killed me. She would have killed both of us."

After a brief silence she said, "We won."

"Yeah, I know."

"Mr. Simons let us listen during Reading and then I listened on the bus."

"Cool."

"All these boys were hanging around my seat trying to hear. I was the only girl listening."

"Did The Gunner say anything about a line drive foul that hit someone in the head?"

"I think so."

"That was right near me."

"This ball hit someone's *head?*"

"No, I didn't get that one. They gave it to the guy who was bleeding."

"Oh. Where did this one come from?"

"One of the ball boys gave it to me after the game."

"Oh," she said. "That's okay. It still counts."

"Yeah."

She handed it back to me, picked up the red marker she had been working with and returned to her design.

"Mom's not here," she said after a while.

"I know."

"She's eating dinner with someone from her office."

"Yeah. Sam told me."

Ruthie outlined carefully along the inside edge of each black border before filling in the rest of the shape, her movements quick and sure.

"He's real hairy."

"So?"

"Even his hands."

"That doesn't mean he's not nice. Was he nice?"

"Yeah, I guess. But I'm not shaking his hand again." She finished the last of the shapes that would be red and picked up a blue marker. "And I'm not letting him be my daddy."

She didn't appear to be upset when she said this; she was simply stating a new rule.

The image of Ruthie wrapped around my father's leg in the driveway came back to me again, and I realized that I hadn't seen her cry once since then. Even that first night, she dragged her pillow and blanket into my room and climbed stoically into my other bed. She didn't ask my permission or say anything at all until she had settled in and noticed the ballgame playing on my clock radio. She asked who was winning, and after I told her she started asking other questions: about where they played the games, how many players were on the team, how they kept score. My father loved baseball and had taken me to the games all the time, first to Forbes Field, then to Three Rivers, but Sam and Ruthie had never come with us. I had to start with the basics, even getting out of bed to draw diagrams that would explain where the fielders stood, fair versus foul, how a force-out worked. For some reason, it all made sense to her right away. But I didn't know what to say to her now.

"I gotta go do my homework," I lied.

She looked up from her paper for the first time since she'd passed the ball back to me. "Since I sleep in your room you could do your homework in here if you want."

"That's okay. There's stuff in my room I need."

"Oh. Okay. See ya."

She put the blue marker down and picked up the next candy bar in line.

My own room was a shrine to the Pirates. For a Pittsburgh boy in 1971 there was no other team. The Penguins were a hapless bunch who dressed as though they belonged in another city in their blue and white uniforms, and the Steelers, looking like anything but a dynasty in the making, had just christened the new stadium with another ugly five-win season. ARCO stations in the area gave out eight-by-ten photos of a different Pirate every week with a fill-up. The year before, they had handed out yellow bumper stickers bearing "Gunnerisms" in heavy black type. My father and I did three things together: went to ball games, played catch and got gas. There was no self-service, so we'd sit in the car together, watching the attendant start the pump. He'd click the trigger on the nozzle into place so that he could clean the windshield, sometimes check the oil, and the combination of the gas fumes and my anticipation made me dizzy every time. Then the attendant would hand that week's glossy across to me and I would hold it on my lap by its outer edges all the way home. Gradually, the photos filled one entire wall of my room, empty spaces left for the ones that had been handed out in the weeks since my father left, and the bumper stickers covered the head and footboards of my beds. If I were writing a story about this little boy, a little boy like me, I would almost surely be tempted by a clichéd image here: the angry child tearing down all evidence of his father's kindness in retribution for his leaving. But for me it had started to feel as if my love for the Pirates was more real than my father's love for me, and I clung to it the way Ruthie clung to her candy bars, the way Sam clung to her anger.

The three of us spent a lot of time the way we did that evening—isolated together in the house, each a stationary point on a silent triangle. In the year that followed my father's leaving there was an almost overwhelming loneliness in every moment that wasn't otherwise filled, and it wasn't just because he was gone but because we were alone in the experience as well. My daughter Allie knows the marital status of every one of her friends' parents. She knows their visitation schedules and even which parents have new lovers. I'm sure that there were other students at Riverside Elementary whose parents had split, but if the circumstance was common, the topic itself was taboo, so that I felt as if I was carrying not only a new burden, but a secret as well.

I found a spot on my bookshelves for the ball, tossed my mitt into a corner and lay down on my bed to read the game program. I was mostly a loner as a kid so baseball was the perfect spectator sport for me. I could sit and watch for three hours, mostly in silence, painstakingly recording all of the signs and symbols and notations, and then I could lie in my bed that night, listening to the train whistles, and relive the game—or any game I'd ever been to—all over again: the simple dotted line from first to third becoming a Clemente headfirst slide; the solid column of three K's in the fourth Steve Blass striking out the side; the "6-4-3 DP" resurrecting the image of an aging Bill Mazeroski, still getting the occasional start at second, and still turning a double play with the quickness and grace of the skinny kid who had won the 1960 World Series with a single swing. Those notations were, in a very real sense, my first stories. And because free agency didn't exist, I felt as if I knew my characters intimately. I could rattle off season and lifetime batting averages, RBIs and home runs for every regular position player, ERA and strikeout-to-walk ratios for every pitcher. I knew their faces and their voices and their superstitions. The 1971 Pirates were the first team in baseball history to field a starting lineup of nine black and Latino players, and I never noticed. They were just The Pirates. *My* Pirates. And would be again the next year, and the year after that. For a boy who had just learned that permanence came in degrees, that was a powerful comfort.

I must have dozed off reading, because my mother's voice woke me.

"Hey kiddo."

I flipped the program upright on my chest.

"Hey."

"Were you asleep?" She put a hand on my forehead and spread her fingers up and through my hair.

"No."

"You're in bed early."

"I'm not in bed. I'm just reading."

"Where's Ruthie?"

"I don't know. Her room I guess."

My mother had been young when she married my father—just a year removed from his classroom—so that she was still in her thirties when he left and still beautiful. Her blond hair was pulled back in a ponytail and when she sat on the edge of my bed I could smell some kind of perfume I'd never noticed before.

"I guess Sam told you where I was?"

"Yeah."

"Is that okay with you?"

"I don't know. I guess."

"I'm sorry I couldn't have prepared you better for this first one. I wasn't even prepared for it myself. It just came up at the office today, and I could have said no, but then I thought, why not, you know?"

"Yeah."

"I mean." She seemed to be searching for a way to explain herself to me and then gave up. "Why not?"

I shrugged mostly because she did, but she took that to be my approval.

"Do you want to hear about it?" she asked, excited now. "My date? God that sounds weird, doesn't it?"

I shrugged again. "I don't care."

"There's not much to tell really. Just dinner and a walk afterwards. Just talking. He's very nice, Mark. Mr. Garabedian."

"Ruthie said he's real hairy."

She laughed and hit me playfully.

"Henry *Graham*. You watch your *manners*."

"Well, is he?"

"Yes. Very. But *very* nice."

"That's good, I guess."

"Yes. Nice is good." She looked at my program and I thought she might notice that it was different from any other one I had, maybe twice as thick, the *NLCS* logo prominent on the front cover, but she just leaned over, kissed my forehead and stood. "I'll let you get back to your reading."

"Hey, Mom?"

"Yeah?"

"Something really weird happened today."

"What?"

"I met a guy with no legs."

"What do you mean?"

"I guess I didn't meet him. But I saw him. Walking down Freeport."

"Walking?"

"Well, swinging. He uses his hands and swings his body forward."

"That's amazing. On Freeport Road?"

"Well, on the sidewalk. And he was bleeding."

"Oh my. From his hands?"

"No. His nose. He fell—" I suddenly realized that going further might get me in trouble. "He must have fallen, I guess."

"How do you fall if you don't have any legs?"

"I don't *know*. I just know his nose was bleeding."

"Hm." She paused and looked at my program, but I couldn't tell if she was really seeing it or just letting her eyes rest somewhere while she thought. "What were you doing on Freeport Road?"

My heart sped up. "Just walking."

"You know I don't like you all the way down there. There's too much traffic and you never know if people are watching—"

"I know, Mom."

"And sometimes there are strange people down there. People just passing through town. Like this man you saw."

"He wasn't passing through, Mom. He lives here."

She looked at me hard. "How do you know that?"

"I don't *know* know it. But he turned up the block at the shoe store."

I could see that she knew I wasn't telling her everything, but I could also see her process that I was there, in bed, unharmed, and she didn't seem to have the energy to pursue the truth in the face of that simple fact.

"Just be careful, will you?" she said.

"I am, Mom."

"And don't read for too long."

"I won't."

"Goodnight."

When she opened my bedroom door to leave, Ruthie was standing in the doorway with her blanket.

"Hi sweetie. How long have you been out there?"

"A minute." Ruthie walked past our mother, climbed into my other bed and got under the covers.

"Did you brush your teeth?"

"Yes."

"Would you like me to read with you for a little while?"

"No thanks. I'm tired."

"Okay. Goodnight. I love you guys."

She kissed me again, then Ruthie, whose eyes were already closed.

"Night, Mom," I said.

After she walked out, pulling the door closed behind her, Ruthie turned her head toward me on her pillow.

"Did you really meet a guy with no legs?" she said.

MAGGIE

Maggie Graham doesn't teach on Tuesdays and she is at the stove putting pasta into a steaming pot when Henry comes into the kitchen. Barefoot in jeans and a short white t-shirt, she is all long limbs and sharp angles in profile: sharp-hipped, sharp-shouldered, the long nose that she hates and Henry loves, even the natural wave in her hair creating curls that don't quite finish but end in abrupt upward swoops. Her left breast does the same, ending in a gravity-defying flourish the doctors told her they couldn't hope to duplicate on the right side, so she decided on one perfect breast rather than two that didn't match. Outside the house, in class, she wears a carefully crafted prosthesis. But at home Maggie is defiantly braless, and Henry sometimes can't help but feel—even two years after the fact—that she is daring him to stare. He would never admit to her that it's still sometimes hard not to.

"Your little friend called," she says without turning.

"I know. I ran into her outside Frederick. She says you were genuinely unfriendly."

"I was."

Henry tosses the invitation and the envelope containing

Natalie's pages onto the kitchen table and wraps both arms around Maggie's waist from behind, resting his chin on her shoulder. "Smells good," he says.

"Thanks. And nice try."

"What?"

"We were talking about your friend."

"My student. Natalie."

"Your student who wants to sleep with you. I suppose that is different than a friend."

Maggie isn't pushing Henry away when she says this, so he knows it's more playful than argumentative. Still, she hasn't relaxed back into him and remains intent on dinner. She puts basil, olive oil, macadamia nuts and garlic in a small food processor and starts it spinning.

"Actually, she doesn't," Henry says over her shoulder, over the noise. "Want to sleep with me, I mean. She told me so herself."

Maggie opens the lid, dips a pinky in to taste, then adds Parmesan cheese and starts the blade whirring again. "Are you really so clueless that you think the fact you are talking with a student about *not* having sex is something that will make me feel better?"

"Sorry, no."

Maggie dips her pinky again, but this time crosses it over her shoulder and directly into Henry's mouth.

"God, that's good," he says. "What is it?"

"Macadamia nut pesto."

"Spectacular." Henry reaches around and takes another finger-full. "How did your work go today? Anything new for me to see?"

"Not yet. I'm starting to regret the size choice, though. It's exhausting. And my former boob is killing me." Maggie stretches her right arm behind her, around Henry's boney rear end and arches back into him, stretching. Long days in the studio, working hard with her right hand, give her an ache that is part real, part phantom. The fact that Maggie has stopped asking the question that would naturally follow—about what Henry himself is working on—produces a phantom pain of its own that they both feel but don't acknowledge. Henry pulls himself away and flips absently through the mail on the kitchen table.

"Where are the kids?"

"Allie's at rehearsal. Walt's staying at the Strummers' for dinner because they're having something '*more normal.*'"

Loren Strummer is the chair of Henry's department and a closet homosexual in the sense that he refuses to acknowledge publicly what everyone already knows. Except, apparently, his southern belle wife, Elvira. He married her at forty-five for appearances (long after there was anyone left at the University who cared) and, for good measure, managed to father Walt's best friend, Alex, shortly thereafter.

"If Walt is using the Strummers as his baseline for 'normal,' maybe we should start saving for therapy now."

"He loves Alex. And you're forgetting the most important thing."

"We get to eat alone without paying a babysitter."

"Yup."

"What about after?" Henry has come up behind her again.

"Everybody's home by 7:30. And we are *not* rushing through this meal."

"What if we go upstairs first? I promise to be quick and insensitive to your needs."

"Your little student-teacher conference got you revved up?"

"Nope. Just you and macadamia nuts."

"Letting the pasta sit will ruin it. Set the table and I'll deal with you later."

"Promise?"

"Promise. There's bread too. And salad."

Henry reaches for a bottle of wine from the small rack above the cabinets, takes down two dinner plates, bread plates and salad bowls and gets out silverware, napkins and wine glasses. He sets two places in one corner of the large, antique dining room table, pours the wine, moves the candles from the center of the table to one end and lights them before dimming the chandelier. Eating in this dining room always makes Henry conscious of their good fortune. Anywhere near D.C. an old Victorian like this one—with its high ceilings and big rooms, the small carriage house out back that gives his sister, Ruthie, her own space—would have been beyond their means even before he left the firm. For the first two years here they had rented. But the release of Henry's second novel coincided with their landlord's decision to put the house on the market, and they used Henry's modest advance as the down payment on a bet that tenure would follow in due course. They'd brought Walt here as a newborn to start their new lives together with his. Now Ruthie seemed to be making a new beginning as well. And even though he'd almost lost Maggie here, the fact that he hadn't—the fact that she had gotten well within these walls—gave the house a power over him that he hadn't fully appreciated until his tenure review had begun. This is the first house that has felt like a home since he'd left a strikingly similar one in Pittsburgh more than thirty years ago, and it would be almost as hard to give up as his job.

"Well, hello there, little miss." The Grahams' aging Golden Retriever, Franny, has limped into the room and is looking cloudy-eyed up at Henry. Her hips have become virtually fused, so that her entire back end does a slow, rocking shimmy with her tail. Henry bends and takes her gray face in both of his hands. "I'm honored that I'm still worth getting up for."

Maggie comes in from the kitchen carrying the pasta and the bread. "My, look at all this," she says, meaning the candles and the wine glasses. "I feel underdressed."

"You will be. Later." Henry takes the food from her and pulls her chair out. "Sit." Franny and Maggie sit in unison, Franny looking as if she expects something for her effort, though no one notices. "Actually, this is all very appropriate. We have something to celebrate. Sort of."

"What do you mean?"

"Stay here."

Henry goes into the kitchen and gets the invitation from the kitchen table and, when he returns, sets it next to Maggie's plate. Her face closes around its center as she squints in the candlelight, then opens again as she realizes what she is looking at. Franny has nudged her way under Maggie's hand and appears to be trying to read.

"Is this...?" Maggie begins to ask.

"Yeah. That's him."

I looked for him everywhere over the next few days. The Pirates lost games one and two in Baltimore, collecting only eleven total hits, four of them by Roberto Clemente, who seemed to be the only Pirate ready for the national stage. Clemente was a mythic figure for me. Brooding and angry and passionate, he almost never smiled, but it was impossible to watch the abandon with which he played baseball—the graceful fury—and not find an abiding joy there. By 1971, he had already won four batting titles, but few outside of Pittsburgh recognized his greatness. I was sure that this Series was going to change that, but so far he was getting no help. I pedaled out my frustrations, up and down the entire grid of Riverside sidewalks, expecting to see the strange half-man each time I banked around a corner onto a new stretch of concrete. And then I was surprised by his appearance in the most likely place.

When he swung out of the wings at the Riverside VFW to announce the fall concert being given by our elementary school chorus standing behind him, he was wearing a cut-off tuxedo and white gloves where the heavy work gloves had been. I couldn't help but feel more worldly than my shocked schoolmates who, despite our strict training, had already dissolved from a troop-at-attention into a muddle of bent, whispering pairs. Even the frantic, off-stage finger-snapping of our new music teacher, Miss Donovan, did nothing to quiet them. The girl standing next to me, Alexandra Tuthill, who was nervous under the best of circumstances, started to hum to herself, something she did when she was trying not to cry. Our Master of Ceremonies didn't seem to notice any of this. He took the microphone, telescoped down to its shortest height, and addressed the crowd like a ringmaster. I thought of the man I had seen a few days earlier, bloodied and solitary.

"Evenin folks. Evenin kids." He turned to us and I could feel the chorus tense in unison. I was small for my age, still years from the late growth spurt that would take me to my current, awkward height, so I was front and center. But he was looking over my head, addressing the group as a whole. Alexandra now had a hold on my left forearm with both of her hands and she had begun twisting them in opposite directions, as if my forearm was a washcloth to be wrung out.

"We're still waitin for the transport from up at the hospital to finish unloading, so I'll take care of a few announcements before the kids get started. First off, make sure the aisles are clear so the wheelchairs can get up front here. These folks are excited about their night out, and it took me a while to get approval for this up the hill, so I hope you'll make them feel welcome. Second, remember, there's no *Bingo & Bowling* this Wednesday night on account of the Series, but we'll be back at it next week. Bowling for the men at Laura Lanes in Harmarville; bingo in the back room there for the ladies. Both start at seven o'clock, and then we all move to the bar together at around nine. Any of you ladies prefer bowling, you're welcome to join us. Any of you gentlemen prefer bingo, be sure to bring your clutch purses."

There was some commotion at the back of the hall as the

double-doors opened, and two women I took to be nurses ushered in our late-arriving guests. The wheelchairs came first, most carrying men John's age or older who were missing one or more limbs. Then came the ambulatories, some dressed in street-clothes, but most shuffled in wearing hospital gowns or pajama pants and robes. Two blind men each had one hand on opposite shoulders of an orderly while their free hands reached out, searching, into the unfamiliar space in front of them. In my memory it's like a scene from a George Romero film. And as they all made their way to the area reserved for them at the front of the room, my classmates got louder and louder. Miss Donovan rushed in from the side of the stage.

"Children," she whispered loudly. "Children, hush."

"Come on in, folks," John was saying. "Make yourselves comfortable and we'll get started." He and Miss Donovan were back to back, almost touching, the top of his head just about even with the place where her white, silk blouse tucked into her plaid skirt.

"Children, look at *me*. Don't *stare*," Miss Donovan hissed.

"That's it. Seats to my right, wheelchairs to my left. Just make a few nice rows with the wheelchairs and there should be plenty of room. Ed, make sure Carmine gets all the way up front where he can see."

"Alexandra, if you're going to cry, please do so in the wings."

"And make sure to split up Vic and Les. They'll talk non-stop and they both forgot how to whisper about five years ago."

"Sing to the back of the room, children, just like we practiced. David Bartholomew, did you hear me? Do *not* stare or I'll pull you off this stage this instant. Alexandra…"

When I remember this evening, I can't help but think what might precede a similar performance at the school our son Walt attends now: sensitivity training of some sort, no doubt, lots of talk about diversity and acceptance, permission slips sent home so that parents concerned about the emotional impact could opt out on their child's behalf. But I'm not sure anything would have prepared us properly for what happened before Miss Donovan could finish her little pep talk to Alexandra, which was that she took half a step back, and, upon feeling a head suddenly planted firmly between her buttocks, arched back so violently that she sort of cartwheeled off the stage. "Scuse me, ma'am," the owner of the head said when they were still in physical contact. And then she was gone.

Having thus lost our tangible and emotional center, the choir members streamed from the risers and pushed to the front of the stage.

"Easy, kids," John said. "Hey, Emma. You'll want to check on her." Miss Donovan's fulcrum looked down at her. "Sorry, ma'am. I get under foot and I'm not real quick at getting out."

"It's all right. I'm all right... I think."

But she didn't look it. Being in the front row, Alexandra and I had managed to get to the edge of the stage first and we peered over the precipice at our proper young teacher who lay splayed on the floor below, one foot turned out at an impossible angle. The entire audience was standing, and both the wheelchairs and the ambulatory patients had come forward to form a semi-circle around her, as if they were now her choir. The only people in the room disinterested in the melodrama were two young amputees who had made their way into a corner to the right of the stage to share a cigarette. Both leaned on crutches, their heads shaved close. One was missing a leg from the knee down, the other from the hip. They looked furtive, unsure of their place in this group, and they passed their cigarette back and forth without speaking.

"Can we please give the young lady some room?" John pleaded. "You're all like a bunch of goddamn rubber-neckers, scuse my French, kids."

Most of the audience members took their seats, and the wheelchairs and other patients backed up in unison as a nurse pushed her way between them.

"I think I'm okay," Miss Donovan said again, sitting up on her elbows.

"Don't move until Emma's taken a look, ma'am."

The nurse crouched at Miss Donovan's side and pressed gently on her ankle. Even I could see that it was swollen already. Miss Donovan winced.

"Probably broken," the nurse said. "They'll want to take care of this swelling before an x-ray. Can someone get me a bag of ice?"

Within a few minutes, Miss Donovan was seated at the foot of the stage, leg propped on a second chair, her ankle wrapped in ice and a dish towel. Food items from the buffet that was apparently to follow our performance (lady fingers, biscotti, pigs-in-a-blanket skewered with cellophane-tipped toothpicks) were spread around her like offerings, and a handful of men from the crowd had pushed our risers to the very front of the stage so that she could direct us from where she sat. I don't remember there ever being a question of us staying to sing. It's what we had spent the first six weeks of school practicing for, and it was our only purpose in being there. But I don't remember what we sang. I don't remember whether we were good or bad, whether the events of the evening brought us together as a group in the way adversity can sometimes do, or gave us a greater focus on what I'm sure were passionate directions from Miss Donovan. What I remember next is the tap on my shoulder afterwards.

"Hey, Mr. Baseball."

We were lining up in the foyer to leave. Everyone was talking at once, the excitement that always follows a performance having been enhanced by the strangeness of the evening and the sense that we had all overcome something together. I had walked the four blocks from my house and had a note permitting me to walk home as well. I didn't have to turn to know who was talking to me. If I hadn't recognized his voice, the sudden silence of my classmates would have told me.

"Didn't I see you on the bus after the game the other day? Got off at my stop too, right?"

I was uncertain whether to be proud or embarrassed that he was talking to me.

"Sure, I remember you," he continued. "Hammerin Hank, right?" He laughed. "You had a glove and a ball. A game program too. I remember wondering what you were doing there by yourself. You a big fan?"

"I don't know. I guess."

"Yeah, so am I. I was at the game that day too."

"You were?"

"Right behind home plate. I got friends in high places. Hey, you got a minute? I want to show you something."

Miss Donovan was directing traffic from a spare wheelchair and everyone started moving toward the doors, Alexandra and a few others looking back at me.

"If you gotta go, we can do it another time."

"No, that's okay. I'm walking home."

"All right then, good. Come on back."

We waited for the other kids to filter out around us, and when the way was clear, I followed him around a corner and back down a long narrow hallway that must have stretched the length of the auditorium we'd just come from. He moved easily between his shoulders, and I had to walk quickly to keep up. When we turned another corner, down a darkened hallway, I lost my bearings but felt as if we must be behind the stage. We came to a set of double doors — swinging doors you might see at the entrance to a restaurant kitchen. Even in the dimness I could see that they were pocked and scratched, and the small windows that would have protected kitchen workers or wait staff from running into one another had been covered over with thick black material. A new lock had been installed less than three feet from the floor, and my host was now reaching into the inside pocket of his tux jacket for a key.

"For privacy, not safety," he said. "Wouldn't want any of my lady friends feelin uneasy."

When the latch clicked, he shouldered his way into the darkened room and held the door for me before letting it swing shut. Everything went black, as though I was encased in the material that covered the door's narrow windows, and as I listened to John moving in the darkness, it suddenly occurred to me that I had disobeyed every standard of care my parents had taught me. He could be looking for a weapon he kept handy for catches such as me. Or maybe he was going to open a trap door that would send me plummeting into the dirt-bottomed pit with the other boys he had captured this way, surviving on Italian cookies and pigs-in-a-blanket tossed down every week or two after catered events. Heat and moisture pushed to the surface of my face, and I started to feel dizzy, no longer certain which way the door was or whether I had heard him latch it closed. It sounded as if he was going upstairs, but that didn't seem right. Then those movements stopped, and the lights switched on.

At first I was disoriented, as though my momentary fear had affected my perception. Then, slowly, the room I was seeing began to make sense. It was an old kitchen, though half of it had been converted to a living room of sorts. It was big enough to have once been used to cook for large groups, but it lacked any of the attributes you might expect to see in a modern, restaurant kitchen. Most everything was made of wood, and everything that could be cut down to his level was: a table with four pillows around it where chairs would have been, a work desk where the telephone sat, a legless couch with two squat end-tables, a television set sitting on the floor. The parts of the room that were at a fixed height—the sink and countertops and cabinets and light switches—were made accessible to him by sets of free-standing stairs and poles: steps to go up, poles to come down. The stairs were like the small three-step sections we sometimes used in gym class, and there was a wide wooden plank laid like scaffolding across the ones that paralleled the countertop, so that he could move along its length without having to continually travel up and back down. The poles appeared to have been borrowed from indoor volleyball nets and had round, heavy bases that would bear his weight without tipping. As my view of the room gradually expanded to include him, he was sliding down one of them next to the light switch he had just flipped.

"So what do you think?" He took off his white gloves with a flourish and tossed them onto the couch. My speechlessness seemed to please him. "I've been working on this place weekends for almost a year, ever since they said they'd let me have it. You must be thirsty from all that singin." He went over to the refrigerator and opened the lower cabinet next to it. In my house (and in every other house I'd ever been in) the lower cabinets were for pots and pans, but this one was full of glasses. (I learned later that he kept his pots and pans in the upper cabinets, next to the stove, so that he didn't have to carry them up the stairs when he was cooking.) He took a glass out and opened the refrigerator door until it bumped the set of stairs just in front of it.

"Coke?"

"Sure. Thanks."

The shelves on the inside door of the refrigerator were full of Iron City beer, but there were a few bottles of Coke next to a cardboard carton of milk beneath the dome light. He took one of them down and opened it on the bottle opener that was attached at his eye-level to the counter. When he held both the glass and bottle out, it took me a moment to realize that, with both hands full, he couldn't bring them to me.

"Come on. Don't be shy," he said.

"Sorry."

"Nothing to be sorry about. Except I can't get my beer until you take these off my hands. There you go." He opened a beer and took a long pull straight from the bottle. "Ahh. I'm always tempted by those commemorative cans, but it just tastes better coming from a bottle." He lifted the bottle toward me.

"To the Buccos," he said. We both drank. "Which reminds me. Come over here." He tucked the bottle into the inside pocket of his tux jacket and began moving toward a partition I hadn't noticed. It was about six feet high, extended seven or eight feet into the room and, together with the existing back and side walls, formed a three sided room that I gathered he used for sleeping. But what he wanted to show me was on the outside of the partition.

Framed photographs of various sizes—some color, some black and white—covered the length of the makeshift wall in a band that ran from just below to just above his eye-level. As we passed along its length, it seemed to create a kind of time-line: photos that must have been him as a boy, almost always wearing a baseball cap; then he's one of a cluster of soldiers smiling in clean, starched uniforms, and then with some of those same faces, grim and beard-shadowed and mud-spattered in tilting helmets; then his legs are gone, with nothing intervening to tell the story, and his arms are around the shoulders of two hulking men, smiling and suspended between them in front of a long mirror-backed bar. I kept expecting him to stop and tell me about these people, but he had a particular photo in mind. Finally, he stopped and pointed and I understood.

"Know who these fellas are?" In the photo, he is in full catcher's gear, mask up, in the midst of three squatting figures in Pirate uniforms.

I pointed to each one. "Manny Sanguillen, Milt May, and…" The last one took me a minute. He was the bullpen coach, but at first I couldn't recall the caption from the game programs. "Dave Ricketts."

"You know your stuff. Very good. Dave's an old friend. He slips me a ticket or two whenever I ask, right in with the Pirate wives, which ain't a bad place to be, let me tell you. I play a pretty mean catcher, thanks to him. I'm not so great on offense, but I walk a lot. Small strike-zone. So, you interested?"

"What do you mean?"

"Wednesday night. First night World Series game ever. You and me and a bunch of beautiful ladies." He looked at me and waited. "Does your mouth hangin open like a fly trap mean yes?"

I closed it and my teeth made an audible click. "Yeah. I mean, yes. I mean, I have to ask my mom."

"I'm sure she'll be wantin to meet me. John."

"Excuse me?"

"John. John Kostka. That's my name. Lots of folks call me Swinger, but my good friends still call me John." He put out his hand as if introducing himself for the first time and we shook. "I could come by your place after school lets out, meet your mom, then we can head down to the bus stop and... What's the matter?"

"Nothing."

"You don't think she'll let you go with me, do you?" He looked neither surprised nor disappointed.

"I don't know," I lied.

"What about your dad?" I didn't say anything, but I could tell he understood. "Look, you leave it to me, okay. I can sweet talk an Eskimo out of her parka, no offense intended. When I'm done with her you'll be lucky if your mother doesn't steal your ticket and go with me herself. Hey." He made me look up from my shoes. "You got it?"

"Yeah."

"Good."

There was a soft knock at the door followed by the appearance of one of the young amputees.

"Sir?" he said.

"Come on in," John said, circling an arm. When the doors swung open the rest of the way, both young men were standing in the hall, balanced on crutches. "Something I can do for you boys?"

"Sir, yes sir," one of them said quietly. "We was told to come back here and talk to you for a little while before we head back."

"You don't look so sure."

"Well. We're here." The one whose leg had been taken from the knee down was speaking for both of them. His friend looked at the floor.

"Fine. I'm glad. My new friend and I here were just finishing up. You boys make yourselves at home." They came further into the room, looking around, as I must have done, like Neil Armstrong on the surface of the moon. They paused next to the truncated couch but didn't seem to know how or whether to sit. John turned to me.

"How about if I stop by tomorrow instead? Give your mother a full day to think about things. We could watch the last few innings of Game 3 together and get acquainted. I got a feeling Blass is gonna pitch us back into this thing tomorrow. Four o'clock about right?"

"Okay," I said. "I guess that would be all right." I told him where we lived and we shook hands again, as if agreeing to stand together against whatever fears my mother might have, and I somehow knew that in forty-eight hours I would be in Three Rivers Stadium watching the World Series.

"You mind showing yourself out while I teach these boys how to sit down?" One of the young men—the one who had done the talking for them—laughed softly while the other fidgeted hand to hand with an open pack of cigarettes.

"Sure."

"Goodnight, Hammer," he called when I'd reached the doorway. I turned back to wave and saw something I hadn't noticed before. From this angle, I could see just inside the first few feet of the section partitioned off as his bedroom. The end of his bed was visible—a mattress on the floor with crisply tucked corners—and at the foot of the bed stood a pair of combat boots, fully laced but untied.

WALT AND ALLIE

Walt comes through the back door from the neighbors' house just as Maggie and Henry are finishing the dinner dishes. Walt is seven, almost eight, and has only recently been permitted to walk home by himself from the Strummers'. When he comes in he has both hands in his pockets and looks mostly at the floor with a conscious nonchalance that belies the pride he feels at his new independence.

"Hey, Mom. Hey, Dad. What is up?" Since he first learned to talk, Walt has spoken in a soft, robotic monotone, and he uses a formal, mostly contractionless dialect, the source of which neither Henry nor Maggie can trace. He also has the low, resonant voice of a much older boy, and the combination makes him sound like a very proper suitor.

"I am very hungry," he says. "Can I have some dinner?"

"Hey, buddy." Henry musses Walt's thick, blond hair.

"I thought you were eating at the Strummers', sweetie." Maggie dries her hands and gathers Walt's face in her palms. He keeps his eyes on the floor as she plants a kiss on his forehead.

"Mom, they said they were having pizza, but it had these little fish on it."

"Anchovies?"

"Yes. I almost threw up." Walt sits down in the center of the kitchen floor next to Franny, who immediately lays her head in his lap.

"Alex likes anchovies?"

"Mom, he loves them. He was picking them out of the cheese and swinging them over his mouth and dropping them in. I literally almost threw up."

"Mrs. Strummer didn't ask you what you liked on your pizza before they ordered?" Maggie looks at Henry as she asks this.

"No, Mom. She did not."

"Jesus, that woman's clueless."

"Yes, Mom. And do you know why else she is clueless?"

"Why?"

"She is also clueless because she thinks that we are moving."

Henry and Maggie share a stunned silence as Walt continues petting Franny.

"What did she say to you, sweetie?" Maggie asks, still looking at Henry.

"She did not say anything. Alex did."

"What did Alex say?"

"He said that his mom said that Daddy might not be teaching here next year and that Alex should start to play with some other friends once in a while just in case."

"And what did you say?"

"I told him to suck on it."

Henry turns away to laugh, but Maggie is immediately crouching, looking Walt in the eye. "Walter Evan Graham! Where did you ever hear anyone say that?"

"Alex says it all the time."

"Do you have any idea what that means?"

"It means to suck on it."

"On what?"

"I do not know. Anchovies maybe. That would be really disgusting."

This time Maggie turns away, toward the kitchen counter, but she does so slowly, and Henry can't tell if she is laughing at what Walt has just said, or processing his earlier revelation. Henry steps between them.

"Don't ever say that, okay buddy? I can't tell you why, but just don't ever say it."

"Okay, Dad. Is it like the s-word and the f-word and the a-word?"

"Yes. Exactly."

"Except sometimes you can say the a-word if you mean a donkey."

"Right."

"And Mom?"

"Yes, Walt." Maggie's hands are on the counter and she doesn't turn around.

"I am still really really hungry."

"There's some pasta left over from what Daddy and I had. Would you like me to heat you up some spaghetti sauce for it?"

"Yes."

"Did you make a plate of the pesto for Ruthie?" Henry asks.

"On the counter. Bread and salad too. Walt, if you want, you can go play twenty minutes of Playstation while you wait."

"Sweet."

Henry seldom misses baseball anymore, except where his son is concerned. Walt is something of a video game savant, and Henry can't help but think—especially today, with the news of John's death—that his own childhood was better spent lying in bed next to the radio. No more active, perhaps, but at least there were real people to root for. Walt would spend eight hours a day in his imaginary world if permitted, so that what he perceives as the meager rations his parents dole out are like treasure trove. He stands now and runs out of the kitchen as if on fire. The fact that Maggie knows that he has likely spent most of the last three hours playing some blood-spattered game in the Strummers' basement is indicative of her suddenly fragile state of mind. Franny rises slowly—front end, then back—and leaves the kitchen to follow Walt.

"You okay?" Henry asks.

"I was going to ask *you*."

"Loren couldn't know anything yet."

"Isn't he chairing your review?"

"That doesn't give him more than one vote."

"But maybe he *knows*."

"He doesn't."

"Then why is Elvira talking to their son about it?"

"Since when did Elvira let accuracy stand in the way of good gossip? Trust me. Atlee says it's too early to tell, and too close to call."

Maggie's eyes widen and, for a moment, Henry thinks that will be the whole of her response.

"You talked to Atlee?" she finally says.

"Yesterday."

"And when were you going to share this information with me?"

"There was no information to share. I told you. It's too early to tell."

"But that *is* information! That's information that says our future is in doubt which, five minutes ago—for *me* at least—wasn't the case. Shouldn't we be out campaigning? Isn't that what people do? Shouldn't you be taking single malt to Loren to thank him for his wife's thoughtful care and feeding of our child? Shouldn't I be screwing *someone*, one tit or no?"

"You read my mind."

"If you think *those* plans are still on, you are not taking proper note of my tone."

"Then let's discuss plans for next weekend."

"What are you talking about?"

"John's memorial service. I think maybe we should go. I should go."

"Now? With all of this going on?"

"He's only going to die this once as far as I know."

"How can you be so flip about this? You love it here. *I* love it here. This is the only place Walt remembers living, and Allie is nothing but a hormone with long hair and braces. Incidentally, if we're moving, *you're* telling her."

As if on cue, Allie comes in through the back door and unloads a backpack onto the kitchen table that drops as if it contains cinder block. She has her mother's sharp features, made even more severe by the fact that her body appears to be expending all of its energy growing upward without any corresponding effort to gain weight, and her height is accentuated by straight brown hair that falls below her waist. After her mother's operation, Allie obsessively researched the possible side-effects of chemotherapy and found an organization online that collects donations of human hair to make wigs for cancer patients. Maggie kept her hair, and Allie continues to grow hers.

"Will someone please explain to me how the whole world is going paperless but I have to bring home five hundred pounds of books? God."

Jolted slightly by Allie's appearance during this conversation, Maggie has turned back to the stove to hide what might be remnants of the topic on her face.

"Hey, sweet pea," Henry says. "How was rehearsal?"

"Okay."

"Rapunzel, right?"

"That was funny the fourth time, Dad. We're doing *The Glass Menagerie*."

"Isn't Tennessee Williams a little dark for eighth grade?"

"The world's a dark place, Dad. Get used to it."

"The light bill is paid, and I'm in my very bright kitchen with two gorgeous women I adore. I'll get used to no such thing."

"Whatever. Hey Mom, is there any food?"

"I'm heating up some sauce for your brother but I'm not sure there are enough leftover noodles. Do you want me to put some more on?" Maggie turns around. "What happened to your hand?"

Two of Allie's fingers are taped together, and she holds them up as if she's just noticing them herself.

"We're doing self-defense in gym. I stoved them on Hannah Corning's sternum."

"Are you supposed to actually *hit*?"

"No. My arms are too long."

"They're perfect, sweetie. Do you want some pasta?"

"Sure. I'll be up in my room. Did anyone call? My cell died."

"Not that I know of, but I've been on the third floor working all afternoon."

Allie starts to re-shoulder her backpack when Franny appears in the doorway between the kitchen and dining room wagging her entire back side. She likely began her trek at the first sound of Allie's voice, but has just now arrived. Allie's indifferent demeanor, which is reserved strictly for Henry and Maggie, disappears instantly.

"Hey, old girl! How's my old girl?" She crosses the kitchen and drops to her knees, taking Franny's face in her hands the same way that Maggie had taken Walt's a few minutes earlier, except that Franny responds by slathering Allie's face with her tongue. "How was your day, huh? Busy? Were you busy missing me all day? Were you? Come on." Allie stands and keeps her hand on Franny's head as they leave the kitchen together.

"Don't you want your backpack?" Henry calls after her.

"Later," comes her reply, already halfway up the stairs. "Come on, old girl. You can make it."

"Hey, Mom!" Now it's Walt, yelling from the den as his eyes remain fixed on the television screen, his thumbs working furiously.

"Jesus. Can we agree that we're not done talking about this?" Maggie says to Henry, handing him a covered plate. "Take this out to your sister, please. Yes, Walt!"

"Mom, I just totally wasted Jabba the Hutt with my lightsaber, and I am now entering Level Five of the parallel universe."

"That's nice, sweetie."

"And Mom?"

"Yes, Walt."

"He did not even see it coming."

Maggie takes a few dishes to the sink and answers softly, under her breath. "That makes two of us."

"Don't worry." Henry puts a hand on her shoulder from behind. "Everything's going to be fine. I promise." He places Ruthie's dinner on a tray, slides the invitation under the salad bowl and leaves the kitchen through the back door.

5

I smelled his pipe the moment I opened the front door. Even though he seldom smoked it, my father somehow managed to keep the aroma fresh so that it hung on him like cologne. Until he left us, the scent didn't just belong to him, but to the house. Now I suddenly realized that the house only smelled that way with him in it.

It had been nearly a month since he'd gone and I hadn't seen or spoken to him. If he had called to attempt either one, my mother hadn't told me. So when I walked into the kitchen and he was sitting at the table reading the newspaper, alone, I felt as though I had gone back in time—that his leaving and my going to the game, the bus ride home, all the way up and through tonight, my strange evening at the VFW, seeing John's boots at the foot of his bed—all of that had been a dream, and that this—my father at the kitchen table—was simply a continuation of the unbroken reality of the family life I had taken for granted. I felt like Ebeneezer Scrooge waking to his second chance, only I didn't know what lesson I had learned or what I had done wrong in the first place.

His wavy brown hair was pulled back in a short ponytail and he was wearing what I had come to regard as his uniform: jeans, a tweed jacket and scuffed cowboy boots. Although it was evening, his face had a redness to it that it always had right after he shaved.

"Hey, sport." He folded the newspaper and set it on the table.

"Hey." I looked around the room, partly because I assumed that someone else must be home, but mostly because I found I couldn't look directly at my father.

"How did your concert go?"

"Okay. Where's Mom?"

"She and Ruthie went to pick Sam up at some boy's house. Sam claimed to be studying with him but your mother seems to think differently. I told her I'd wait for you."

"Mm."

"Mm? That's it?" My father turned toward me in his chair and slapped both faded blue knees twice with his hands. I stayed where I was. "You always going to be this friendly now, or just this first time?"

"I don't know."

"No. I don't suppose you do." He opened his paper again and I saw that he was reading the sports pages, though his glasses were tucked into his shirt pocket. Remembering this detail now, I think he must have been nervous, only pretending to be interested in the paper, but it never occurred to me to think of my father that way then. To me, he seemed both the man I missed so desperately and a complete stranger at the same time.

"Can't hit a lick, can they?" he said. "Except Clemente."

"So far."

"I wish I thought it was going to get any better. Four twenty-game winners on that Oriole staff. We've never seen pitching like this."

"Blass is gonna pitch us back into this thing tomorrow," I said, repeating what John had said to me just a few minutes earlier.

"I hope you're right, sport. Come here." He folded the paper into one hand and held the other out to me. I remember the power of that simple gesture. It held the gravitational force of memory. I couldn't ever remember *not* going to my father when he put his hand out that way, and I started toward him out of both habit and longing. I'd like to think I was able to hold back because of some kind of loyalty that seemed to be required of me in this new game between my parents, but mostly I knew that I would cry if he folded me in that arm, and I didn't want that to happen. I felt strangely as if I were trying to make a first impression on my own father, to assert myself in some way. When he saw that I wasn't going to come to him, his arm dropped. "Anyway," he said.

"She went on a date," I injected into the silence that followed. "Mom went on a date." I said it to hurt him, but it seemed to have the opposite effect.

"Really? That's great. That's really great. Who was it?"

"Mr. Garabedian."

My father laughed. "The guy from the office with the forehead that starts about here?" He laid his index finger halfway between his brow and his own hairline.

"He's nice."

"I'm sure he is, sport. When was this anyway?"

"Wednesday. While I was at the game." Again, I said it to hurt him, or at least to make him feel guilty, but neither registered on his face.

"Good. I was hoping those tickets wouldn't go to waste. Who'd you go with?"

"No one. I went by myself."

He laughed. "No, really."

"I *went* by my*self*." After my two failed attempts to get a reaction from him, I couldn't help but feel proud of the momentary look of disbelief that crossed his face. "Mom doesn't know. You're not gonna tell her, are you?"

"How did you get there?"

"The bus. Are you gonna tell her?"

"And what did you do with my... What did you do with the other ticket?"

"Nothing. I still have it."

"Jesus." He shook his head and smiled with half of his mouth. "Didn't take long for you to become the man of the house, did it?" When I didn't say anything, he reached into the inside pocket of his jacket and I hoped he might smoke his pipe, something he never did inside unless my mother was out of the house. Instead, he took out two tickets and placed them on the kitchen table. "Guess I won't be taking you to your first post-season game after all. First World Series game though. That's something. What's the matter?"

"Nothing."

"Look, I'm sorry about the game, okay? Your mother wouldn't answer my phone calls and I didn't want to just show up. But then when these fell into my lap, I figured what the hell?"

"The night game?"

"You got it. Boxes, third base side. History right in front of us."

"It's a school night. I don't know if Mom will let me go."

"I already got the okay. How could she say no, right? I'm picking you up at five and we'll get dinner somewhere. I mean, if you want to go. You don't look so sure."

"No, I want to go."

"Then what's the matter?"

"Nothing."

"Hey, this is hard for me too. You think I don't miss seeing you guys every day?"

"You haven't seen us once."

"I told you. Your mother wouldn't return my calls. She's mad, and I don't blame her. It's going to take a little while for all of us to get used to this, but everything's going to be fine. I promise. Okay?"

I nodded.

"That's my sport. Hey, I've been picking up the photos for you."

"What?"

"At the gas station. I think they saved some of the best ones for last. Oliver, Stargell, maybe Clemente. I'll bring them Wednesday night."

"Okay."

"Great. Like I said, we'll pick you up around five."

"We?"

"Yeah."

"Who else is coming?"

"My friend Jeanine. I thought it would be a good chance for you to get to know her a little bit. I think you'll really like her."

He was smiling, but I felt as if he had just struck me.

"The girl from your class?"

"She's not a girl, sport. She's a grad student who came back to school after working for a few years. And her father's the one who gave her the tickets, so I can't exactly tell her to stay home."

"Oh."

The back door opened and Ruthie was the first one through, jumping over the back of the kitchen chair my father was sitting in and wrapping her arms around his neck from behind, her feet suspended over the white tile floor.

"Daddy! You're still here!"

Sam came in behind her and didn't even look at him, followed by my mother.

"Of course I am, sweetie. You didn't think I'd leave without saying goodbye, did you?" Sam snorted and I realized this was the first she'd seen him.

"Hey Sammy," he said. "How'd the studying go?"

Without turning toward him, Sam said matter-of-factly, "Didn't Mom tell you? We weren't studying. We were fucking."

"Mom! Sam said the f-word!" Ruthie sang as she dropped to the floor.

"I'm right here, Ruthie. I can hear. That's lovely, Sam."

"Well, that's what you think, isn't it? I mean you just show up there without even calling, and then I'm being hauled up from the basement like a fucking criminal—literally—and—"

"Sam," my father interrupted. "Don't talk to your mother—"

Sam turned to him for the first time, her face in a rage I hadn't seen since the day he left. "No. *Fuck* you, Dad. You don't get to tell me what to do anymore, least of all how to treat my mother."

My father stood. "Listen, I'm still your father—"

"You're my father because you fucked Mom before she graduated and got stuck with me, just like you're doing to this new one."

"That's enough, Sam."

"No, Dad. It's not even close."

"Sam." Now it was my mother, and she was nodding toward Ruthie, who was starting to cry softly.

"Shit," Sam said. Then she left the room without looking at any of us.

Ruthie shuffled sideways and put her head against my father's waist and he laid his hand over her ear. My mother turned to the dish rack on the counter, opened the cabinet above her head and started stacking glasses inside. From the living room, the sound of the stereo needle being carelessly dropped and then scratched across the surface of a record preceded the plaintive rasp of Janis Joplin's voice into the kitchen, the volume absurdly high. My mother had to shout to be heard.

"I think you should go now!" she said.

Ruthie

The carriage house where Ruthie has been living for the past three years sits no more than twenty-five paces from the main house, a distance of some comfort to both parties, though for different reasons: Henry knows that he is close enough to his sister to respond to any emergency that might arise; and Ruthie, despite the proximity, has her own four walls which, admittedly, sometimes emphasize her solitude, but more often help her to feel more like a neighbor than a burden to her brother and his family. When the previous owners of the property added an attached garage to the main residence, they renovated the carriage house into a two-story living quarters for an elderly relative with an intercom connection to the house and an electric stair to the second floor. Ruthie's doctor would prefer that she walk the stairs herself for the exercise, but there are days when the numbness in her right foot is such that she doesn't trust herself, especially coming down.

Ruthie is five feet, three inches tall and weighs two hundred and twenty pounds, down from two hundred ninety when she moved in, something she is proud of. She would be the first to admit that the year after her father died was a self-destructive one. Her small psychotherapy practice, which had already dwindled to almost nothing during her father's illness, disappeared entirely and, having no one to take care of—neither her patients nor her father—she neglected herself as well. She ate her way through most days, ignoring her diet, only sporadically checking her insulin levels, all leading to several frightening seizures, extended hospital stays and, finally, a firm directive from her brother that she move in with them. When she first arrived it was hard for her even to cover the distance between the two houses. Now, most nights, she walks around the block with Henry, sometimes with Allie, and the dog. Because Franny doesn't move any faster than Ruthie, Ruthie doesn't feel that she slows them down much. And although she is winded and running with sweat when they drop her back at her front door, she no longer experiences the tightness in her chest that used to accompany every small exertion. She can't drive because of her foot, but she has no trouble getting from the parking lot into the Wegmans anymore, and she goes with Maggie once a week, shopping on her own in a motorized cart provided by the store.

Most nights, Ruthie cooks for herself, though Maggie insists on sending a plate out to her on the days she doesn't teach—Tuesdays and Fridays this semester—and on Sundays Ruthie walks over to the main house for dinner, bringing with her the salad or the bread or one of the tasteless (to her way of thinking) desserts she is allowed to eat. This being a Tuesday, Ruthie is sitting in her recliner working on a mosaic when Henry arrives with dinner.

"That you?" she calls. She is tiling a glass lampshade. Vines in shades of green and yellow surround a small white unicorn with a prismed horn. She removes her reading glasses and lets them fall to her chest before pushing the rolling table aside.

"If you mean me, then yes." Henry appears in the doorway holding a tray.

"Goodness, I could smell that as soon as you opened the front door. What is it?"

"Macadamia nut pesto."

"Am I allowed to have that?"

"Lots of *good* fat."

"Unlike this stuff." Ruthie grabs her midsection and pulls.

"Did you take your insulin?"

"Half an hour ago."

"What was your glucose?"

"One-ten."

"Good." Henry exchanges his tray for the one holding Ruthie's mosaic and pushes the table back over Ruthie's midsection. He stands looking down at the dome of cut glass. "This is beautiful," he says.

"It's for Allie's room. I'm hoping to grout it tomorrow."

"She'll love it. Water?"

"Please."

Henry sets the mosaic on the end-table next to the couch and goes into the kitchen. He takes a glass from the cabinet above the sink, fills it with ice and water, then opens the refrigerator and takes the low-fat vinaigrette from the shelf inside the door.

"Dressing?" he asks, holding the bottle up as he re-enters the living room.

"Lovely, thanks."

He hands the bottle to her and stands, fidgeting, as she pours. He picks up a framed photograph from the end table, an adult Ruthie and their mother smiling on either side of a baby-faced Pirate player he doesn't recognize, clear skies and palm trees in the background. Then he sits on the front half of one of the couch cushions, elbows on knees.

"You don't have to stay," Ruthie says.

"Just for a minute." Henry nods toward her tray. "There's an envelope there."

Ruthie lifts her salad bowl. "I didn't even see. What is it?"

"Open it."

Ruthie slides her reading glasses into place and takes the invitation out of the envelope. It's only a few seconds before she registers its meaning, and her eyes fill immediately. "Oh," she says, the tips of her fingers touching her lips.

"It just came today."

"How old would he have been?"

"Seventy-something, I think. One or two."

"That's amazing, isn't it? Living that long, the way he was."

"Yeah."

"I won't even get close."

"Ruthie."

"It's just a fact. But who would have thought it then?" Ruthie puts the invitation down and laughs. "Do you remember when Dad took all of us to the World Series?"

"Not one of those tickets was his."

"Why does that matter?"

"Sorry. It doesn't."

"Anyway. Do you remember the look on his face when we picked John up at the VFW?" Ruthie laughed. "I swear I could see the crowns on his back teeth in the rearview mirror."

"I remember he didn't like John from the moment he met him."

"Well. It was a hard time for everyone."

"Really? How was it hard for Dad?"

"You think he didn't miss us? Because I happen to have it on good authority that he did. For the rest of his life."

"A dying man examining the wreckage."

"An unpleasant luxury to which you will be entitled one day too."

"This is old ground for us, Ruthie. I just wanted you to know about John." Henry stands as if to go.

"You're sounding more and more like Sam," Ruthie says.

"Because it turned out she was right."

"Right about Dad, or right to be angry?"

"Both."

"It's never worthwhile to be angry about someone's nature. It's wasted energy."

"Better to be naïve?"

"Is that what you think? That just because I never stopped loving him that I kidded myself about him?"

"You used to talk about him coming back all the time."

"Henry, I was eight years old when he left. We *both* talked about it at first." Ruthie spins a fork of pasta, puts it in her mouth and chews slowly. "Mm. And things turned out okay for you. That woman can flat-out cook."

Henry manages a smile and sits again. "You're right. On both counts. I'm sorry. Thinking about John has me thinking about Dad is all."

"For someone who has changed his life the way you have, it's funny how you think everyone stays the same. You know your sister is thinking of having a baby?"

"Sam?"

"Mm hm."

"Now? She's almost fifty."

"It's been done. And if she can't, they may adopt."

"I'm shocked."

"Of course you are."

"What's she going to do about Save the Whales or the Redwoods or whatever it is she's saving these days?"

"Strap the kid to her back I'm sure." Ruthie takes another bite and picks the invitation up again as she chews. She laughs at what she is reading. "Are you bringing food or a six pack of bottles?"

"I was thinking you might be interested in going with me if

Maggie wants to stay behind. Even if she doesn't."

"I'd love to." Ruthie looks at the date again. "I'll have to change my flight down to Mom's. I'm supposed to leave next Friday. Last week of Spring Training."

"Already?"

"I was thinking you might join me this year. They've got lots of young talent."

"You mean lots of cheap salaries."

"Sitting on the first-base side in the shade at McKechnie Field in March there is nothing but possibilities."

Henry smiles. "Sucker."

"Deserter."

"Can I get you anything else before I go?"

"You could bring Walt. He'd love it."

"He hates baseball."

"Has he ever been to a real game?"

"And he's got school that week."

"You didn't answer my question."

"In case you hadn't noticed, we're three hundred miles from the nearest major league city."

"What about the Binghamton Mets? They're less than an hour away."

"I thought we were talking about Spring Training?"

"We're talking about your son growing up without baseball. It's not healthy."

"Okay, Doc. Is our time up for the day?"

"Fine. Be that way. Thank Maggie for me, will you?"

"Sure."

There is a soft knock at the door followed by the sound of the latch turning.

"That will be your other child," Ruthie says. "Could you quickly slip that lampshade into my bedroom please?"

"Sure."

When Allie enters the room she is a different girl than the one who came home from rehearsal not twenty minutes earlier. She is smiling, carrying a plate in one hand, a script in the other.

"Hi, Aunt Ruthie," she says.

"Hello, angel. What happened to your hand?"

Allie holds up her taped fingers. "Self-defense."

"I'm sure it was."

"Will you run some lines with me while I eat?" She lays her plate on the coffee table and sits on the couch cushion from which Henry has just risen.

"Certainly. Who am I tonight?"

"Jim O'Connor."

"Oooh, that cad."

"And maybe a little Laura too."

"I'm not sure I can be too convincing as the fragile waif, but I'll give it my best shot. *Ah'l put lots of ay-ah in mah voyce.*"

Allie laughs. "*I'm* the fallen southern belle, Aunt Ruthie."

"You should have gotten Laura. You're better than what's-her-name."

"Pamela. And how do you know?"

"Because you're *good*." Henry comes back in from the bedroom. "She's really *good*, Henry."

"I know. Don't stay too late, okay sweet pea?"

"I won't."

"And could you bring Aunt Ruthie's dishes back with you when you come?"

"Sure."

Henry leaves the room but slows his pace in the small foyer, enjoying the sound of his daughter and his sister talking. If there are difficulties associated with having Ruthie live with them, they are more than offset, in Henry's mind, by the buffer role she has been able to play during Allie's adolescence.

"Who's playing Jim O'Connor again?" he hears Ruthie ask.

"Nathan."

"He's the cute one, right?"

"Big time."

Henry lets himself out quietly and begins the short walk back to the house. Only last week there was still snow on the ground, but now the air feels even warmer than it did this afternoon, and he wonders if they might get an early spring. In the lighted kitchen window Maggie is finishing the dinner dishes and Henry stops to watch his wife. Her face, so animated in the presence of others, falls of its own weight into the deepening lines around her mouth. She lays the large pasta pot in the drainer and then leans heavily on the front edge of the sink, staring out toward Henry but seeing, he is certain, only her own reflection in the darkened pane.

Before the huge regional high school was built, the building that became Riverside Elementary had been the local high school. Erected just after the turn of the century, it was an imposing, cavernous three-story stone structure with heavy front doors flanked by pillars as big around as oaks that reached upward all the way to the eaves beneath the slate roof. Everything about the school was meant for people much larger than ourselves, and it felt almost as though the older students were still there, mocking us. The iron backboards that rose from the asphalt playground had chain-link nets set at NBA regulation height. The shelves on the insides of the tall, narrow lockers were too high for most of the younger students to reach. The hallways were dark, wide, high-ceilinged concrete and marble throughways that echoed with unchanged voices that all sounded female, and stepstools stood next to the water fountains. In the first floor boys' bathroom there was a giant stain of a star on the marble wall—as tall as I was—that had been pissed there by a high school boy at least ten years earlier, the lines dripping like tears where his urine had seeped downward before drying. When I visit my own children's schools—with their primary-color-coded floor plans, carpeted common areas and "No-Bullying Zone" posters—I do not pine, in any way, for what others perceive as *the good old days*.

But one luxury we had that doesn't seem to exist anymore was the option of putting school on hold for more important events. Apollo launches and splashdowns, LBJ signing the Civil Rights Act, Nixon's Inauguration, Eisenhower's funeral, even the occasional solar eclipse had all been reason enough during my years at Riverside Elementary to wheel every television from the AV room into the cafeteria/auditorium so that we could share the experience together. The Pirates being in the World Series was no different, and no one was about to miss the weekday games just for the sake of the curriculum. At one o'clock sharp we were called, floor by floor, to file in to watch the game until the buses arrived. The fact that the Pirates were down two games to none only made our participation more important, and extra credit was handed out like candy at the doctor's office to kids wearing Pirate caps and jerseys or making signs that could be hung around the classrooms or in the hallways.

The entrance to the cafeteria resembled the entrance to a theatre-style auditorium, since that's exactly what it had been for the fifty years before the high school merger. Two sets of double doors, one stage-left and one stage-right, opened onto upward sloping ramps that passed beneath the low-slung balcony overhead. Once up and inside the room, the floor pitched gradually downward to a stage that had a full proscenium and heavy gold curtain. Overhead light came from two enormous, gothic lanterns that hung from the ceiling two stories up. The cafeteria tables were always set perpendicular to the stage, not parallel, I suppose so that some of the younger kids wouldn't lose their balance and fall backward off their stools. During important assemblies and evening school programs the tables were folded and pushed back up under the balcony, replaced by hundreds of folding chairs. But since there hadn't been time for that today, we sat as we did at lunch, pitched slightly sideways.

I saw Ruthie stand up at a table down front and she waved when she found me. Her teacher placed her hands gently on Ruthie's shoulders to sit her back down. Then I could hear the third and fourth graders (whose rooms were on the second floor) entering the balcony above us. Once they were settled, the televisions were turned on and Riverside Elementary was at the World Series.

Even from our vantage point at the back of the cafeteria it looked from the very first pitch like John was going to be right. Blass was unhittable. He worked both sides of the plate with a precision completely at odds with his free-wheeling limbs that all seemed to fling out in every direction from the center of his body at the moment of release. He was mesmerizing, and the entire student body hung on every pitch, even kids who probably hadn't watched a game all season. This was different. This was important, and everyone knew it. But remembering John's prediction also made me remember his promise: that he would stop by to sweet-talk my mother into letting me go to the game with him, and suddenly I could think of nothing but him arriving at our house before me, sprouting from the little patch of grass next to the driveway as she pulled in from work. My mother came home early on Tuesdays and Thursdays and was not only completely unaware of John's offer to take me to the game, but didn't know that my contact with him had gone beyond the brief sidewalk sighting I had told her about. For all I knew, she'd call the police. When my bus number was finally called in the bottom of the fourth, Blass still had a no-hitter going, and I bolted out the front doors and down the concrete stairs as if being first on the bus would get me home faster.

"Did you see Blass?" Ruthie said when she got on.

"Yeah."

"I *love* him."

She sat down and looked at me without saying anything for a while, waiting, I'm sure, for me to tell her to go sit with her own friends, but I was too distracted.

"You okay?"

"What?"

"You just *ran*."

I shrugged. Ruthie looked at me for a while, waiting. When she saw that she wasn't going to get any more of an explanation, she turned her little transistor radio on and the kids around us leaned in close.

I stopped at home just long enough to get my bike and then I pedaled as fast as I could, skidding to a halt just as John was coming down the wheelchair ramp outside the front door of the VFW. The tux from the night before had been replaced by the same leather harness and work gloves he'd been wearing the day I first saw him.

"Hey, Hank. I was just comin to see you."

I nodded, trying to settle my breath. "I can't come to the game with you," I blurted. He looked amused rather than hurt.

"I thought you were gonna let me talk to her at least. I told you, I can sweet-talk a—"

"I'm going with my dad."

"Oh." He shrugged. "Okay. I must have misunderstood you last night. It seemed to me like maybe your father wasn't around."

"No. He's around."

"Good. I'm glad to hear that. It just seemed funny, you goin to that game by yourself last week." When I didn't say anything, he cocked his head back toward the door. "You want to come in and watch? Blass is pitchin a beauty, just like I said."

"Yeah. I know. But I gotta go. I promised my sister I'd watch with her. And maybe my dad. He said he might come home early."

"Okay. No problem. Hey, tomorrow night, why don't you both come say hello? Section 41, right behind home plate. There'll be a beautiful lady in your seat."

"Okay. Maybe." I put my foot on the right pedal and got ready to push off.

"And kiddo?"

"Yeah?"

"You stop by here any time, all right?"

"Okay."

At home, Ruthie was already settled in on the couch with the game on, and my mother was starting dinner in the kitchen. Sam, freed from her after-school babysitting duties on the days when my mother was home to greet us, was already at her boyfriend's house. I sat down beside Ruthie.

"Where did you go in such a hurry?" she asked.

"I left something at the concert last night."

"What?"

"Nothing."

We watched quietly for a while as Blass mowed down one Oriole batter after another, working fast. I don't remember him shaking Sanguillen off once, and the quick, loose, slinging motion that snapped his head back with every pitch was like a three-second video on a constant repeat loop. He couldn't miss.

"Why doesn't The Gunner sound excited?" Ruthie asked. "Blass is clobberin them."

"That's not Bob Prince. It's Curt Gowdy."

"Who?"

"Curt Gowdy. He announces for NBC."

"Where's The Gunner?"

"On the radio."

"I don't like this guy. He doesn't even sound excited."

"You said that already."

"But he doesn't."

"He's not supposed to root for one team or the other. He's supposed to stay neutral."

"That's stupid. Why would you watch baseball if you didn't want someone to win?"

"It's his *job*, that's why."

"It's The Gunner's job too. I'm going upstairs."

"But don't you want to *see*?"

"This feels weird. I'm going up to listen." She pushed herself off the couch.

"Just wait a second, will ya? I'll go up and get it next commercial."

So that's how Ruthie and I stumbled upon what I later learned was the routine in nearly every household in Pittsburgh that October. We set the radio next to the television, turned the volume down on Curt Gowdy and listened to The Gunner call the Pirates. *His* Pirates. And when Frank Robinson finally solved Blass with a home run in the seventh to pull within a run, Prince sounded as though he was personally offended, his slag pile of a voice barely rising above a foul-tip call.

The game only gave the illusion of being close. In the bottom of the same inning, Clemente led off with a come-backer to Cuellar at the mound that should have been an easy out. But Cuellar seemed surprised by Clemente's trademark sprint to first—even on sure outs—and he threw high, pulling first baseman Boog Powell off the bag. Flustered, Cuellar walked the struggling Stargell on four pitches, and big Bob Robertson came to the plate. Robertson didn't have a single hit so far in the series and he had already struck out twice against Cuellar, so when the count went to one ball and one strike and Murtaugh saw Brooks Robinson playing deep and hugging the line at third, he sent in a signal for Robertson to bunt the runners over. When Robertson gave no indication of having seen the sign, third base coach Frank Oceak went through the motions again. Still nothing from Robertson, who hadn't been asked to bunt all season. Clemente, who had seen the sign, raised his arms over his head from second base to call timeout, but it was too late; Cuellar was already into his windup. Robertson drilled the pitch deep into the seats in right-center field for a three-run homerun, and the game was as good as over.

"*You can kiss it goodbye!*" whooped The Gunner and Ruthie in unison. A yelp came from the kitchen too, and I realized that my mother had been watching on the black and white portable.

"Did you see that?" she called. As if her voice had carried it, I smelled the chicken pot pie, my mother's specialty and Ruthie's favorite.

"We saw it, Mom!" Ruthie answered. "Can we eat in here?"

Clemente crossed the plate, then Stargell, then Robertson. Stargell was laughing and said something to Robertson, which he repeated later for a reporter: "Nice bunt."

My mother emerged from the kitchen carrying a stack of place settings. She was wearing an apron over green bell-bottoms and a white tank top. "No. We're eating in the dining room tonight, but we'll wait until after the game. Can you both please set the table during the next commercial?"

After Jackie Hernandez grounded out to end the seventh, Ruthie and I raced to the dining room and divided labors so that we wouldn't miss anything. Whenever Ruthie set the table, she insisted on making place cards for everyone and deciding on the seating arrangements. She went into the kitchen and came back with a pencil and four recipe cards. "I get to sit next to Sam tonight," she said. "Mom's on the end and Sam and I are on this side."

"You can sit next to her every night, as far as I'm concerned," I said.

My mother came in carrying the water glasses we only used when we had company. I noticed that she was wearing makeup.

"Sam's staying at Matthew's for dinner."

"But there are four plates."

"Mark... Mr. Garabedian is joining us. Won't that be nice?" Ruthie stopped writing. "Here, I'll help you spell it, sweetie. Just erase Sam and put Mr. Garabedian in that chair."

Ruthie dropped her pencil. "I'm not sitting next to him."

"Well then just switch with Henry."

"I'm not sitting across from him."

Blass already had two strikes on the first Oriole batter in the eighth but Ruthie wasn't listening.

"Don't be silly, sweetie. There are only four of us. You're either going to be sitting next to him or across from him."

"Not if I sit at the other end."

"Ruthie."

"What if Daddy comes home and sees him!?"

"Sweetie, Mark is just my friend. And we've talked about this. Daddy's not going to be coming home."

"He came home last night!"

"That was just for a visit. And to tell Henry about the game tomorrow night."

Ruthie's eyes got wide and she turned to me. "You're going to the *game*?" I looked down and straightened a fork on its napkin. "With *Daddy*?"

"What? Was I supposed to say no?"

"Sweetie, I don't think Daddy even knows you like baseball now."

"Yeah. And they only have one extra ticket anyway," I said.

"*They*?" Ruthie and my mother asked in unison. I found another fork to adjust.

After a while, my mother just said, "Shit," and then Ruthie started to cry. It wasn't like the night before, when my father and Sam had been fighting. This time, Ruthie was angry.

"He *always* gets to go!"

"Ruthie, don't be so dramatic. This is his first game."

"No! When Daddy lived here, he *always* took Henry. Just because he's a boy. Now he finally comes home one day and Henry gets to go again. And Daddy's taking his girlfriend instead of me. It's not fair!"

"You think *I* want to go with her?" I asked. "But she's the one who got the tickets."

"Then let *me* go! You got to go *last* week."

"No he didn't, Ruthie. No one went last week."

"Oh yes he did!" I looked at her hard, but it was already too late. "He went by *himself*. On the *bus*!"

By now, every utensil on my side of the table had been surgically aligned, and I felt my mother's eyes boring through the top of my head.

"He *what*? When was this?"

Ruthie stopped crying. She seemed to suddenly regret her revelation and spoke quietly. "That night you went out for dinner with Mr. Garba... Mr.... the hairy guy. He went by himself, Mommy. And there was another ticket."

The silence that followed may have lasted only a few seconds, but by the time the doorbell rang, delaying my execution, I had invented and discarded at least a dozen possible explanations. Ruthie bolted for the stairs.

"We'll talk later, young man. Ruthie! You come down and at least say hello, do you hear me?" Ruthie stopped halfway up the stairs, dropped back down and ran into the living room where she picked up the radio, pulled the plug and made for the stairs again. My mother reached for her as she passed, but Ruthie ducked and was already at the top when the doorbell rang again. "I'm not kidding, Ruthie! I want you down here. Henry, answer the door." She removed her apron, wiped quickly at her forehead and the sides of her nose with it, and hung it over the banister. Then she took half of her ponytail in each hand and tugged them apart, cinching it tight. By the time

I opened the door she had come up behind me and put her hands on my shoulders. Her grip was tight and close to my neck, as if she would have preferred to have been strangling me.

"Hello, Mark," she said. "I'm so glad you could come."

"Hi, Beth. You look beautiful." Mr. Garabedian held a bottle of wine in one hand and clutched a mishmash of wildflowers in the other. He looked like a cartoon of a nervous suitor. And Ruthie hadn't exaggerated. Even dressed in his suit from work I could tell he was the hairiest guy I'd ever seen. The backs of his hands were black with it and a tuft was creeping out from behind his tightly knotted tie. His face was red and freshly shaven but a dark shadow already showed beneath the surface. The hair on his head was neatly trimmed but started just a few inches above his heavy eyebrows, like he was wearing a hairpiece that had fallen forward. "And this must be Henry." He made a motion to shake my hand but he couldn't quite figure out how to shift the flowers without scattering them everywhere. I let my own hand drop as obviously as possible. "Your mother has told me a lot about you. She's very proud of you."

My mother's grip tightened at the base of my neck. "Thanks," I managed.

"Henry, could you please run upstairs and see if your sister's ready yet?"

"Okay."

"Mark, why don't you follow me into the kitchen while I finish dinner. And we'll get those lovely flowers into some water."

I went upstairs. From behind Ruthie's closed door The Gunner called a come-backer to Blass for the last out in the eighth. The crowd was on its feet for him as he left the mound and I could scarcely hear Prince's lead-in to the break. Then it was his voice again, clear and pre-recorded, reciting the wonders of Hillshire Farm's Hickory Smoked Sausage. I knocked.

"Go away."

I opened the door and went in. Ruthie sat on the floor surrounded by chocolate bars, one half-eaten already in her hand.

"Close the door," she said. I did and then sat across from her.

"One more inning," I said.

"Yeah."

Neither of us said anything as we sat and listened to the Pirates go quietly in order in the bottom of the eighth. It was almost as if they wanted to get Blass back out there as quickly as possible to finish them off, which he did: 5-1 Pirates, and a complete game three-hitter for Blass. We were back in it and I was going to the game that could tie the Series. Ruthie turned the radio off. She had finished her chocolate bar and was tearing open another.

"We're having dinner in a few minutes."

"So?"

My mother called from the bottom of the stairs in a voice that sounded nothing like her own. "Kids! Come on down. Time for dinner," she sang, both cheerful and pleading. I stood and waited for Ruthie. I don't know whether she heard the same thing in our mother's voice that I did, but the fight had gone out of Ruthie. She carefully stacked all of the chocolate in a shoe box and slid it under her bed.

"You ready?" I asked her.

"I guess."

Down in the dining room my mother had solved the seating crisis in our absence. We hadn't thought of putting Ruthie in the big armchair at the head of the table because she never sat there, but that's where her place card was, with my mother to her left and me to her right. Mr. Garabedian would sit next to my mother on that long side of the table, neither next to, nor across from Ruthie. If Ruthie was particularly pleased with the seating arrangements, she didn't say. She climbed into the armchair that dwarfed her like a throne, sat back, crossed her legs (which stuck straight out) and crossed her arms.

"Here, honey. Let me scootch you in a little."

"I'm not a baby, Mom."

"I didn't say you were. You just seem a little far away."

"Only babies get scootched."

"Fine. Scootch yourself."

Ruthie climbed out of her chair, turned to face it and pulled it toward her, ducking, until both she and the heavy arms she was tugging were under the table. Then her head reappeared and she pulled herself up as if through an open manhole cover.

Mr. Garabedian, who had seated himself by then, said, "My, you *are* a big girl." I immediately felt sorry for him.

"You only say *that* to babies too," Ruthie said.

"Ruthie."

"It's true, Mom."

"Well, Mr. Garabedian doesn't have any children so I don't think he's familiar with that little *rule* of yours."

"You don't have any kids?"

"No, I don't. I've never been married."

"How old are you?"

"*Ruthie.*"

"It's okay, Beth. I'm not sensitive about my age. I'm forty-three."

"How come you never got married?"

"Oh, I don't know. I never met the right person when I was younger, and then I started my own business and got too busy."

My mother had begun dishing steaming spoonfuls of pot pie onto everyone's plates. "Mr. Garabedian owns the insurance company I work for. He's always there when I arrive in the morning, and he's still working when I leave every day."

"How come you got to leave early today?" Ruthie asked.

"Ruthie Graham. If you're going to spend the entire meal being rude to our guest, you can just go back upstairs to your room." Had it not been for the pot pie, I think she would have done just that, but even with two chocolate bars in her stomach, Ruthie didn't want to miss her favorite dinner. She started eating and we were all quiet for a while.

"This is delicious, Beth. Most of my dinners come in a block of ice."

"My daddy's a professor," Ruthie said. "He's really smart."

"Ruthie."

"What, Mommy? That's not rude. It's just true."

"It's your tone and you know it. Why don't you just eat quietly for a while. We haven't heard anything from Mr. Baseball over there yet."

Mr. Garabedian looked at me, relieved to be momentarily freed from further exchange with Ruthie. "So who's your favorite player?"

"Clemente."

"Even I know him. He's beautiful to watch. Graceful."

"I guess."

"So you like the Pirates, then?"

"Yeah."

"A little too much, apparently," my mother said. "Seems he caught a PAT bus to the stadium last week so that he wouldn't miss the game his father was supposed to take him to."

"I think that shows initiative," Mr. Garabedian said. "I'm not much of a sports fan, but if you're willing to take risks to do something you love, I think that's great."

My mother laughed. "If I didn't already know you don't have kids, I'd know it now. We haven't discussed the particulars of his punishment yet, but after tomorrow night, I don't think he'll be leaving the house unchaperoned for a while."

"What's tomorrow night?"

"He's going to the game with his father."

"It's the first World Series night game ever," I told him. My mother smiled, pleased, I think, that someone was making an effort to engage her guest. Ruthie, reminded of the slight that had sent her up to her room, decided to engage him as well.

"If you had three tickets to the World Series, who would you take?"

"Well, I don't know. I've never even been to a regular game."

"Me neither!"

"Do you like baseball?"

"I love it."

"Then I'd take *you*."

"Who else?"

Mr. Garabedian looked at my mother, then at me. "I don't know. That's a tough one."

"*He's* already going," Ruthie said, nodding in my direction.

"All right. Then I'd take you and your mother."

"My daddy's taking Henry and his girlfriend."

"You have a girlfriend?" Mr. Garabedian asked me.

"*No*," Ruthie said. "My *dad's* girlfriend."

"Oh."

"Do you think that's fair?"

"Ruthie," my mother interjected.

"I'm just asking."

"But we've been over this already. They're *her* tickets."

"How can *you* be on her side, Mom? You're supposed to *hate* her."

"I've never met her."

"But she stole our daddy." Ruthie said this softly, and the sudden, stark contrast with the spirited tone of the rest of her argument up to this point quieted everyone.

"She didn't steal anything, sweetie," my mother finally said. "And I don't want to talk about this now."

We ate in silence, looking at our plates, until the front door opened and Sam strode into the dining room pulling Matthew by the hand.

"Oh shit," were her first words.

"That's nice, Sam. You remember Mr. Garabedian, don't you?"

"Yeah, sure."

"Hello, Sam."

"Aren't you going to introduce him to your friend?" asked my mother.

"This is Matthew."

Matthew nodded once, quickly, and the bangs that were covering his eyes jumped out, then settled back. "Hey," he said. His right hand stayed in Sam's and his left scratched at a pimple on his chin.

"We left Matthew's because his house was like crawling with people. Can we go upstairs?"

"Excuse me?"

"We ate at Matthew's, Mom," Sam said, already sounding exasperated. "We just want to hang out." Then, seeing the look on my mother's face, her tone changed. "And we don't want to interrupt you guys or anything."

"Yeah," added Matthew, nodding.

My mother's hand went to her forehead as if taking her own temperature. "Door open. No music."

"You won't let me have the stereo in my room anyway."

"No radio."

"What do you think we're going to do up there with all of you—"

"Sam. Please."

Sam turned and pulled Matthew back out into the hall.

"Nice seeing you again, Sam," Mr. Garabedian called. "Nice meeting you, Matthew." It sounded like Matthew might have grunted something in response but they were already around the corner.

My mother shook her head at Mr. Garabedian and gave him a tired smile. "I suppose you admire her initiative."

"She's got spirit," he said.

"Oh, she's got that going for her all right."

We finished eating and cleared the table, and then while Ruthie and I watched TV in the living room, Mr. Garabedian and my mother stayed in the kitchen to finish cleaning up. I kept the volume low, wanting to know what was happening in there, but all I could hear was running water and clanking dishes. Once in a while, one of them said something but too low for me to discern any actual words. After a while the water shut off and Mr. Garabedian came into the living room to say goodbye to Ruthie and me. My mother followed him into the hall and they both said goodnight, and then my mother was back in the living room, standing next to the couch.

"He has to get up early tomorrow for work," she said, looking at the television. Then she sat down next to Ruthie and, reaching around her to find me as well, took us both in her arms. "You guys have school tomorrow, and you, Henry Graham, have a big night out. Go on up and I'll come tuck you in in a minute."

It was still early, but neither of us argued. Upstairs, passing Sam's room, I could see her sitting on the floor with Matthew, their backs against her bed, shoulders touching, fingers laced. I was focused on their hands and didn't see her see me.

"What're you looking at?" she said.

Ruthie and I got ready for bed. She brought the radio back into my room so that we could listen to the talk shows. The same callers who, the night before, had already counted the Pirates out of the Series, were now sure they'd win it. Never mind that the Orioles were the defending World Champions and had won more than a hundred games three years in a row. Never mind their four twenty-game winners. Never mind that, for the historic first night game, the Pirates would be starting the most unfortunately named pitcher in baseball, Luke Walker, who had spent most of the season living up to his name. I turned to remind Ruthie, to warn her against listening to all of this talk, but she was already sleeping. I thought about what she'd said the first time my mother had gone to dinner with Mr. Garabedian—*I'm not letting him be my daddy*—and I figured it must have been an exhausting night for her.

I don't know what made me go back downstairs except that it still wasn't my usual bedtime and my mother hadn't come up to say goodnight. Only an inch of dim light was visible at Sam's door when I passed, and I could hear my sister's breath coming heavily through her nose. There was no sound coming from downstairs, and I wondered if it was possible that my mother had gone to bed with Matthew still in the house. But the lights were still on and when I rounded the corner of the kitchen doorway, my mother was sitting at the table crying.

I think I expected her to be embarrassed, to pick up a napkin and turn away, make some excuse about fighting a cold, anything but what she did, which was to look right at me and smile, tears still filling her eyes.

"Hey there," she said.

"What's the matter, Mom?"

The smile never left her face but she wasn't trying to hide anything with it. And that made me feel different, older, as if she was forgetting, just for this moment, that I was a child.

"Nothing and everything, if that makes any sense," she said.

I nodded, mostly because I thought I was supposed to, and went back upstairs.

I went straight to Ruthie and touched her shoulder. She opened her eyes, slowly at first, then wide when she saw me.

"What's the matter?" she said.

"Nothing. Do you really want to go to the game with Dad tomorrow?"

"Are you kidding?"

"Because I think I might know where to get another ticket."

STORIES

Henry is sitting up in bed reading Natalie Currant's pages, and Maggie is curled sideways, facing away from him. Whatever sense of romance accompanied their dinner together has been lost not only to Henry's revelation about his tenure review, but to feeding Ruthie and the children and overseeing homework and Walt's nightly bedtime ritual. Henry isn't resentful because the mood has left him as well. His only regret is that he didn't try harder to coax Maggie upstairs while she was cooking, make love to her while they were alone and wide awake and playful. Like any otherwise happily married couple, the greatest enemy to their intimacy is routine.

This is another part of their routine—Henry reading his students' work while Maggie sleeps beside him in the crescent of light that reaches her from his bedside lamp. A hyperkinetic ferment by day, Maggie can sleep through an air raid. Henry, on the other hand, expends his daily allotment of energy with a seeping evenness that requires an hour or so of work in bed before he is drained enough for sleep.

For most of the years of their marriage that work had been

writing. Even a sentence or two. A few words written before sleep almost always grew into something more in the morning, as if Henry's dreaming self turned them over and over and pushed them out from their center like clay. But since Maggie's diagnosis, it has been impossible to find importance in stories, especially his own. His student's work still carries weight because of its significance to them; Henry's stories have stayed in remission even as Maggie's cancer has entered it. She knows it but won't push him; he's aware of the timing but won't admit the connection. So this unspoken fact lies here between them every night, neither one willing to accept the guilt that would accompany giving it voice. It is easier, instead, to admit this new routine; easier to rationalize that reading is more conducive to sleep than writing anyway.

But tonight, Henry is more alert than usual. His glasses, which always make him appear awed by what he is reading are, this time, revealing the truth. And as though disturbed by something audible in his animation, Maggie is restless.

"Are you almost finished?" she asks her pillow.

"Jesus this is good."

"What?"

"I mean it could use some trimming but it's really good."

"Your little friend?"

"Yes. I mean, no. Yes, it's Natalie's."

Maggie rolls toward him. "A story?"

"The beginning of a novel, I think. It opens with a girl visiting her mother in jail. Care to guess why?"

"Her mother killed her father for bedding a student."

"No. Her mother has just been jailed for an old murder, convicted by twenty-year-old DNA evidence. Turns out the mother killed a pregnant woman and stole her baby."

"The daughter."

"Yeah."

"So the daughter is staring through the prison glass at the woman she's lived with all her life who killed her real mother."

"Five pages in."

"Sheesh."

"Yeah."

"But can she write?"

"She's underplaying it just right so far. This opening scene focuses on all the mundane details: the echoes from the cellblock, the tattoo on the back of the neck of the guard who leads her into the visitation room, the smell of stale smoke on the telephone receiver she picks up. The reason why she's there—what her mother did, or, not her mother I guess—those details are dropped in with no more emphasis than the description of the chicken wire in the glass between them."

"Has she shown this kind of talent before?"

"She's better than most. But nothing this focused, this tight. I can see why she was so anxious for me to read it."

"I promise I'll be more impressed in the morning. Or more jealous, maybe. More something."

"Do you want me to go downstairs?"

"Do you mind?"

"No."

Maggie's eyes are already closed again when Henry kisses the side of her face and rolls away to turn off the lamp. In those first seconds the room is blind-black, and he has to use his hands to search his side of the bed for Natalie's opening chapter. Then he hears a rustling and his forearm brushes against a stack of pages in mid-air. Maggie is holding them out to him. "Thanks," he whispers, then feels his way around the bed and out into the hall.

Five steps below him on the landing where the stairs turn back on themselves to disappear under Henry's feet, the huge stained glass window floats silently, glowing dimly with moonlight, and for the second time tonight Henry is struck by how much he has come to love this house. This time he recognizes that his nostalgia has deeper origins than the slim possibility that they may have to leave it. This house reminds him of his childhood home: the one that has been so much on his mind today; the one that his father left. And when his mother finally decided that the rest of them should do the same, he had no real sense of the courage that took. It wasn't until almost thirty years later, when he quit his job and uprooted his own family to come here, that he gained some appreciation for his mother's bravery. When they arrived on campus Henry had never taught, and Maggie had done nothing *but* teach — for ten years, at their local high school, where the one hundred-plus students per semester exhausted any energy that might have gone into her own work. So they came here as a "package deal," with a simple but elegant plan: Henry would use his writing to make a new career as a professor, and Maggie would use this new version of her old career to make time for her art. Until his recent meeting with Atlee, it had mostly worked just like that, and somehow the house had seemed to nurture them both. It felt big and wise around them, its drafty windows and groaning floors and ticking radiators like constant reminders that they were not alone.

Henry stands listening to his house now, staring at the stained glass window until it starts to move and disorient him. When he finally flips the switch to the chandelier at the base of the stairs, the light bursts up from below like a silent explosion, instantly draining all of the color from the window.

Henry teaches both contemporary fiction and creative writing. The former he could mostly do without. It's not the material, which he chooses himself — DeLillo, Russo, Alice Munro, Toni Morrison, Tim O'Brien, early Irving — but the way the University expects him to talk about it: thematically, structurally, debating what "school" the writer might fit neatly into, none of which (he is almost certain) concerned any of the writers themselves. He likens it to asking a food critic to review the new French bistro based on a detailed reading of the recipes. Which is why Henry asks his students (often enough that they eventually begin to finish the sentence for him), "But what does it *taste* like?" Setting aside style and structure and theme, why does one story move them while another doesn't? He considers being privy to the nerves and longings of his students — most of whom will never write another word once they leave here — to be just that: a privilege. The course catalog calls his workshop "Writing Longer Fiction," but Henry understands that there is very little that comes out of a college student that can truly be called fiction. They all have the sense that their common experience is unique, that their adolescence (always spent in the company of an incomparably dysfunctional family) stung more sharply than others, and that their emergence from it constitutes the achievement of a lifetime. It is his assurance that they are all correct in this belief — that much of what is worth writing about in their lives has already happened, and that those experiences *are* worthy of art — that creates the connection between Henry and his students he's not sure he could do without.

Downstairs, before he has even managed to settle himself on the living room couch to begin reading again, footsteps creak lightly above, followed by the sound of Walt's bedroom door opening. Walt is a light sleeper and often finds a reason to come downstairs when he hears one of his parents — usually Henry — moving through the rooms below him. Tonight, as quiet as Henry has been, it's almost as if the light itself, with no more brightness than smoke by the time it seeps under Walt's door, is what has wakened him. As the footsteps descend the stairs, Henry tries to look as though he has been busy for some time. Walt views a parent with free time as an invitation to fill it.

"Dad?" Walt has been sleeping on his left side and looks as if he's standing in a strong wind from that direction.

"Hey, buddy. Who's doing your hair for you these days?"

"Dad, we did not check on Freddie before bed." Walt's low voice is further deepened by a sleep-filled throat.

"What, buddy?"

"We always check on Freddie before bed and we forgot."

Relative to expected life-span, Freddie the goldfish is even older than Franny, and Henry is hoping for a teachable moment that might help smooth Franny's eventual passing for Walt. They look in on Freddie together every night, but this evening's tension eclipsed their routine. Henry rolls off the couch, takes Walt's hand and they walk together into the kitchen where Freddie's small plastic tank sits on the counter.

"Is he dead yet, Dad?"

"Not yet, buddy. He looks close though. He's sort of got that Nemo one-fin thing going."

"How long would you guess that he has to live?"

"I'm guessing a few days, tops. What do you think about flushing him now and saving everyone the suffering? A formal burial at sea."

"No. I want to watch him."

"But he's dying, buddy."

"That is life, Dad."

Henry shakes his head, mostly at himself, because his own son is a complete mystery to him. He was certain that Freddie's death would devastate the boy, and instead he is waxing philosophical.

"True enough. You got me there."

"What is it like to be dead, Dad?"

"I can't say for sure. I can only guess. But since it happens to everyone, I'd guess it's not too bad. Nice even."

"Can you visit the earth?"

"I don't know. That would be pretty cool, wouldn't it?"

"Yes. Do you sleep in heaven?"

"I don't know that either. Sleep is mostly to rest your body, so maybe you wouldn't need to. Or maybe your soul needs rest too."

"Yes, Dad. My soul sometimes gets really tired. Do they have first grade?"

"I don't know. I doubt it."

"Because everyone in heaven is really old?"

"Mostly."

Walt appears to consider this for a moment. "Did you ever know anyone who died?"

"Sure."

"Pap Pap?" Walt was just four when Henry's father died, and he'd only met him a few times, but he always talked about his grandfather as if he'd been an omnipresent member of the family.

"Yes, Pap Pap."

"When am I going to die?"

"Oh, not for a very long time."

"Twenty-five years?"

"Much longer than that. You won't die until you're a grandpa or even a great-grandpa."

"So Grammy is going to die soon?"

"I didn't say that. Don't tell your mother I said anything like that, okay buddy?"

"Okay." He looks away from Freddie and up at Henry. "When I die, will you be there up in heaven?"

"Most definitely. I'll die way before you do."

"But I do not want you to die, Daddy!" Walt starts wailing, and Henry scrambles to comfort him before Maggie hears.

"No, no, buddy! I'm not going to die for a very long time either." He pulls the boy into his arms, flummoxed, again, by his inability to read his own son, and he wonders whether Freddie's slow demise is bothering Walt more than he's willing to admit. Walt settles down and looks at the tank for a long time without saying anything, and

Henry is waiting for him to start crying again, but he doesn't.

"Dad?"

"Yes, Walt."

"Are we really moving?"

Ah, so there it is, Henry thinks. He is quiet for a moment, carefully considering his options this time, before deciding on some version of the truth.

"Not that I know of. I mean, anything's possible, but if I were a betting man, I'd bet we're staying right here." Walt hasn't stopped looking at Freddie and, even as Henry puts a hand on his shoulder, sprinkles some fish food onto the surface of the water and watches as the flakes flutter down around his pet.

"Okay, Dad," he says after a while, and Henry takes him back upstairs.

Walt's room is always organized chaos. In the corner by his bed, for easy nighttime access, he has stacked his Pokedexes, encyclopedias of all the Pokemen, their powers and what they can evolve into. He keeps a few other books in his bed with him at all times, usually a kids' graphic novel and a magazine, maybe a gadget catalog. On his walls there are Pokemon posters that surround and draw attention to a much larger poster of Yoda in an action pose with the caption: "Do or do not, there is no try," and it occurs to Henry for the first time that, like Walt, Yoda never uses a contraction. Scattered on and around Walt's old train table are his lightsabers, his Nerf dart gun armory and all of his Bionicles, organized by their current level of consideration for inclusion in his indoor recess battle repertoire. His Nintendo DS is plugged in and charging on his desk, tiny game chips strewn about. Under the desk are all of the stuffed animals and matchbox cars that he never plays with anymore but won't part with.

Once Walt is under his covers, Henry kisses his forehead, tells him goodnight and turns to go.

"Dad?" Walt says.

"Yes, Walt."

"Can you do a magic trick?"

"You're a staller, you know that."

"Really quick."

Henry takes a coin from his pocket, holds it up between a thumb and two fingers, covers it with his other hand, then opens both and it is gone. It is the only sleight he ever learned, and it took him most of the first six months of Walt's life to make the visual effect seamless. He reaches under Walt's pillow and shows him the coin. Walt takes it.

"Goodnight. I'll see you in the morning, okay." Henry starts to leave again.

"And a story."

"Walt."

"I am not even sleepy."

"That makes one of us, buddy. And I've still got work to do."

"Just a quick one."

"It's late, buddy."

"A Swinger story."

Henry laughs and wonders whether Walt's request is coincidence or flawless strategy. He has stopped being amazed by his son's ability to gather information without ever appearing to pay attention.

"You know, tonight would actually be a perfect night for a Swinger story." He sits on the side of Walt's bed. "Any one in particular?"

"We have not done the Amputee Ball in a long time."

"Ah. One of my favorites."

"Mine too. It gives me a little bit of the creepies."

"With the standard intro or without?"

"With, please." Walt smiles and his arms come out from under the covers to press the sheet and comforter tight to his sides. He reaches for the blue stuffed Pokemon that sits on his nightstand.

"Manaphy will listen too," he says.

"Okay. As a long-time loyal listener you are well aware by now that there is a man who seems to be everywhere at once. He is a brilliant surgeon..."

"That is the power that he needs this time."

"...an accomplished gymnast, an amateur but not amateurish magician, a better story-teller than the poor substitute who sits before you now, and a better catcher than Johnny Bench, or even Manny Sanguillen."

"He used to play for the Pittsburgh Pirates, right Dad?"

"Right. But there is one thing you should know about this man..." Henry stares at Walt and brings his face slowly closer until their noses almost touch.

"Come on, Dad, say it!"

"...He has no legs."

"Not even a little bit, right?"

"And do you know why?"

"Because he does not even need them."

"That's right. He doesn't need them because his arms are so strong that he can spring forward ten feet at a time and land with the grace of a leopard descending from a tree. He can battle up to four two-legged schoolyard bullies at a time, emerge unscathed, and be back at the hospital operating on a dying woman within the hour. He is a double-back-flip of a man in a world where there are no spotters. He is..."

Walt shouts into his father's long pause: "The Swinger!"

"Shh."

"Sorry."

"After a long week in which he has already dispatched a gang of roughnecks who had been tripping kids as they got off the school bus, the Swinger decided to spend his Friday night doing something special for a group of people close to his own heart. The event had started out being just for veterans, men who had fought in one of our country's many wars, but as the years went by it had grown to include anyone who had lost a part of themselves through any kind of sickness or accident. Husbands and wives were welcome too, but they had to give up the use of a limb for the evening, and there was sturdy twine available at the door for just that purpose. The Swinger had attended this event for many years."

"But he has a big surprise for them this time, right Dad?"

"Yes, he does."

The Amputee Ball

The Amputee Ball was held every year around Halloween at the big VFW social hall in Riverside. Many people on the outside didn't understand the event and found it tasteless or, as some listeners have said, a little bit creepy. But to those who founded it, it was a way of celebrating their distinctiveness. When the phantom pain struck, it was as though what had once been there—a hand, a foot, an arm, a leg— was now merely invisible, as if a cartoon character might throw a bucket of ink and reveal it again. The Amputee Ball was meant to commemorate what was both gone and insistently lingering.

The Swinger had attended this event for many years, and the surprise he had in store for them this night had taken all of that time to prepare. In his secret laboratory, using human cells, he had grown miles of blood vessels, yards of skin, stacks of cartilage, and pound upon pound of bone, muscle tissue and fat. Like a sculptor, he had crafted arms and legs, hands and feet, some delicate, some thick and heavy, some with downy, light hair, some with coarse black pelts. For years, he had been tirelessly cataloging the needs of everyone in attendance, surreptitiously taking photos and measurements so that no one would be left out or disappointed by the results: Mario would get a powerfully muscled right arm that would enable him to wield the huge forty-ounce bat that had once been the scourge of the local softball league; Etta would get long fingers on a right hand that would join her left at the piano again; and Hal, whose wife loved to dance, would get two nimble legs. Unlike Dr. Frankenstein, the Swinger didn't aspire to make a whole human being; he simply wanted to make a few human beings whole.

On the night of the ball he carefully reversed the cryogenic freeze of each limb and transported them, on ice, to the back room at the VFW that would serve as his operating theatre. As the guests arrived, the ones who were to receive new limbs were told to line up by a heavy black curtain for their door prizes. There was lots of chatter as folks caught up with one another, the good and bad times that had passed since they'd last been together, though little was said about the bad, except, "Well, can't complain," or "I guess gettin up every morning is better than the alternative." But no one suspected that lives were about to be changed until Hal, a man who had been living legless in a wheelchair for nearly twenty-five years, emerged from behind the curtain, walking. There were tears in his eyes as he stretched the new limbs before him, turning them left and right. He ran his hands along the muscled thighs, over the knee joints and around to the calves. Others in line crowded around him, and the realization of what was about to happen rushed through the crowd, as Hal skipped to the dance floor with his joyful, disbelieving wife.

One by one, the attendees of the Amputee Ball disappeared behind the curtain. The Swinger worked in a blinding whir of motion, never tiring, never faltering. Blood vessels that had been clipped and shriveled dead ends for years opened into fresh pathways, hearts pumped a little harder to help blood rush to new extremities, bringing them color and life, and the wounds healed as quickly as the Swinger's rapid-fire stitches passed through them. It took longer for the patients to undress and then dress again than it did for the

Swinger to finish each procedure, so that sometimes three and four exited the operating room at once, often holding hands. The dance floor quickly became raucous, with men proudly rolling up sleeves and pant legs, and women unabashedly hiking skirts to show off their new possessions. The dancing reached a fever pitch when the DJ shut down his equipment for the night and Etta sat at the piano playing ragtime, with both hands, at a tempo that might threaten the heart of a marathon runner.

When the Swinger himself finally emerged from behind the curtain, it was a shock for the crowd to see him push his way through on tired arms. He had changed out of his scrubs and into the tuxedo and top hat that had become his familiar trademark at this event. At first, the room erupted in applause, but then went quickly quiet. The Swinger now looked out of place, the effect even more telling because he was struggling to move, the exhaustion showing both on his still-smiling face and in the uncharacteristic shuffle of his torso against the wooden floor. The crowd watched in silence until a woman, younger than most of the others in attendance, came forward. A murmur spread through the gathering because everyone realized at once that she was unfamiliar and wondered how the evening had passed without anyone noticing her. She was tall, pretty in an unpretentious way, and she bent down and put her hand to the side of the Swinger's face as if they were old friends, maybe more. Her hand seemed to glow where it touched his skin, and the eyelet hem of her sheer white dress fluttered on a draft of cool air coming in from the foyer.

"What about you?" she said.

The Swinger's chest was heaving from his hours of exertion, and it took a moment for him to register her presence.

"Naw," he said. "The tux wouldn't fit anymore."

Everyone laughed quietly.

Then the Swinger himself seemed to see this woman, a girl really, for the first time, and he looked up at her, puzzled and amazed. She looked very much like someone he had known once, but altogether different at the same time. If she had been the self-conscious type she might have sensed that the eyes of everyone in the room were on her. She appeared quite whole. There was no twine restricting any part of her body, though her pale limbs now matched the luminosity of her dress, so that it didn't seem that string would do anything but pass through them.

"Do you have a husband with you? A boyfriend, maybe?" the Swinger asked. He spoke haltingly, unsure of himself.

"No. I'm here alone," she said.

"But do you know..." The Swinger seemed to be struggling for a way to tell the girl politely what everyone else in the room was thinking. "Everyone here has lost something," he said finally.

"I know," she said. "I lost you."

The crowd parted for them to pass and he followed her out onto the floor. When she turned and laid one hand on his shoulder, her radiance passed to him, and Etta began playing a slow waltz.

TALK

Henry kisses Walt's cool forehead, pulls the sheet up around his shoulders and heads back downstairs to finish reading. It takes a moment for The Amputee Ball to leave him, but soon Natalie's work has drawn him in again. As always, he reads with a pen in his hand but, page after page, he is not writing anything. Near the end of the stack his face begins to change. Perspiration appears above his top lip and he swipes at it with his tongue. He looks up, clears his throat and continues. When he sets the last page next to him, face down, he stares at it, his lips slightly parted. He takes off his glasses and dabs at his forehead with the back of his arm. Why did she show that part to him—only him? He looks at the cell phone number written on the back of the manila envelope; then he looks at his watch.

Upstairs, Maggie still can't sleep. The ache on her right side has traveled and her right hand is under her nightshirt, the middle three fingers flat and together, moving out from her nipple in concentric circles in a pattern she repeats so often that she sometimes finds she has finished without consciously registering the results and has to start again. When Henry comes in the diffused remnants of the light from the downstairs hall are just enough to reveal her, left hand over her head, pressing at the tissue under her armpit. He reaches behind him, around the corner, and flips the switch down.

"Everything okay?" he asks into the darkness.

"I don't even know why I do this. Depending on the day, I can convince myself of almost anything."

"What about today?"

"Today it just hurts like a mother."

"But no lumps."

"Like I said, there are days when I can convince myself that smooth means one big lump. But no, I don't feel anything."

Henry sets his glasses on the nightstand next to his side of the bed and climbs in. He lies on his back, arms outside the sheet straight down at his sides, and stares at the ceiling. His eyes have adjusted and there is a yellow glow to the air above him from the clock beside Maggie.

"Did I hear Walt come down?" she asks.

"Freddie."

"Ah, yes. Freddie the Indestructible."

"He's looking more and more mortal all the time."

"Did he eat?"

"Depends on your definition. If it's one that involves actively coming to the surface in search of food, then no."

"What else is there for a fish?"

"Some of the flakes rained down close enough to his mouth that they got sucked in when he breathed."

"Doesn't sound good."

"No."

They are quiet for long enough that an unseen observer would assume that they have decided to go to sleep.

"So what will we do?" Maggie finally asks.

"Hm?"

"If they don't want you to stay."

"I don't know. I haven't thought about it."

"How can you do that?"

"What?"

"Not think about things. Important things."

"Like I said. We don't know anything yet. There will be plenty of time."

"Jesus." Maggie's hands go to her head in the dark. "Aren't you angry? I mean these people are *idiots* and they get to decide *you're* not good enough?"

"They haven't decided that yet."

"But just the fact they're *considering* that. There shouldn't be any question, should there? I mean, it's nothing but jealousy, pure and simple. You have books. You have students who love you. What more could they want?"

"It's a process. And from what I gather from Atlee, never a very simple one."

"But shouldn't we at least be *thinking* about what we might do?"

"Sounds like you have."

Maggie says nothing at first and Henry has to coax her. "Go ahead," he says.

"What if we stay?"

"What do you mean? I thought we were talking about the other."

"I mean, even if they don't *want* you to stay, what if we stay?"

"Just live here?"

"I could keep my adjunct position so there'd be a little money from that. You could write, maybe open a solo practice on the side, be the small-town lawyer you wanted to be in the first place. I could start trying to sell a few pieces, alumni weekends, that kind of thing. Maybe even take a few to Elsa in New York, see if there's any interest there."

Henry laughs. "All of this since dinnertime?"

"*Someone's* got to think about this stuff."

"Do you have any idea what that would be like for me?"

"Yes."

"Running into George and Loren in the frozen foods at the Grand Union? You dealing with Elvira every time Walt and Alex want to play together? I'd be the annoying little neighborhood kid who won't go away."

She continues as if she hasn't heard him. "You could start your own little workshop down in the dining room, charge five hundred bucks a kid on top of the tuition they're already paying, and you'd suck their crappy little fiction program dry. You know that, don't you?"

"Mag. Hey." Henry reaches across the mattress and lays his hand on her hip.

"Shit," she says, her voice catching. "Shit, shit, shit."

"Hey."

"I don't want to start over again. Do you understand that?"

"Yes."

"We started over *here*. I got sick *here*. I got well *here*. I learned to work again *here*. If it comes back I don't want to be in some strange place. I don't want to be away from that studio, upstairs, all that light. I don't want a new oncologist, a new waiting room with strange people. I don't want my kids figuring out how to grieve in a new school."

"It's not coming back."

"Don't change the subject. And don't talk to me like I don't know my own statistics. We all know them. You think Allie's still growing her hair for some stranger?"

Henry lets out a long breath. "Okay."

"Okay what?"

"Okay, we'll talk about it."

"We are talking about it."

"We'll talk about it more. When the time comes. This will be something we'll consider doing, something we'll see if we can make work."

"Thank you."

They are quiet, and again the silence lasts long enough that it feels as if they have decided on sleep as the way to end their conversation. And, again, it's Maggie who breaks the silence.

"So how was the rest?" she asks. And although they haven't really been fighting, her tone is that of a peace offering.

"Hm?"

"The rest of the story. Natalie's story."

"Chapters."

"Chapters."

"Fine."

"Fine?"

"Yeah."

"When you left here you were thinking it was more than *fine*."

"It's good. I mean it's very good. It's just not my thing, you know? All that intrigue."

"Oh."

"All that sex."

"Yeah. Not your thing at all."

"Which probably means she'll make more money than I ever will."

"You've done fine."

"*Fine*."

They both laugh. Maggie rolls toward him, straddles him and sits up in the soft golden light.

"My, look at you," he says.

"Yes, do. Look at me."

"I thought this was off."

"I did promise."

"Yes, you did."

"And I've got to stay ahead of the competition."

"No competition."

"Look at me, I said."

Maggie pulls the nightshirt over her head, and her one perfect breast falls into Henry's waiting hand. His right thumb brushes gently over her nipple, which hardens to his touch. The thumb on his other hand avoids the smooth, horizontal scar. Henry would never admit this, but his eyes avoid it too. Maggie reaches behind.

"My. Such a Boy Scout," she says.

"Reporting for duty, ma'am."

"Is this left over from the story...?"

"Chapters."

"Chapters. Or just for me?"

"You really think this could have survived your recent interrogation?"

"Sorry."

"Either way, it's just for you now."

"Mm." Maggie takes him out and runs her fingernails along the length of him. "So what happened? In the story. Chapters." She is whispering, smiling, eyes closed.

"Something we've never tried."

"Something we *should* try?"

"Maybe."

"Mm." She takes him in her hand and squeezes and Henry lets out a grunt of pleasure. "You don't mind same-old same-old for now, do you?"

"No, ma'am."

Maggie slides him easily inside and bears down hard.

7

I don't remember it being a conscious decision not to tell anyone but Ruthie what our extra passenger looked like. I just told my father that a friend of mine had a spare ticket to the game and had offered it to us on the condition that we give him a ride. There was no reason for my father to suspect anything unusual until I told him where to stop.

"Your friend lives at the VFW?" he asked.

"He just moved there. He used to live up at the hospital."

"How old is he?"

"I don't know."

My father and Jeanine exchanged looks across the front seat. Jeanine was young and pretty, with a blond ponytail she flipped by always turning her head more quickly than necessary. Other than that, she was nothing like I had expected. She was soft-spoken and kind and seemed comfortable with Ruthie and me from the beginning. If anything, she reminded me of a younger version of my mother, and when she and my father got married a little more than a year later, their wedding photo looked eerily like the one that, until recently, had occupied one of the side tables in our living room. It would be a while before I understood that my father had excellent taste in the women he ruined.

He had left his little sports car at the house and borrowed my mother's station wagon for the game. Ruthie and I were in the middle seat, and in the "way-back," as we called it, the third seat had been stowed flat. My father tossed a couple of blankets back there to carry with us to the stadium. It would be late by the time the game ended, and he said that Ruthie and I could lie down on the way home. When we pulled to a stop outside the VFW, I told him to beep the horn.

When John Kostka pushed his way out through the front door, Jeanine's sharp intake of breath was audible. My father hadn't been looking, and when he turned and saw what Jeanine was seeing, he leaned across the space between them, as if getting closer might help him make sense of it.

"Jesus Christ," he said.

That made Ruthie sit up on her knees and look out the window on my side. "Is that him?!"

"Who?" my father asked.

"The guy with no legs!"

"Ruthie, I think it's safe to say he's a guy with no legs. But why is he coming toward our car?"

"Because he's my friend," I said. Maybe it was just the fact that I was enjoying my father's shock, but I felt none of the self-consciousness I had experienced when John spoke to me among my classmates. I rolled down my window with one hand and waved my baseball glove at him with the other.

"Hammerin Hank!" John called. "A backstage entrance would be easier if you could flip er open for me."

I got out, went around and swung the tailgate open. When I looked inside, both my father and Jeanine were facing directly forward, ponytails motionless, looking as if someone was checking their posture. Ruthie was hanging over the back seat, facing me and smiling. The back of the car was higher than any first step, but John pulled himself up and in without effort.

"Whoa!" said Ruthie.

"Hey there, missy."

"Hi!"

By the time I closed the tailgate and ran back to my own seat, Ruthie and John were just about nose to nose.

"Sit down and face front, Ruthie," my father said.

"Your name's Ruth?" John said, sounding incredulous.

"Yessir."

"Now that's good luck if I ever heard it. And we need it with Walker on the mound tonight. You know you got about the greatest baseball name in history?"

"I do?"

"Babe Ruth. The Bambino. All-time home run king. Never anyone like him before or since." He hooked his thumb toward me. "Except maybe Hammerin Hank here."

"Cool."

My father glanced at John in the rearview mirror. "I'm Ned Graham," he said. "And this is my friend Jeanine." Jeanine raised a hand in greeting and looked as if she might turn around but stopped halfway.

"Nice to meet you," she said over her shoulder.

"John Kostka. I appreciate the lift. As Hank knows, I'm usually stuck with public transportation."

The introductions complete, we sat there, the car idling but not moving, no one saying anything. No one ever called me "Hank," and I thought at first that might have been the source of the uncomfortable silence.

"What're we waiting for?" asked Ruthie. "Let's *go*."

My father cleared his throat and Jeanine looked his way quickly, flipping her ponytail. Then she flipped it back again and reasserted her gaze straight ahead.

John reached over the seat-back in front of him and touched my shoulder. "You didn't warn them, did you?"

I shook my head.

"Well now, that's just cruel." He smiled.

"It's not that," said my father, finally turning to face us. "It's not your..." He paused, appearing to choose his words carefully. "How did you meet my son?" he asked, with a suspicion I didn't understand.

"On the *bus*, Daddy," Ruthie volunteered, as if our father had failed to see the obvious.

"Excuse me?"

"That's right, sir. I met your son on the bus home from the game last week. Then he and his classmates came to entertain the folks at the VFW the other night and we got better acquainted."

"Is that right?"

"Yes, sir. I figured he must love baseball to go to a game by himself, so I showed him the picture of me with Manny Sanguillen and Milt May and Dave Ricketts."

"He's the bullpen coach," I said.

"He's the one gave me these tickets. Which reminds me. You got that ball?"

I reached inside my glove and showed it to him. "Got it."

"Great. We just might be able to get you an autograph or two."

"Well," my father said. "We appreciate the ticket."

"My pleasure."

"Dad, did you bring those ARCO photos? Maybe I could get those signed too."

"Sorry, I forgot them. The players aren't going to be standing around signing autographs at a World Series Game anyway, sport."

"Let's *go*, Daddy," said Ruthie. "I don't want to miss anything."

We pulled away from the curb, my father and Jeanine quiet in the front seat, John perched above and between Ruthie and me in the back. I didn't understand the tone of my father's questions then, assuming he felt awkward because of John's appearance. Ruthie, for her part, didn't feel awkward in the least.

"Did you always have no legs?" she asked.

"Ruthie," said my father.

"No, that's a fair question," John said. "Had em and lost em. Almost twenty years ago now."

"Did it hurt?"

"Not when it happened. I'll tell you the truth, Miss Bambino, I don't remember much of that. But afterwards, yeah. Still does once in a while. Sometimes my feet hurt. Isn't that somethin? Never have to cut my toenails though."

Ruthie laughed.

"So, you go to lots of baseball games, do you?" he asked her.

"This is my very first one."

"Your first baseball game is a World Series game? Where you gonna go from here? You're gonna be bored silly if you ever go to an April game against the Expos."

"No I won't. I love baseball. I'll just sit in the sun and keep score. Henry taught me how."

"Now there's a worthwhile skill people just don't learn anymore. You get maybe two minutes of highlights on the news, but if you can keep score you can see the whole game again."

"My dad taught me," I said, hoping he might join the conversation.

"Do you color in your homeruns or just draw the line all the way around?"

"Color them in."

"Me too. How about a called third strike?"

"Backwards K," my father said stiffly into the mirror. I nodded.

John put one gloved hand on my head, one on Ruthie's. "I'm with the right crowd," he said. "What do you think of the stadium?"

"A travesty," my father said.

"Yup. A baseball diamond inside a football stadium. Not a considered sightline to be found. One of these days they're gonna realize what they've done and they'll knock that place down and build Forbes Field all over again. And that carpet they play on..."

Jeanine finally spoke. "Don't get him started on the Astroturf," she said. "You both sound like a couple of old men."

"Just sensible ones," John said. My father looked at the road.

Jeanine's father had given her the company parking pass for the private lot that ringed the outer walls of the stadium. We had a bright yellow tag that hung on the mirror, and the parking attendants and security guards just kept waving us through until the stadium loomed over us. This was the first sporting event of any real import in Pittsburgh since Bill Mazeroski had ended the 1960 Series against the unbeatable Yankees with the most famous homerun in baseball history. Maz was still my father's favorite player, despite the fact that he seldom got into the lineup anymore, and every time Dave Cash failed to make the pivot at second on a tough double play, my father would start calling for Maz.

As soon as I got out of the car a cold charge of anticipation went through me. Crowds streamed up the concrete ramps on either side of us, chants of "Let's go Bucs" flaring and dying like an orchestra warming up. Vendors hawked hats and shirts and pennants, and the Goodyear Blimp, something I'd only seen on television, hung above, underlit by the stadium lights, putt-putting like a toy. I opened the rear door for John who handed the blankets to my father then rolled to his stomach and slid down and out.

"This is what it's all about, Hank. Can you feel it?"

"Yeah."

"People who don't live in sports towns don't understand. You just don't get this in Des Moines. Let's go."

We funneled into the moving crowd and up the ramp, Ruthie holding on to my father's hand but looking back and smiling at John about every ten seconds.

"Daddy, he's keeping up with us, can you believe it?" she said. "And we have *legs*."

"Don't stare, Ruthie."

"Can I get cotton candy?"

"It's not the circus, Ruthie."

"Well, *some* kind of candy then?"

"Sure. Let's at least get to our seats first, okay?"

"I bet his muscles are *huge*. Are your muscles huge?" she asked, turning to John again. Our pace slowed to a shuffle as we neared the turnstiles. John lifted his torso off the ground and held himself there.

"Come check for yourself, Miss Bambino."

"Oh my gosh!" Ruthie exclaimed, both hands gripping John's arm through his heavy flannel shirt. "It's like a *leg*!"

"Gets the ladies every time."

"It's like a leg, Daddy. Come and feel."

My father tugged Ruthie back gently and set her in front of him. "Get in line, sweetie. We're almost there."

"You got your ticket, missy?" John asked. Ruthie looked panicked until John held up both hands and pulled them apart as if pulling a piece of taffy. A ticket gradually appeared in the space between his fingers, and he handed it to her.

"Whoa!"

"You keep track of it now. I can't do that again."

Once we got to the front, the ticket-taker called John by name and pushed the turnstile for him as he sidled his way through. His seats were straight ahead, behind home plate.

"Where are you?" he asked my father.

"Sixty-six. Row D."

"Nice. You can spit on Hebner from there. Your boy and I are right here in forty-one. Row F. We can meet and switch it up halfway through if you like. It's a hoot watchin the pitches come in from back here."

I could see the hesitation in my father's face, even if I didn't understand it.

"I want a turn to sit with him, Daddy," said Ruthie.

"We'll see, sweetie. Forty-one F?"

"That's it. You'll be able to see us from where you are."

"I'll stop over in a few minutes after we get settled. If that's okay with you."

"Happy to have you. Just tell the usher you're comin to see me. They're careful about who comes into this section because it's mostly team complimentary tickets."

When we parted I could feel my father turning around to watch us, and I remember having what I thought at the time was a revelation: my father was jealous. He was jealous of my friendship with John. Jealous of the time I would be spending with him. Even jealous of our seats. Knowing now that I was wrong makes the memory of that moment no less powerful for me. I remember standing very tall in his gaze, aware of my shoulders in a way that felt new, thinking of the empty seat next to me the week before and the strange series of events that had led me to fill it with this unlikely man swooping along beside me.

"You okay?" John said, turning to me and, perhaps, I think now, sensing the change.

"I'm great," I said.

ADVICE

When Henry arrives, Atlee Sproul is already at their usual corner table, halfway through his first drink. The food at Milligan's is famously mediocre, but the Wednesday lunchtime bartender pours a three-finger neat shot that nearly makes Atlee weep. Henry never drinks at lunch, but he tolerates the tasteless vinaigrette and limp fries for his friend who has no idea how bad the food is since he never eats this early. Atlee has an unspoken agreement with the university schedulers that he doesn't teach before two o'clock.

But Atlee is no sloppy drunk. In fact, at fifty-nine, he is still the most ardently discussed and sought-after faculty member in the department. His eyes are clear and sky blue, and the alcohol gives his face a year-round ruddiness. He has managed to escape the drinker's paunch by eating next to nothing.

Atlee stands. "I was just toasting to your health."

"I'd return the gesture if I thought you needed it," Henry says.

Unlike so many of the younger professors who pull a tweed jacket over whatever they used to wear before they got hired, Atlee's fits him like a thick skin. And as long as the temperature stays below sixty, he invariably wears a fine wool or cashmere sweater underneath, so that when he stands to shake Henry's hand, he looks as if he might burst the shoulders and chest of his coat if he tried to button it. Truth be told, Henry has always been somewhat jealous of his friend's effortless manliness, and he concentrates hard on returning Atlee's strong grip.

"Good health is as simple as fresh air, good scotch and plenty of exercise," Atlee says.

"I've been meaning to ask with whom you've been exercising. Seems like it's been a while since you've mentioned anyone in particular."

They sit.

"A lovely young lady of Dutch descent called Astrid. Legs that begin at her sternum."

"I don't think I know her. Grad student?"

Atlee nods. "I have my scruples."

A waiter appears beside their table and fills a water glass for Henry but not for Atlee.

"Can I get you anything else to drink, Professor Graham?"

"No, just the water will be fine. Thanks."

"Ready for a freshener yet, Professor Sproul?"

"Just bring mine with lunch." When the waiter looks hesitant, Atlee clarifies. "With *his* lunch," he says.

"Yes, sir. Do you know what you'd like, Professor Graham?"

"I'll have half a chicken salad sandwich and whatever the soup is."

"Split pea?"

"Yes, that's fine."

"Gawd," says Atlee. When the waiter has gone, he lifts his glass toward Henry and sips. "You know, assuming you're asked to hang around here, one of my long-term goals is to turn you into a proper scotch drinker."

"Not going to happen. I can't bear the stuff."

"Neither could I when I was your age. But I worked at it."

"I've never understood trying to develop a taste for something your palate rejects."

"How was cunnilingus for you the first time?"

"I think that's a new record for you."

"What?"

"Maggie says it never takes you longer than ten minutes to reference a specific sex act, no matter the company or the context."

"Please don't mention your spectacular wife and sex in close proximity or I'll not be able to concentrate. And you're ignoring my point. Some things are worth the effort. Like teaching."

"Scotch is to oral sex, as oral sex is to teaching?"

"Precisely."

"But I loved teaching from the first day."

"And that's part of your problem. If you'd bitch about your students once in a while like the rest of us, maybe our friends on the committee would be afraid of losing you."

"Speaking of which, I told Maggie what you said."

"About what?"

"The review. She's scared to death."

"Bloody hell, why would you tell her now?"

"I had no choice. Loren's wife is apparently discussing the matter with their seven-year-old. Walt came home from a play date asking if we were moving."

"Did you know that Loren pads his pecker? I caught him stuffing a codpiece in the gents' once after a piss."

"Maggie just doesn't understand their hesitancy. And neither do I, I guess. I know my student evaluations are good because I see those. And unless you count chapbooks..."

Atlee blows a short, sharp raspberry.

" ...I've published as many books as anyone in the department." Henry seldom raises his voice, and no one other than Atlee and Henry's own family would recognize that he is raising it now. "I know the funding is there, and no one else is up for at least three years. So what's the problem?"

Atlee sits forward, takes up his glass and sips. When he sets it back down, he wraps both hands around it and stares into the brown liquid as if it will show the future.

"Do you want me to tell you the truth?"

"Yes."

"You write *accessible* novels."

"And?"

"And someone casting stones—unfairly in my opinion—might even derisively describe them as *feel-good* novels. And feel-good, my friend, is a state of being our esteemed colleagues view as unattainable in a world in which their own pitiful rants persistently take up residence in the *Last Chance* bin." Atlee finishes his drink in one quick toss and sets the glass down. "Look. Academics in general—and ours in particular—tend not to respect books that people actually read. Frankly, I thought you'd have figured that out by now."

"So it's helpful to my career as a teacher to write books just so long as I don't sell very many."

"The fewer the better. It just means your writing is misunderstood by the general public. Like Loren's."

"Loren's novel didn't sell because it was unreadable."

"You know that, and I know that. But I have it on good authority that when Loren saw you popping off on your book tour that summer..."

"I went to Pittsburgh—my home town—and to Cleveland."

"...and then heard you getting interviewed on some hard-to-tune-in station on one of the far ends of the dial, he couldn't bear it. The unfairness of it is just too much because your writing is so *simple*."

"Is that what you think?"

"Yes, I do. It's simple, and it's lovely. I wouldn't have lunch with you otherwise."

"You're not eating."

"I didn't say I was."

Henry's soup and sandwich arrive along with Atlee's second scotch. They are one of only a few tables of diners, though the bar is full of men on lunch break from the pet food plant just outside of town. They bring with them a faint smell of peat.

"I've always wondered why you stopped trying," Henry says between spoonfuls of soup. "Poetry, I mean."

"I'm not any good. Unfortunately, I *am* an excellent reader, so my failures as a writer became apparent rather quickly. That's where Loren and his lot have gone wrong. They're all smart fellows when it comes to everything but their own work. They're capable of wasting hours and countless bottles of good whiskey arguing over who is a post-modernist and who isn't, and yet they can't understand what makes their own writing so wretchedly lifeless. If you could give them a serum that made them forget they'd written it?—told them a student had handed it in?—they'd skewer it. I got tired of skewering my own stuff."

"Why not work at it?"

"Like scotch and cunnilingus, you mean?"

"Can we stick with scotch as the analogy of choice?"

"You can develop taste. You can't develop talent. The only difference between me and the rest of them is that I'm enough of a realist to know I don't have much. Cheers." Atlee lifts his glass, takes a longer swig than usual, then closes his eyes and smiles. "Which reminds me. It's about time for you to get back to work."

Henry is taken aback but tries to hide it, looking down at his lunch. "What do you mean?"

"It's been long enough. She's going to be fine. Write something. Anything. Write a 'How To' on how to develop a taste for pea soup. Just put some words together and throw them in the rubbish."

Henry has recovered but still doesn't look up at Atlee.

"How do you know I'm not working on something now?"

"Come on. Give me at least a modicum of credit for human insight. I thought maybe that was what you asked me here to talk about."

"No."

Henry eats while Atlee drinks. During his first couple of years on campus these lunches had been at least twice weekly events during which Henry had relentlessly mined Atlee's teaching knowledge and instincts. Whatever his other failings Atlee was deeply devoted to his students, and Henry was immediately drawn to him as the one colleague who might help him to stop waking at five a.m. every morning obsessing over his lecture notes. "The hour is ungodly, of course," Atlee had told him, "but if the fear of making a fool of yourself in front of them ever leaves you, it's time to quit." They pass a few minutes in silence before Atlee turns back to Henry.

"So we never have lunch more than once a week anymore and I always call *you* these days. We already talked on Monday about the status of the review. I don't believe you've asked me here to grill me on my dormant writing career, and you're apparently unwilling to talk about your own."

"Guilty."

"I never have more than two drinks before class, but if we're still sitting here when I finish this one I'm going to have no choice. So out with it."

Henry has taken a bite of his sandwich and chews slowly.

"Did you ever have Natalie Currant?" he finally asks.

"When you say '*have*'..."

"As a student."

"Yes."

"Since you've invited it, do I need to ask the follow-up?"

"Strictly student-teacher. And I can't imagine it will ever be anything different."

"Why do you say that?"

"That one scares me. Aside from the fact that she's still an undergraduate, she's too smart. Spectacular ass, mind you. Why?"

"She gave me some pages the other day. Outside of class. It's the first few chapters of a novel, but she didn't want the class to read it. Just me."

"And?"

"And it's really good."

Atlee lifts his drink and swirls it to show Henry how much time he has left.

"The girl in the story, the narrator, finds out some startling facts about her lineage, that her mother is dead, that the woman she thought was her mother killed her real mother. Then on her way home from the prison she walks into the first bar she sees, starts talking to the first man she sees and drags him into the ladies' room."

"She's got my attention."

"And they have intercourse."

"Naturally."

"Anal intercourse."

"Instead of, or in addition to?"

"Instead of. And quickly, violently."

"Yes, then what?"

"*Then* what? There needs to be more?"

"I guess I'm not sure what your question is."

"What do you think it means? That she would show that to me. Just me."

"You mean do I think she wants to drag you into the ladies'?"

"Yeah."

"Yes, I do. They all do."

"I'm serious."

"So am I. Maybe not all, but lots. Certainly more than the *none* you have naively maintained. Look, they've read your books, right?

So they know you're sensitive as hell. They see you're not the best-looking guy around, no offense, and figure you've had to work at it. You think any of these Long Island footballers know what they're doing? The girls here are positively frantic for a man who can do it right. Trust me. I've made a career out of it."

"But why *that*?"

"Anal sex is the new abstinence, gaining fast on the high school hummer in a district near you."

"You're kidding."

"I never kid about such things."

"How do you know that?"

"In case you haven't noticed, I am plugged into today's youth."

"But the way she described it. I mean, they all write about sex, right? They think they invented it. But this was different. This was..."

"Arousing?"

"Well. Yes."

"Pffft. Leave it to you."

"What?"

"To fall for a student for her *writing*."

"I haven't *fallen* for anyone. I'm just not sure what to do. We can't talk about her chapters in class, but I'm not comfortable talking to her about them alone."

"Like I said. She's too smart."

"So what would you do? Wait, I should rephrase that. If you were *me*, what would you do?"

"Take it head on."

"Meaning?"

"Meaning, she thinks she knows how you'll react, and so far she's right. She thinks you'll be knocked off a bit, embarrassed. So talk to her like it's any other piece of writing. Be her teacher. Look her straight in the eye with the most neutral look of concern you can muster and ask her precisely *why* her protagonist crams a stranger in her pooper."

"I don't know if I can do that."

"Which is precisely what she thinks, and precisely why you should. That and the fact that if you fuck up, I'm coming for your wife." Atlee finishes his drink and holds out the empty glass. "*Then* you'll have something to write about. Time's up."

Before we had even settled into our seats, Game 4 was already looking like a blowout.

"Goddamn Luke Walker," John said. "He ain't worth a crap, scuse my French."

Walker gave up quick singles to the first three batters he faced to load the bases, and then Sanguillen let a low pitch skip under his glove and all the way to the backstop to allow the first run to score.

"How do I score that?" I asked, trying to concentrate on my program instead of what was happening on the field.

"PB-35, Belanger to second, Rettenmund to third, Blair scores."

"Is that an earned run?"

"Wouldn't think so but it is. Walker deserves it anyway."

John was shaking his head but it only got worse. Walker managed to record just two outs before getting pulled—sacrifice flies by Brooks Robinson and Boog Powell that scored the second and third runs.

"Here comes Murtaugh already," John said. "This crowd's gonna let Walker have it."

Sure enough, as soon as Pirate Manager Danny Murtaugh took

the ball from Walker, all of the energy I'd felt gathering on the ramps outside was released in a merciless rain of boos. Into that atmosphere, tall and skinny as a foul pole, trotted Bruce Kison, a twenty-one-year-old rookie who'd just been called up from the minors in July.

"I like Kison," I said, struggling to sound positive.

"He's gonna be a good pitcher one of these days, but he's gotta be ready to mess his drawers right about now."

Kison managed to get Davey Johnson to ground to Hebner right in front of Ruthie and my dad, and the Pirates jogged off the field to less applause than the stadium organist, Vince Lascheid, had received during the pre-game introductions. Lascheid himself launched into a spirited rendition of the Beatles' *Help*!, as another one of the Orioles four twenty-game winners, Pat Dobson, warmed up for the bottom of the first. My father appeared next to us in the aisle.

"Everything okay over here?" He looked at John who was perched toward the front of his seat so that it wouldn't fold up on him.

"Is the score the same over there where you're sittin?"

"I'm afraid so."

"Then no, everything's not okay, but we're not givin up yet, are we, kiddo?"

"Nope."

"Good man."

I saw my father glance at the two empty seats next to us and I could tell he was thinking of staying. Before he could say anything a beautiful young black woman holding a toddler stopped at our row.

"Excuse us."

My father moved aside and the woman smiled when she saw John. "Hey there. Shangalesa asked if you were going to be here, didn't you, sweetheart?" The little girl pretended to hide her face, but she made sure she could still see John.

"Hey, Paula. This is my friend, Hank. And this is his father, Mr.

Graham. Gentlemen, this is Paula Ellis, Dock's wife."

The volatile, free-spirited Ellis had been my father's favorite pitcher ever since Ellis's wild, eight-walk no-hitter in San Diego the year before, and there was an uncomfortable pause before he recovered himself and took the slim hand being offered.

"Nice to meet you," he finally said. Paula Ellis slid in front of us and sat in the seat next to mine with her daughter on her lap. "Well," my father continued, looking somehow defeated by her arrival, "maybe I'll stop back to see how you're doing in a few innings, okay sport?"

"Sure."

"Do you want me to bring you anything? A hot dog maybe?"

"No thanks."

"No need to worry about us," John said. "The usher who showed you down here. Tony. He takes care of all my concession runs for me. Only takes a few bites on the way back."

"Well. I might stop back just the same if it's all right with you."

"Anytime."

A minute after my father left, I spotted him walking down the ramp of his own section. Ruthie stood when he reached their row and asked him something. My father pointed and Ruthie eyed along his arm until I stood and waved and she found us. Ruthie waved back with both arms, jumping like a cheerleader. If I didn't know better, I'd have thought she didn't know the score.

"Is that your sister?" Paula Ellis asked.

"Yeah."

"She's welcome to sit here if she'd like. Shangelesa will probably sit on my lap the whole game, and we can move down one."

"That's okay. I don't think my dad will let her come over."

"Well, if he does."

"Thanks."

Dave Cash walked to start the Pirates' half of the first and the crowd tried to muster some enthusiasm. Then Hebner popped harmlessly to the shortstop and Clemente struck out.

John rubbed his rough, scarred face. "Christ Almighty. Even Clemente."

Stargell was due up next, and although he had been the most dangerous homerun hitter in the league all season, he had gone oh-for-fourteen with six strikeouts in the playoff series against the Giants and seemed beleaguered by the pressure. In the Series so far, he had just one single. When Stargell stepped to the plate, Shangelesa reached into my lap and picked up my game program.

"Shangelesa. Mind your manners," her mother said. "I'm sorry, young man. I forgot to buy a program and she loves to find her daddy. Willie is Dock's roommate on the road, and she loves him too. Seeing Willie must have reminded her."

"It's okay. I can catch up between innings."

Stargell looked at ball one.

Shangelesa turned the pages of the program by pushing them with the palm of her small hand until she found the full-page photo of her father on the mound. Her mother seemed to know what she'd want next and reached into her purse for a pen.

Stargell swung wildly and missed.

Shangelesa shook her head at her mother and pointed to John. "Him," she said.

"What's that?" John asked.

Paula laughed. "She never stops talking about the magic pen. She won't take mine. You don't happen to have it with you, do you?"

A groan went up as Stargell looked at strike two and turned away in disbelief.

"I don't need to have it with me, do I, little missy? We just have to find it."

John held his hands up and, just as he had done with Ruthie's ticket, pulled a ballpoint pen from the empty space between them.

He handed it to Shangelesa who thanked him quietly, then began to scrawl small, misshapen hearts on her father's picture, concentrating hard.

"Nice work," John said. "You're makin better use of that program than we are."

Certainly, even then, I wasn't superstitious enough to believe that the way the game turned at that very moment had anything to do with Shangelesa Ellis. In the coming years, her father would divorce Paula. He would struggle with and conquer addiction. He would admit that his 1970 no-hitter had been thrown under the influence of LSD, and that both his intense focus and his wildness that day had been products of a euphoric, constantly shifting perception. But on this day, Shangelesa knew only one truth about her father, and she was recording it carefully, meticulously.

Stargell stepped back in, down two strikes, and resumed his distinctive pinwheeling ritual: a loose, rhythmic spinning of the bat that marked the time it took Dobson to look in to get the sign. It was a routine that had intimidated pitchers all season, but one that had seemed nothing but wasted motion in October. It finished with a one-handed, two-spin flourish as Dobson entered his windup, and when Stargell laced a double to the gap in right-center field, the crowd, almost as surprised as it was jubilant, stood and roared as Cash scored from first.

"Well what do you know!" John yelled, clapping me on the shoulder.

Paula Ellis leaned close to my ear to be heard. "You want to write that down?" she asked, moving to take my program from Shangelesa.

"Don't you *touch* that thing!" John shouted over the noise.

Almost before the stadium had settled, Al Oliver doubled to the exact same spot and Stargell scored, an unmistakable look of relief on his face as he crossed the plate.

Everything had changed. The swiftness with which that could

happen in a sport that so often gave the impression of indolence was what I loved most about baseball. Suddenly, the stadium vibrated under our feet. The same voices that had tormented Walker's exit not ten minutes earlier found a note together a full octave higher and held it there as big Bob Robertson came to the plate. Even when Robertson grounded weakly to the pitcher to end the inning, the crowd rose and bellowed and whooped as if to make amends for its earlier loss of faith. *Now we remember*, we all seemed to be saying at once. *We came here because anything can happen.*

And, that night, it did. In the third inning, with Hebner on first, Clemente drilled an outside pitch down the right field line. When it cleared the wall and bounced off the facing beneath the bleachers, Clemente's sprint toward second slowed to a homerun trot amid the delirium.

John pulled a clean handkerchief from the front pocket of his harness and shook it over his head. "We got em reelin now!" he said.

No one had seen the umpire in right field signal that the ball was foul.

The argument that ensued was like nothing I had ever seen. Clemente, Murtaugh and first base coach Don Leppert all converged on the right field umpire as though they were oppositely charged ions. Clemente had to be restrained and dragged away. Leppert kept inserting himself between Murtaugh and the umpire, but every time it looked as if Murtaugh was headed for the dugout he'd turn and come back for more, and soon the first and second base umpires joined in as well. I don't know how long it went on but I remember wishing I could hear Prince. "An old fashioned rhubarb," he would have called it. From twenty yards away, where he was being held, Clemente was still shouting, and he didn't stop even when Murtaugh finally retreated to the dugout, didn't stop as he walked, as slowly as possible, back to the batter's box, where he picked up that bat that always seemed longer than any other, and stepped in. He twisted and craned his always creaky neck and I could see his lips still moving, looking out to right field, his eyes like slits. And then, mid-sentence it seemed, he laced a single into right, sending Hebner to third. Clemente stood on first, hands on his hips, facing the umpire in right field, oblivious to the deafening cheers. Two batters later, when Al Oliver drove Hebner home to tie the game, it sounded like the stadium might come down around us.

After that, the baby-faced Kison attacked the Orioles as if channeling Clemente's anger. He was merciless with his inside fastball, hitting three batters and knocking two others to the dirt. One pitch was so high and inside Sanguillen never touched it, and everyone in the first seven or eight rows of our section flinched or ducked as the ball struck the netting in front of us. Paula Ellis instinctively hunched to cover Shangelesa, who was still hard at work and only looked up to see what all the nervous laughter was about. You'd have thought she was trying to crack a secret code.

Kison, three months removed from the minors, pitched six shutout innings, giving up only two hits. In the seventh, another seldom-used rookie, catcher Milt May, pinch-hit for Kison and drove in the winning run. John pronounced it "the darndest game I've ever seen," and when it was over, Shangelesa quietly handed the pen back to John, closed the program and placed it on my lap, as though her work was done.

"What do you say, sweetie?" her mother asked.

"Thank you."

Paula stood, shifting Shangelesa to her hip, and they slid out into the aisle while the crowd was still standing and applauding.

"Will we see you tomorrow afternoon?" she asked John.

"Nope. This is it for me for the Series. I'm sure I'll be around come spring."

"Well, you take care. Nice meeting you, Hank."

I've always been slightly embarrassed that I didn't offer to let

Shangelesa keep that program, but I couldn't imagine going home without it. I still have it, the scoring filled in later with some help from the newspaper, and I take it out and look at it every few years and think about trying to find her, maybe send it to her, but the same thought stops me every time: What if she doesn't want to remember? If there was such evidence of my sister Sam's unconditional love for our own father, she wouldn't want to be reminded. It would only get in the way of the bitterness she has worked so hard to cultivate. Ruthie, on the other hand, would welcome that kind of confirmation, I think, even in her current state. She's beginning now to lose feeling in her right foot, the diabetes progressing slowly but steadily, and she has been told that she could be facing an amputation within five years. Still, her bitterness has always been more like longing—a longing she finally satisfied when she got to nurse our father into his grave—and if such a concrete record of her childhood feelings for him existed, I think she'd want to have it.

Ruthie was the first to appear next to us, bounding down the aisle, followed by Jeanine, and then my father.

"Can you believe we *won*?"

"Told'ya you were good luck, Miss Bambino."

Out on the field I could see someone wearing an NBC jacket trying to stop Clemente for an interview, but he shook his head silently and continued into the dugout.

"You got that ball, Hank?"

I held it up.

"We'll be as quick as we can."

My father put his hands on Ruthie's shoulders. "It's late, Henry." I knew what he was going to say, but I couldn't believe it. "We should be getting Ruthie home."

"I'm not tired," Ruthie volunteered.

"Ned," Jeanine said.

"What? It's past eleven on a school night, midnight by the time we get home even if we leave right now."

"Dad. The *locker* room."

"Do you know what your mother will say if I bring Ruthie home at one o'clock in the morning?"

"I'm *not* tired."

"We'll take the bus," I said.

There was a long silence.

"Excuse me?"

"You go ahead and we'll take the bus. John can walk me home from our stop."

"I'm happy to do that, Mr. Graham."

"Are you kidding? You expect me to put my son on a city bus with a stranger at midnight?"

"He's not a stranger, Dad."

"Night's different. I understand that, Mr. Graham."

"Professor."

"Scuse me?"

"It's Professor Graham."

"Yes. I should have remembered that. Professor."

"How old are you, Mr. Kostka?"

"I'm thirty-nine."

He was younger than my father, which was a shock to me. I looked at him closely and realized that although there was gray in his hair, in his thick eyebrows, it was the crooked nose and all of the tiny scars that aged him.

"And why does someone your age want to be friends with my son?"

Not knowing the accusation implicit in my father's question, I didn't understand the anger in his tone.

"Honestly?" John said. "He looked like he needed a friend. Like maybe he was goin through a tough time."

"And you think that's your business?"

"No, sir. That's your business. But he came to that game last week by himself. By himself in downtown Pittsburgh. When I offered him the ticket to this game, offered to take him, I didn't have any reason to know you were around."

"No. I'm sure you didn't."

"What's that supposed to mean?"

"I think you know."

"Yeah, I do. I was just givin you the benefit of the doubt. That's the way I am with people I don't know."

"Ned," Jeanine said.

My father looked out over the field and put his hands in his pockets.

"We'll wait here," he said.

John and I made our way down to the very bottom of the aisle and then turned left along the roof of the visitor's dugout, in front of the front row of seats. When we got to the point where the railing began, John signaled one of the grounds crew who helped him through, and then we crossed right over the on-deck circle, down the dugout steps and into the tunnel beyond—a secret place to nearly everyone else in the world. It was dark and damp and narrow and we had to go single file, but as soon as we entered I could hear the exuberant voices of the players echoing toward us, growing louder with each rhythmic scrape of John's leather harness against the concrete floor, and no moment in my life before or since has ever felt as much like a waking dream. When we rounded the corner into the locker room the television lights blinded me at first, but I could hear Prince's voice above the others. And when the crowd in front of us moved in just the right way, there they were, in a cleared-out semicircle washed in white light, my two heroes, seated in front of a locker and leaning close to hear one another above the clamor, Prince calling Clemente "Bobby," an Americanized familiarity no one else dared, Clemente briefly allowing the beautiful smile he guarded like privacy to break across his face. Clemente distrusted everyone in the media except Prince, who spoke Spanish and was like a father to the Pirates' Latino players. Early in his career, certain writers had quoted Clemente phonetically, belittling his scattered English, so that he'd stopped talking altogether and was labeled a malcontent. But here he was, laughing easily with Prince—about the homerun argument, no doubt—and speaking freely. Then the crowd closed again and John was motioning me to follow him.

"Do you think they'd sign my program too?"

"I don't see why not."

He found Dave Ricketts who shook my hand and then led me right to Manny Sanguillen's locker. It was the perfect place to start. Sanguillen was famous for his smile and his infectious laugh, and although his English was worse than Clemente's it wasn't hard for him to figure out what I wanted. He signed my ball, then took the program, found his picture and signed that too. He said something to John I didn't understand and John laughed. Then we moved on.

"What did he say?"

"He asked how my boy got to be taller than me so fast."

We went from locker to locker, John introducing me, joking with the players. He told Dock Ellis how their luck had changed as soon as his daughter had found his picture in the program, and Ellis smiled and said they might have to take her to Baltimore with them. Then came Cash, Hebner, Oliver, Davalillo, Robertson, Kison, Blass, Moose, Stargell, all of the men I'd been studying since I could read. We skipped Luke Walker. Even Mazeroski, who was still pinch-hitting and playing the occasional game at second, signed for me and, at John's request, took an extra ball from his locker and signed it as well. I remember every detail—the echoing voices, the laughter, the broad, wet backs, the smell of sweat and mildew and after-shave— and yet none of it seemed real in the heavy basement air.

By the time we got near Clemente's locker Prince and the

television cameras had gone. Clemente sat facing away from us, alone and bare-shouldered. He twisted his neck, first right, then up and around and left, just as he did at the plate, and then he slumped forward briefly, elbows on his knees, crossed himself, and sat back up. If he felt us watching, he gave no indication. In what was still a crowded room, he gave the impression of being entirely alone.

"Go ahead," John said softly.

"I can't."

"Do you want me to get it for you?"

"Do you know him too?"

"No. But I could ask."

"That's okay."

"You sure."

"Yeah."

"You're not going to be sorry?"

"No."

"It's just a signature. I'm sure he'd do it."

"I know. We should go. They're waiting."

"Okay then. You got lots of good ones."

"Yeah. Thanks."

"My pleasure."

Back out on the field Ruthie waved when she saw me come up out of the dugout. She and my father and Jeanine had made their way up the third base line and were waiting at the spot where we'd climbed through earlier. The grounds crew had taken up all of the bases and covered the infield, and the same crew member who had led us down to the tunnel helped John back into the stands. I handed Ruthie the ball.

"This is for *me*?"

"I got my program."

"Whoa!"

"Ready?" my father said. "It's late."

John tossed the ball Mazeroski had signed to him. "Thanks for waitin, Professor." Then he turned and called to the crew member who had turned away and was just about to cross the third base line. "Hey, Chuck. You mind takin our picture?"

"Happy to."

John pulled an instamatic camera from the pocket of his harness and handed it back through the railing. I looked at him.

"You had that the whole time?"

"Yeah, why?"

"Why didn't we take pictures in the locker room?"

"We're guests, not gawkers. Take it from someone who gets looked at a lot. Gets tiresome." John pulled himself up into a front row seat, got turned around, and motioned for us to surround him. "Come on. Squeeze in close, everyone."

ALLIE AND RUTHIE

"*All pretty girls are a trap, a pretty trap*," Allie Graham says to herself in the mirror. "*And men expect them to be*." She gathers her long hair, twists, piles it on top of her head, looks sidelong, raises an eyebrow and kisses the air. Franny is on the floor at Allie's feet, thumping her tail.

Allie knew from the beginning that she was too tall to play Laura Wingfield, that it was Laura's mother, Amanda, or nothing. And most of the time she doesn't mind. She tries hard to embrace her height onstage—in a way that's impossible in the hallways of Panama Middle School—to help portray Amanda's haughtiness. And she is even aware, sometimes, of what feel like maternal instincts as she fixes Laura's hair and readies her for the arrival of her long-awaited gentleman caller. It's when he makes his entrance that Allie's ability to be anyone other than herself disappears.

Tryouts were a formality for Nathan Emery since everyone knew he'd end up playing Jim O'Connor. He may or may not be the best-looking boy in the eighth grade, but he has a presence and an easy confidence that make the distinction irrelevant. It is unoriginal to have a crush on him but Allie can't help herself. And as soon as he appears as Jim, the confusion of being a teenage girl trying to play a vapid middle-aged woman who is trying to recall her days as a desirable teenage girl is too much. At that moment, Allie wants nothing more than to be Laura, sitting there on the couch, touching shoulders with Nathan as they examine the tiny glass unicorn.

"*Oh, be careful!—if you breathe it breaks*," Allie says to the mirror, Laura's lines coming just as easily as her own, her right shoulder tingling cold. "*Hold him over the light. He loves the light.*"

She takes off her sweater and fingers the small pink flower at the center of her scoop-neck undershirt. She only wears a bra when she has gym class, and even then only so that the other girls will see her wearing one. Taking down one cotton strap, she places a palm under her budding nipple and pushes up, trying to cup volume behind it. She does the same on the other side, her taped middle fingers scratching her white skin. Then she tries both at once.

"Nice tits, Graham," she says in her own voice. Franny looks up at her. "Not you, old girl." She opens a drawer, finds her favorite hooded sweatshirt and climbs inside. "Come on," she says.

She walks slowly down the stairs so that Franny can keep up, and then they make a U-turn together, pass through the kitchen and out the side door. Thursday is one of her days to walk both Franny and Ruthie, and though she complains about the chore it's mostly out of habit. She did dread it in the beginning, when Ruthie first arrived. Ruthie was so slow then, like a cripple really, and it took so much of her energy, so much of her concentration, just to put one foot in front of the other that conversation was impossible. Ruthie's breath would start to come fast before they'd even reached the sidewalk, and if she talked at all it would only be to apologize: "I'm... sorry, sweetie... Why don't... you two go on... around the block... one time while I... rest a minute." That first year Ruthie wore a huge men's sweat suit that had to be rolled at the cuffs and sleeves and a white elastic headband to keep the perspiration from burning her eyes, and Allie was in constant fear of being seen by her friends with this odd, hunched, shuffling figure.

But as Ruthie shed pounds, Allie shed her embarrassment. And as Ruthie regained the ability to walk and talk at the same time, Allie found that she had a confidante. It wasn't that she didn't trust either of her parents, but with them there was always the threat of judgment, and even when they didn't judge, they seemed to feel the need to advise. Allie didn't want advice; she just wanted someone to listen, and that's what Ruthie did. As Allie approaches the carriage house, Ruthie appears in the doorway.

"I was just coming to get you," she says. "You girls think you can keep up with me tonight?" Ruthie rubs Franny's gray face.

"We'll try, Aunt Ruthie."

Ruthie burned the sweat suit in a joyful ceremony after losing fifty pounds and on this evening wears a long loose skirt and a button-down sweater that ties at the waist. Her sneakers are new and white.

"How was rehearsal, sweetie?"

"Fine." Allie puts out a hand to help her down from the stoop but Ruthie waves her off.

"I'm okay."

"We were supposed to run scene six today."

"Does that mean our gentleman caller was present?"

"Yeah, but we never finished scene five. It sucked having him there watching me the whole time. Amanda is so pitiful and clueless in that scene. I'm brushing Tom's hair like he's my little girl, wishing on the *'little silver slipper'* moon. God. Did people really used to talk like that?"

"I doubt it."

"And with Nathan sitting down in the front row and me up onstage? I felt like twelve feet tall."

"Do you know how lithe and beautiful I'd be if I could spread these extra pounds out over the five or six extra inches you've got?"

"You look great, Aunt Ruthie."

"You're sweet. And a terrible fibber." They have reached the first corner and turned down Fourth Street, both matching Franny's stilted but steady pace. The sun has just fallen below the hillside behind them where the campus now lays in shadow, taking with it the uncharacteristic warmth of the day, and Ruthie wraps her wool sweater around her and cinches the belt tight. "I can't wait to get to your Nanna's next week. I can't get used to how late spring comes up here."

"I'm *so* jealous. My skin is so pasty white my blackheads look like whisker holes on a cat."

"What blackheads?"

"*I'm* a fibber? Look at these things." They stop and Allie brings her face close to Ruthie's. Franny looks up, apparently confused by the early rest stop, and Ruthie goes momentarily cross-eyed before pulling back.

"I'd need my reading glasses," she says. "Anyway. I tried to get your father to join me. How about you?"

"We'll be down next month. Easter's late this year so spring break is too. And the play's the week before. Will you be back in time?"

"Wouldn't miss it."

They walk in silence for a while, Franny panting between them, each short breath visible for an instant. When they aren't talking Allie has learned to keep Ruthie in her peripheral vision, watching her speed, looking for the telltale drop and swoop of Ruthie's head that means her limp is worsening and that they need to slow down, but she seems strong tonight.

"Aunt Ruthie, can I ask you something?"

"Anything at all."

"How come you never got married?"

"That's my girl. Small talk's a waste of time."

"You don't have to tell me if you don't want."

"There's not much to tell. I never met the right person, and then I was taking care of Pap Pap and here I am."

"Were you ever in love?"

"That's hard to say. I loved someone once. But if your definition of being in love requires two people then no, I haven't been."

"No. You can definitely be in love by yourself."

Ruthie smiles and touches Allie's shoulder. She can't talk for long stretches while they walk, and her breath quickens now. Allie waits before continuing.

"Daddy says it's Pap Pap's fault. You not being married and being... having the problems you have."

"Being fat you mean? It's okay. I've got mirrors."

"Yeah. I guess."

"If saying it's his fault means he did it on purpose, then I disagree. Pap Pap was who he was, just like the rest of us. But yeah, watching the man you love most in the world leave your own mother, then watching him leave three others the same way could make you a little wary. I'd spend more time psychoanalyzing myself if I weren't such an easy case. I ate to avoid love so that it couldn't ever leave me again. Ooooh. I need to catch my breath."

"Sorry." They are midway around the block when they stop. Franny sits and seems glad for the rest herself this time. "Then why did you go to live with him?"

"He was alone, he was my father, and he was dying. That and the fact that I think your Nanna would have left Florida to move in with him if I hadn't. She didn't need him leaving her twice."

"She would have done that?"

"She loved him. When she said '*for better or for worse, til death*' she meant it, even if he didn't."

"What was it like, living with him?"

"Your father thought I was crazy. So did your Aunt Sam. But I wouldn't give that time back for anything. We talked, we ate together, went to ballgames, all the stuff I missed with him as a kid."

"Why didn't we visit him? Why didn't Dad?"

"Your mom was sick then."

"Oh."

"I don't think your dad had room in his heart. Why are you so curious about your Pap Pap all of a sudden?"

"Just the way you and Dad talk about him makes sense all of a sudden."

"How's that?"

"With Nathan. Lots of things I see tell me he isn't someone I should be in love with."

"But it's not really about the pros and cons, is it?"

"No."

"You're figuring this out a lot sooner than I did."

"I have lots of time to think while he's paying exactly no attention to me."

"Sounds like maybe that's a good thing."

"Aunt Ruthie."

"I'm not just trying to make you feel better. Promise." Ruthie runs a hand the full length of Allie's hair which reaches almost to the hem of her sweatshirt. "You ready for the homestretch?"

"Ready."

"Let's go then. Remind me that I've got something for you when we get back."

The second half of the walk is always work for Ruthie, though Allie has noticed her pace improving steadily. Once they turn up Third Street they are silent but for the huff of Ruthie's breathing which now keeps time with each step and the dip of her right shoulder into her bad foot. She'd have lost twice as much weight by now if it weren't for her foot. She's been strict, almost militant, about her diet but she just can't exercise the way she'd like. A stationary bike, Allie thinks, maybe for her birthday in May. When they round the final corner onto Emerson, a rising full moon peers between the trees in the darkening sky.

Inside the carriage house Ruthie strips off her sweater and dabs at her face with a handkerchief.

"Help yourself to a drink and get a bowl for our friend there. I'll be right back."

"Okay. Thanks."

"And would you pour me an iced tea?"

"Sure."

Allie gets iced tea for both of them, puts sugar in her own and sets a bowl of water down for Franny who laps at it with enthusiasm. When Allie takes the glasses into the living room, Ruthie is already coming out of the bedroom carrying the lampshade.

"I was going to wait until after the play to give this to you, but I think it's just as appropriate before."

Allie takes it from her, turning it fully around in her hands.

"Oh my God, Aunt Ruthie, it's beautiful!"

"Here, let's see how it looks over the light. I've been waiting."

Ruthie removes the shade from the table lamp next to her recliner, replaces it with the mosaic and turns the switch. The yellow and green vines glow softly around the bright white body of the unicorn, whose prismed horn throws its spectrum to the wall behind them.

"It's *awesome*, Aunt Ruthie. I love it."

"I'm glad. Break a leg. Speaking of which, I need to sit." Ruthie lowers herself slowly into her recliner and reaches down to flip the lever that elevates her feet. "Ahh. And you've probably got homework to do."

"Not really." Allie sits on the end of the couch closest to Ruthie.

"No?"

"We've sort of got a free pass right now with the play. As long as we do okay on the tests."

"My, aren't we special."

"I was wondering if I could ask you one more thing."

"Sorry. I didn't mean to steer us toward small talk. Shoot."

Allie pauses. "When Mom was sick, did Dad ever talk to you about her dying?"

Ruthie laughs. "Good Lord, child. I hope your school opts for a musical comedy next time."

"I'm sorry. It's just that until you said what you did about Dad not having room to think about both Mom and Pap? I'd kind of forgotten how bad it was around here for a while."

Ruthie nods. "I know."

"So. Did he?"

"Yes. Yes, he did. He didn't talk to you?"

"No. We talked about her being sick and what was going to happen before she got better, that the chemo was going to be hard and that she might lose her hair. But we never talked about her dying."

"You were younger."

"I don't mean I'm mad at him for not talking to me. It only took one Google search and I *knew*. It just always made me sad that he didn't have anyone to talk to, you know? He just seemed so numb all the time, like as soon as he got up he couldn't wait to go back to bed. I thought maybe since you were his sister, and since it was sort of your job to talk to people about things anyway, that maybe he was talking to you."

"He was. All the time. He'd call and I'd talk about Pap and he'd talk about your mother, and then we'd both cry, and then we'd both laugh about how all we did was cry. We were a pair, I'll tell you."

"Good. I'm glad you were."

Franny limps in from the kitchen and lays her chin on the arm of Ruthie's chair. Ruthie strokes her face. "Funny you should bring up my old job, because now you'll be the first to know. I'm thinking about starting to see a few patients again."

"Really? I think that's great. You'll be Dr. Ruth!"

"God, you know about her?"

"Everyone does."

"Don't tell your father that."

"Trust me."

"Anyway, I'll probably start off seeing them here at the house, if it's all right with your father, until I can make enough to be able to afford an office. I've got to update my certification and then get licensed here in New York, so it's going to be a while. But I've been thinking lately that I might be ready."

"No doubt, Aunt Ruthie. You go, girl."

Allie puts her fist out and they bump knuckles.

9

At dismissal, we burst from the building as if there had been a loss of cabin pressure. Nellie Briles had been doing an unlikely but pretty fair Steve Blass imitation for four innings, and we rushed to the buses in the hopes that our own energy might inspire our drivers to whisk us quickly home, as if the lumbering pace of the bright yellow beasts was a daily choice they could unmake for us, just this once. Ruthie had her transistor radio for the ride home, and the only voice that could be heard over the chuffing of the bus engine the whole way home was The Gunner's.

When Ruthie and I bolted into the living room, Sam was sitting on the couch with a boy I'd never seen before. He was smiling at her with red, sleepy eyes and only looked away for an instant when we appeared. The stereo was blaring and the television was off.

"What about the game?!" I yelled over the music.

Sam swung the leg that had been over the new guy's knee back to her side of the cushion. "Mom's watching it over at The Missing Link's house. He closed the office early."

I turned the stereo down. "No. I mean *here*."

"We're not into it." It was the new guy talking but he was still looking at Sam.

"Stop staring, Gino. You're creeping me out," she said to him. "We're not into it," she said to us.

"Does Mom know you have a boyfriend here?" I ventured.

"Gino's not my boyfriend."

"I'm not?"

"No."

"Then go up to your room and let us have the couch," I said. "We won't tell."

"Yeah," Ruthie chimed in.

"We're listening to music."

"We could go up to your room," Gino said. "I'm cool with that."

"Yeah, you wish."

I grabbed Ruthie's hand and pulled her out of the living room and toward the front door.

"Wherever it is, do your homework!" Sam called.

Gino thought that was the funniest thing he'd ever heard, and he was still laughing as I pulled the door closed behind us.

I put Ruthie on my handlebars, figuring she'd never keep up on her own bike. When I slammed on the brakes in front of the VFW, she popped off and kept right on running for the entrance. I passed her on the stairs and led the way through the hallways and back to John's apartment.

"Well, get on in here then," he said after we'd nearly beat the door down.

"Whoa!" said Ruthie, running straight for the nearest set of steps and then sliding down a pole.

"I don't know what you did last night, little missy, but everything Murtaugh touches right now turns to gold. Can you believe Briles?"

John had the radio and the television on, the television volume turned down. Both were in a commercial break. Before we'd even left school, the Pirates were leading three to nothing. Briles was a journeyman pitcher who hadn't pitched in two weeks—hadn't even been taking his regular turn in the rotation toward the end of the season—but he had given up just one harmless single in the second and, after a homerun by Bob Robertson, had driven in the Pirates' second run himself. Briles had a habit of falling on his chest after each pitch, but every ground ball seemed to hop over or dodge around him and right into an infielder's glove. The third run was scored by Gene Clines, a speedy backup outfielder who had walked to lead off the inning, and who had started in center field just to give Al Oliver the day off after the late night game. John was right. The magic from the night before had somehow survived.

Three Rivers Stadium appeared on the TV screen at the same time that Prince's voice came through the radio.

"Hey, that's what *we* do!" Ruthie called from the top of one of the sets of stairs. Her arms were wrapped around a pole, ready to slide. "We don't like that TV guy either."

"I don't mind Gowdy," John said. "It's the color guy, that Tony Kubek. I can't stand him." He swung over toward the refrigerator, took two Cokes from the inside of the door and pried them open under the countertop.

"How come?" Ruthie asked.

"Kubek played shortstop for the Yankees in the '60 World Series. Virdon hit him in the throat with a bad hopper in the eighth inning of Game 7 and he had to come out. Kubek was in the locker room cooling with the Yankees' victory champagne when Maz hit the homerun to win it. He's hated the Pirates ever since. I can't listen to him. Come get these, will ya?" We each took a Coke and I went to sit on the couch. Because the legs had been cut off, my knees were above my lap, and I must have looked awkward.

"Stretch em out, Hammer. Make yourself at home," John said, settling himself next to me.

"Can I sit up here?" Ruthie asked. She had climbed the stairs next to the refrigerator and was walking along the scaffolding that paralleled the counter. She was holding her arms out and looking down as if she were on a balance beam two stories up.

"Wherever the karma takes you, Miss Bambino. But I reserve the right to move you if Briles wakes up from this dream."

But he didn't. Briles kept flopping to the dirt after every pitch, and the Orioles kept hitting balls right at someone. Clines wasn't done either. His only hit in the entire Series was a triple in the fifth, and Clemente, who was continuing to use the Series to build his own legend, drove him home. Ruthie paced back and forth across the scaffolding. She'd been standing when Clines tripled and was afraid to sit down until John tossed her a pillow and assured her it wouldn't be bad luck. She sat on it only during commercials. When it was over, Briles had thrown a two-hit, complete game shutout, and Sanguillen embraced him as if they'd just won the Series. Ruthie finally came down and celebrated by circling the room over and over, up the stairs and down the poles, singing *"The Bucs are going all the way, all the way, all the way."* John popped open a bottle of Iron City, slid it into his pouch and swung back over to the couch.

"I'd offer you a sip to celebrate, but your father doesn't trust me as it is."

"That's okay. I tried some of his once. I didn't like it."

"Probably some fancy foreign beer, no offense. This here's the nectar of the Gods." He took a long pull on the bottle. "Ahh. What're you two doin for dinner?"

"I'm not sure," I said. "My mom isn't home."

"I'll whip somethin up for us."

"That's okay."

"No trouble. I hardly ever get to cook for more than one."

"Hey, who's this?" Ruthie called. I was sure she was looking at the wall of pictures John had shown me on my first visit, but when I looked over the back of the couch she wasn't there. That's when

I realized she had gone back behind the partition and into John's bedroom. I could see just a sliver of the bed and, right there in the open, were the combat boots I had noticed on my first visit. It was as though they had appeared the instant Ruthie asked her question.

Something changed in John's face.

"Come on out of there, missy," he said.

"But who is it?"

"You always go snoopin in people's bedrooms without askin?"

"Sorry." Ruthie peered around the corner. "I didn't know it was a bedroom until I was in it. There's no door."

For a moment I didn't think John was going to say anything. Then he sighed deeply, put his beer in his pocket. "Come on," he said. I followed as he swung heavily across the room. My attention was fixed on the boots, and I passed close enough to touch them. It wasn't until Ruthie spoke that I looked away and followed her gaze.

"Is that you?"

Unlike the outside of the wall, the inside held just one photograph, centered above a small dresser. In it, a young man in uniform stood next to a barefooted girl in a white summer dress. Her outside heel was off the ground, that knee kicked in toward the man, and while he was looking at the camera, she was looking up at him.

"Yeah. That's me."

"Whoa!" said Ruthie. "You were *tall*."

But it wasn't just his height that made it hard to see John in the photograph. The short-cropped hair, the smooth, clean-shaven face and almost pointed nose. Everything about him seemed narrower, less substantial, especially his shoulders, which didn't quite reach the sharp corners of his jacket. His dress shirt, buttoned to the top, didn't appear to touch his neck at any point in its circumference. If the uniform had ever fit him, it didn't when this picture was taken. We all stood and looked at the photograph in silence for a while, and John gradually seemed to recover himself.

"*Suddenly*," he sang softly behind us, "*I'm not half the man I used to be*." He laughed softly but Ruthie and I kept staring. "Pretty handsome guy, huh?" he said.

"Yeah," said Ruthie. "Is that your girlfriend?"

It was, of course, the question that begged to be asked but also the one John had undoubtedly feared the instant he realized what Ruthie had been looking at in his bedroom. I never could have asked it. But Ruthie's uncomplicated curiosity had charmed John from the beginning, and he answered as though he'd meant to show us this picture all along.

"That was my fiancée. Kathy. Never been happier in my life than this exact minute you're seein here. I couldn't look at it for a long time, but then that started to seem like a waste. When I moved into this place, I put it up."

"Didn't you marry her?" Ruthie asked.

"No. She died."

"Oh." Ruthie paused. "When?"

"Six months after this was taken."

"How did she die?"

John turned away from us and started pulling himself back toward the living room.

"Come on," he said. "Enough history. We got some celebratin to do."

So that's what we did. Ruthie scampered back and forth across the scaffolding like a squirrel on a wire, helping John make spaghetti sauce. I set the low table and poured two more Cokes and a beer. He called it "Italian food Chinese-style," all of us sitting on pillows, John chattering like a shortstop.

"Okay, questions. Who's got a question to start us off? No? Okay then. Beatles or Stones?"

"Beatles," Ruthie said immediately.

"Why's that?"

"I like Paul."

"Good enough. Your turn then."

Ruthie thought for a moment.

"*Brady Bunch* or *Partridge Family?*"

John smiled. "*Partridge Family.*"

"Why?"

"Shirley Jones versus Florence Henderson ain't even a fair fight. *Mary Tyler Moore* or *That Girl?*"

It went on like that for a while, mostly between John and Ruthie, who basked in his attention and bestowed on John all the warmth she'd denied our mother's dinner date just a few nights earlier. I don't think I realized until then how much of what I craved from my father I was now getting from John. But watching Ruthie beam and laugh and lean into every word, I saw myself too. Eventually he turned and drew me into the conversation.

"Hammerin Hank. What's your opinion of our president, Richard Millhouse Nixon?"

"I don't know."

"You don't know? Rule number one for U.S. citizens: You must have an opinion about your elected officials."

"He's okay, I guess."

"He slouches," Ruthie said.

"Right you are, Miss Bambino. I don't trust slouchers."

"And he sort of looks like a sad dog. His cheeks are all floppy."

"Excellent observation. More bread for anyone?"

"Me, please," said Ruthie.

I looked at all of the crusts spread around the outside of her plate on the table. "You're only eating the middles again, Ruthie."

John handed the bread to me to pass to Ruthie. "That's okay," he said. "There's plenty. Send those crusts my way, Miss Bambino. I'll eat them. More spaghetti?"

"No, thank you."

"Okay then, Hank. What about the war?"

"Hm?"

"Vietnam. Stay in, or get out?"

This wasn't "*Star Trek* or *Lost in Space?*" and I froze.

"Umm..."

"You should know—those statistics you hear on the radio every morning? Those are real people. Some of them came to hear you sing the other night." There was a brief silence for the first time since we'd sat down. "Well, I'll tell you what I think. We shouldn't have been there in the first place, and now we shouldn't be leavin. Same as the one I was in. We got no idea how to fight these kinds of wars but we keep tryin. It's hubris, is what it is." He shook his head and we all ate quietly.

My childhood memories of the war are precisely as he stated them that night: the daily casualty statistics on my clock radio as I got dressed every morning: how many killed, how many wounded, then on to the sports, weather and traffic. It was nothing like the wars we were starting to learn about in school. There was no rhythm to it, no ebb and flow, no sense of what we were trying to win, no movie-house newsreels or fight songs. It was just data. Low numbers were a good day; high numbers were bad. Ruthie broke the silence.

"*I Dream of Jeannie* or *Bewitched?*" she said hesitantly

John hooted.

"Thanks, Miss Bambino. Almost forgot this was a celebration. Let's ask your brother. You go for the pretty mom or the one in the silky outfit who seems to be missin a navel?"

I blushed and shrugged. Too many people had mentioned how much our mother looked like Elizabeth Montgomery for me to think of "Samantha" that way, but I had a powerful boyhood crush on Jeannie that had everything to do with my weekly hope that her belly button might peek out from beneath her flimsy elastic waistband.

Ruthie was too focused on John to notice my discomfort.

"Were you ever a real magician?" she asked him.

"You mean like up on stage? No. I never had that Big Trick."

"What do you mean?"

"The stuff I do, sleight of hand, only works up close where you can see every slip-up. Those fancy magicians all have that one big trick they end with. Like levitating a pretty girl or making her disappear from a big box and then reappear at the back of the theater. The trick that makes everyone cheer and forget how ordinary you were, how many mistakes you made before that."

"I like your kind of magic."

"Thanks, missy."

"Why are there boots next to your bed?"

I tensed immediately but Ruthie had her head cocked like a quizzical puppy, unaware that there was anything jarring or inappropriate about her question. To her it was just part of the game we had been playing all night: you thought of a question, and you asked it. John himself appeared unfazed.

"You noticed that, huh?" he said.

"Yeah."

"Kinda creepy, ain't it?"

"A little."

"You ever learn anything in school about how the ancient Egyptians used to bury people with the things they'd need in the afterlife?"

"No."

"Well, they did. I just want to be ready is all."

"I like that. I'm going to take my magic markers with me."

The television was still on, the volume down low, and when the local evening news started playing highlights of the game, John smiled and shook his head.

"Can you believe we're goin back to Baltimore leadin this thing? We got no business beatin these boys. It's 1960 all over again."

"Don't jinx it!" said Ruthie.

"There's no jinxin these boys, missy. This ain't the Steelers we're talkin about."

An Invitation

Henry rarely loses control of a workshop but this one is going particularly badly for Evan Hobbs, Friday afternoon's final author, and Henry feels powerless to stop the onslaught. Or, perhaps, *disinclined* is the word he would choose. His conversation with Atlee brought on two straight days of uncharacteristic crankiness, and the story up for critique is, by any standard, awful. Moreover, there is the matter of Henry's own attention, which he is working hard not to divert to Natalie Currant. He has yet to talk to her about her chapters, and she has been sitting at the far end of the table, directly across from him, without once looking up.

The leader of the ongoing attack on Evan's story is Parker Philp, a gifted sentence writer who consistently rejects Henry's contention that perfect sentences strung together don't make a story. Parker is typical of many of the male students who take Henry's workshop in that he doesn't want to write nearly as much as he wants to be a writer. He has adopted the aloof, sardonic manner he believes to be required and wears a lot of black while producing very few pages. Henry's customary patience with students like Parker derives from his belief that some will come back to writing like Henry did—as adults with something to say.

"I mean, the setup isn't awful," Parker is declaring. "You get the kid to the beach fire with his babysitter, just the two of them, she's hot as hell, he's nervous, the night sky hangs over them like a fucking blanket of clichés, but still, something could *happen* here. And then he throws *up*? Are you fucking *kidding* me?"

"But that's what *happened*," Evan protests.

"Check the syllabus, dude. This isn't *Memoir*."

"Plus you're not supposed to be talking, Evan."

Paula Price is the self-appointed monitor of workshop protocol, and this is her first and only contribution to the critique.

"And *he's* not supposed to be addressing me directly," Evan reminds Henry. Henry nods at Parker.

"Okay, okay," Parker continues. "So *he*, Evan, the author, sets this up, with all of the myriad fucking places it could go—a confession of love, an awkward, unsuccessful pass, a pity kiss, she shows him her fucking tits, I don't know—and then his narrator just yack-yawns all over his LL Bean shorts and goes running into the lake? What a fucking copout."

Henry holds his hand up. "We've got it, Parker: you don't like the choice; and '*fucking*' is your favorite adjective today."

"I was offended by it," says Miriam Klink.

"There's a shocker," says Parker.

Miriam is the leader of the Student Christian Coalition. Her last story was about her kitten.

"Not the throwing up part. I actually felt really bad for the narrator when that happened, and I thought he was going to explore his shame over some of the improper thoughts he'd been having about her. But then when her boyfriend comes to the house and they have premarital sex? I just thought the rest of that scene, what the boy sees, went way too far."

"Are you fucking kidding me?" Parker again.

"So you weren't offended at all by the girl's virginal blood right there on the carpet?"

"Yeah. I was offended by its *triteness.*"

"All right," Henry cuts in. Evan hasn't looked up from his story during this last exchange, and Henry knows he has to try to bring him in from the ledge, though he has some difficulty mustering his usual enthusiasm for the job. "Since we're almost out of time for today, can we at least agree that Evan has attempted to address certain themes and emotions that are worth writing about? Jealousy, insecurity, coming of age, unrequited love."

"Yes," says Natalie Currant, looking right at Henry. He freezes momentarily, his eyes big in his glasses, and hopes no one has noticed.

"Would you care to elaborate, Natalie?"

"No." She looks back down and makes a show of writing something.

"All right then. Anyone else?"

Parker is shaking his head. "So we're supposed to give the writer credit for trying to address universal themes? That happens automatically, doesn't it? Just about anything you can think of comes back to love or sex or death. But if he can't *execute*, it's all wasted."

"We've had some version of this discussion before, I think, Parker. At this point in your development, I don't think it *is* all about the execution. I'm just pointing out that Evan is looking at the world like a writer, and that it's an important first step. The rest is largely a matter of practice, trial and error, ruthless revision, all of the things we've been talking about all semester."

"So talent is irrelevant?"

This was a topic Henry avoided whenever possible, mostly out of compassion.

"The necessary talent, Parker, is for empathy as much as it is for language. Together, you and Evan might make a pretty fair writer someday."

Parker looks stunned before blowing a short, defiant burst of air. "Who put Tabasco in *your* Cheerios?"

"Who's up next week?" Henry asks. Three students raise tentative hands as everyone begins gathering their belongings. Evan sits, motionless and silent, shoulders hunched, his arms covering his story on the tabletop. Most days Henry would now be taking the chair next to his, treating wounds, but Natalie isn't moving either. The others pass Evan and place ink-filled copies next to him. The chatter that normally accompanies this exit ritual is absent.

"Thanks," Evan says a couple of times.

"I have office hours Monday morning if you'd like to stop in, Evan. I've got a few thoughts on where you might go with this in revision. I've jotted a few notes on my copy that you might consider before we talk."

Evan accepts the pages. "Thanks," he says again. Then he pushes himself up, tucks the stack of paper under his arm and walks out. Henry and Natalie are alone.

"Do I make you uncomfortable?" she asks.

"Is that your intent?"

"Yes. I've been uncomfortable for three days waiting to hear from you."

"I'm sorry."

They are still sitting at opposite ends of the seminar table and look like a caricature of an old rich couple having a tense, wordless dinner.

"Do you know what it feels like to give your work to someone you trust and then have him go silent?"

"Actually, I do. And you're absolutely right. I should have called. And I almost did, but—"

"But?"

"Well, it was late when I finished."

"Come on. I'm twenty-one. Do you know what *late* is for me?"

"I thought of that."

"And?"

Henry is conscious of the fact that this conversation isn't going at all the way Atlee had advised. But he is not Atlee. He is again aware that Natalie seems older than his other students, and he is certain that she would see through any pretense he might attempt. "The truth is the prospect of talking to you about it was a little unnerving."

"Why?"

Henry dips his chin and looks at Natalie over the top of his glasses, shrinking his eyes.

"Oh, that," she says.

"Yes. That."

"Should I have warned you?"

"Maybe that's standard fare at places like NYU, but up here in the great gray north it's mostly broken hearts, dysfunctional families and the occasional kitten."

"Do you see why I didn't want to let this group at it?"

"They might have surprised you."

"The only surprise would have been Miriam not calling for an exorcism at my apartment. She keeps this picture of her family at the beach on her dresser? She's wearing a bathing skirt."

Henry laughs. "And no tan, I'm betting."

"SPF 50 on Longboat Key. All week."

They both laugh and then are quiet. Natalie seems to be waiting.

"Have I said yet that it's good?" Henry finally asks.

"No."

"It is. Very."

"Good for this class, or just good?"

"Just very good."

Natalie's face opens and her eyes shimmer until she blinks. "Thank you."

"Don't overvalue my opinion. There are those—some right

down the hall—who think I don't know a heck of a lot about good writing."

"They're jealous."

"I doubt it."

"How's that going. The review."

"You know about that?"

"The students always know who's up for tenure. Sometimes there's betting."

"What's the early line on me?"

"I'm not aware of any activity. I can't think of anyone who'd want to bet against you."

"Mr. Nice Guy."

"A little edgier than usual today, though, I must say."

"Yeah. Sorry. I've had a lot on my mind, I guess."

"Parker Philp is an asshole who's been begging for a dose of reality. When you lumped him in with Evan, he looked like he'd been shot."

"I shouldn't have said that."

"Look, most everyone on this campus has been coddled since birth. Someone needs to tell them the whole *'you can be whatever you want to be'* line is a load of crap."

"I've just told you that you could be a writer."

"You did, didn't you?"

"Yes, I did."

Natalie smiles again and stands. "Do you have a few more minutes?"

"A few."

She walks the length of the table and takes the chair immediately around the corner from Henry. "I don't want to *unnerve* you or anything," she teases.

"No, I'm okay."

"But can we talk about it? That last scene? Because I had a very specific purpose in writing it."

"And what was that?"

"Tell me your reaction first."

"It made me feel, I don't know, *guilty,* in a way, reading it."

Natalie laughs. "Lucky wife."

"How does that follow?"

"There are men in your department who would have read that chapter and immediately come to find me. You felt guilty about being aroused by a piece of writing that was meant to be arousing. Why do you think I felt safe showing it to you?"

Henry shrugs.

"Look," Natalie continues. "Now it's my turn to be honest. I wanted you to read this because I wanted to see how far I could push what little I have to work with. I don't exactly have a lot of experience to draw from. My parents love me and I love them. I don't recall either of them ever missing a single dance recital, chorus concert or soccer game that any of my sisters and I were in. As long as I kept my grades up, I had almost no restrictions. I could go to parties where my parents knew there would be alcohol as long as I promised to call home for a ride if I needed one—no matter what time of night—no questions asked. We take family vacations and have fun. My mother knows my taste in clothes so well that I never have to return a Christmas present. My parents and I share an *iTunes* account, for Christ's sake. They're incredible people. But sometimes I feel as though I've been ruined by all that contentment. I know that sounds like the ultimate self-absorbed, over-privileged lament, but don't we all crave a little pain? Isn't it possible that the range of emotions we're required to exercise growing up affects our range as adults? I can't do rage because I've never had to. I can't do despair or rejection or even rebellion. It's hollowing in a way. But sex? I think I got my first porn spam when I was ten. Sex I can do. I don't think there are kids in the middle sexually anymore. You've either grown up with free rein on the web, in which case you've seen, read, and probably typed things your parents never thought about until they were married, or you're Miriam and don't have a clue. So I guess I'm exercising. I'm seeing if I can extend what I *do* know into emotional places other writers go, writers with more emotional baggage than I'll ever be able to pack. There. Whew."

"Whew."

"Did that sound rehearsed?"

"Not at all."

"Good."

"And I don't disagree, by the way. My parents split up when I was eleven, but I was still basically Parker Philp as an undergrad. Beautiful middle-class sentences full of sound and fury, signifying nothing."

"So what changed?"

"Having kids. My sister getting sick. You know. Life."

"Your wife?"

Henry fidgets, shrugs. "That's different."

"I'm sorry. I didn't mean to..."

"No, it's all right."

Henry looks at his watch.

"Do you have to go?"

"Yeah. I do. Sorry if I haven't been much help."

"No. You have. But can we talk more?"

"Sure. I'm in the office Monday morning, though I expect I'll be seeing our friend Evan then."

"I was thinking about tomorrow. We're having a small social at the House. It'll be quiet. We can find a corner. Maybe even take a plastic cover off a couch."

"I thought you hated that place."

"I make an exception once in a while. Can you stop by?"

"I don't know."

"Bring her."

"What?"

"I know what you're thinking. Bring your wife. Around nine?"

"I'll see what we're doing. The kids. You know."

"Stop worrying, Professor," Natalie says as she stands to go. "I'm not in love with you."

After Natalie leaves, Henry is packing up his shoulder bag when Loren Strummer peers in around the corner of the classroom doorway.

"Got a minute, sweetie?"

Loren is one of a dying class of married gay men who think that marriage, by itself, hides his secret from the world. In all other aspects of his life Loren unabashedly flames. His head freshly shaved, salt and pepper goatee precisely trimmed, he is all in black: mock turtleneck, linen pants and shoes that resemble ballet slippers. He walks in like a mime—toe, heel, toe, heel—hands clasped in front around a rolled piece of paper. He is the Department Chair because he is the only person everyone can agree on: they all dislike him equally.

"Come in," Henry deadpans, Loren already standing in front of him.

"Who's your little friend?"

"Hm?"

"The tall lovely who just left by herself."

"Student. Natalie Currant."

"Talent?"

"Yes, actually."

"Hm. I don't think I've had her in class."

Henry wonders if he is playing dumb. Natalie dropped Loren's Intro to Fiction Writing class after two weeks during her freshman spring to pick up Henry's.

"Is there something you wanted, Loren?"

"Oh, yes. Quick question. Did you leave any publications off your CV?" Loren jiggles the paper he is holding between thumb and index finger up around his ear like a bell.

"What do you mean?"

"Essays, criticism, stories in any of the lit journals you may have considered unimportant?"

"No."

"So it's just the novels then?"

"Yes."

"Graduate degrees?"

"Just the J.D."

"Well, you're not teaching law here, are you?"

"No."

"No. Okay then."

"Okay?"

"Yes."

"That's all you came in to ask me?"

"I'm just crossing and dotting all the proverbials. Making sure your chances are as good as they can be."

"Right."

"Oh." He says this as if he has turned to go and then, remembering something, has doubled back, but he hasn't budged. "And you might want to scoot on home and have a chat with little Walter."

"What are you talking about?"

"Elvira called. Something about a swordfight gone wrong. Sounded like good clean fun to me, but she was in a *state*."

"Thanks, Loren. Any more professional or parenting tips before I go?"

"Nope. Toodles."

"Toodles."

On his way to the stairwell, Henry looks into Atlee's office and is surprised to find him there. He is facing away from Henry, standing at his tall, mullioned window, looking out at the quadrangle below. "Almost four-thirty on a Friday?" Henry says by way of greeting. "Everything all right?"

"Ah, Henry," Atlee says, turning. "Just the man I was hoping might happen by."

"I just had the oddest conversation with Loren."

"Careful, my man. That's a difficult benchmark."

"He wanted to know if I had published more than '*just the novels*.'"

"Have you?"

"No."

"Bugger."

"You knew that."

"I thought there might have been a story or two, or book reviews perhaps."

"What's the problem?"

"At today's meeting he was on about how you'd only been published once since you arrived here."

"It was a novel for Christ's sake, not an essay in *Bloom*."

"And I assured everyone you were hard at work on another." Atlee sends a mock glare toward Henry.

"Oh, perfect. Thanks."

"Don't worry too much about it. He's just fishing."

"For what?"

"For something he can latch onto to sway one or two others to his way of thinking."

"Which is?"

"He can't stand you. You must know that by now."

"But why?"

"Other than what we talked about at lunch the other day? Have you looked in on one of his workshops lately?"

"No."

"It's Loren and four students who couldn't get into yours. The only person he hates more than you is me, but he knows he can't get rid of me."

"But if you can see what he's doing, doesn't the rest of the committee see it as well?"

"Of course they do. That's why I said not to worry."

"Then why are you looking at me like that?"

Atlee turns back to his window and clasps his hands behind him. His white hair tapers to a sharp line just above the collar of his jacket, the straight edge freshly shaved, and his broad shoulders strain at the seams. Except for the tweed, he looks from behind more like a general surveying his troops than an aging professor.

"Do you mind if I turn the tables? Ask you for a bit of advice?" he finally asks.

"After almost seven years I think you're entitled."

"I'm not quite ready to name names, so can we just keep it in the hypothetical for now?"

"It's your office, Professor."

Atlee turns his head and shows Henry his profile. He lifts his chin so that he appears to be sniffing the air to test that it will properly carry the import of what he is about to say.

"What if a man, about my age, suddenly decides that he is in love for the first time?"

"*What?*"

"For the first time in thirty-odd years anyway."

"You're in love?"

"Hypothetically."

"Not with your student of the month, I hope. Astrid?"

"I made her up. Haven't had a student of the month in months. Almost a year. And in any event she's irrelevant to our hypothetical—which involves a man who is in love with another man's wife."

Henry pauses. "You didn't mention that part."

"I'm parceling out my details for dramatic effect. As a writer, you should know something about that. A colleague's wife."

"Atlee, what are you confessing to me?"

"Nothing. I told you. I'm asking for your advice."

"My hypothetical advice."

"Precisely."

"About whether or not you should pursue a trusted colleague's wife?"

"I didn't say that I was pursuing, and I don't particularly trust anyone."

"Not even me?"

"No one is who they appear to be, so trust is mostly misplaced. People talk about it as if it's an absolute, but it comes in degrees. It's more like hope, really."

"So I should simply *hope* that it's not my wife you're in love with?"

Atlee turns full front for the first time during this exchange. "Since, as you said, this is one time in seven years, can this be about me?"

"Sorry."

"It's all right. I suppose I didn't really want advice anyway. Just wanted to hear myself say it is all. See what it would sound like."

"And?"

"Scary as hell."

When we got home from John's that night I heard, for the first of many times, my sister Sam having sex in her bedroom. It was after eight and our mother's car was still missing from the driveway. Downstairs, both the stereo and the television were off, but I could hear Sam's radio playing through the ceiling. There were other sounds too, sounds I didn't fully understand but somehow recognized as being part of something that, finally, put my older sister out of reach.

"You wanna go upstairs?" Ruthie asked.

"No."

"Why not?"

"Sam's up there."

"So?"

"I think that guy is still here too. Gino."

"She's not allowed to have the door closed. Let's go check." Ruthie turned toward the stairs and I had to grab her by the shoulders.

"Just stay down here, okay?"

"Why? She wouldn't let us watch the game. I don't care if she gets in trouble."

"Just *listen* to me, Ruthie." I raised my voice and it startled her.

"Okay. You don't have to yell."

"Stay down here."

I turned the television on to try to keep her from asking about the noises coming from above us. Flip Wilson was prancing across the screen in a wig, heels and short skirt, dragging a man by his tie.

"Ooh, don't change it," Ruthie said. "I love Geraldine."

"We'll take da booth in da back in da corner in da dark," Geraldine told the *maître d'.*

After a while there were footsteps on the ceiling, then on the stairs.

"Can't we just chill for a minute?" Gino was asking.

"I told you, you have to go."

"But I wanna meet your mom. I hear she's hot." Gino laughed.

"Fuck you."

"No, seriously. Shouldn't she meet your new man?"

"You are *not* my *man.*"

"Coulda fooled me."

They were in the hallway, around the corner from us now.

"Look, you're not my boyfriend, okay? And if you tell anyone— and I mean *anyone*—that you are, or if you tell *anyone* what happened here, I can promise you it will never happen again. Just ask Matthew. Got it?"

"Okay. Geez." Gino was quiet. "Can I call you?" he finally said.

"What for?"

"I don't know. So we can, like, *talk.*"

"What part of not being my boyfriend don't you understand, Gino?"

"Man, I don't get you at all."

"Now you're catching on. Come on. Before my mom gets home." The front door opened.

"See you at school?" Gino said.

"Yeah. Sure."

The door closed and Sam strode with purpose into the living room.

"Either of you say anything to Mom and I'll tell her you left for four hours without telling me where you were going."

"You wouldn't let us watch the *game*," Ruthie protested.

"Doesn't matter. You were still MIA for four hours."

"We were just at Henry's friend's house. He made us dinner and he has no legs."

"What are you talking about?"

"We're not going to say anything," I interjected.

"Did you eat?"

"I just *told* you," Ruthie said.

"Mom claims to be helping Boss Hairy clean up after his party. She'll be home by nine to put you guys to bed."

"Is he coming here?" Ruthie asked. "Because if he tries to kiss me goodnight I'll sock him one."

"I don't think you have to worry about that, Ruthie. I don't think she likes him that much."

"Then why is she going on dates with him?"

Sam's face softened a little at that, the muscles in her cheeks letting go and pulling her eyes down with them. "I'm going to straighten up my room," she said.

And when she left she was, in many ways, gone from us for good. Maybe it had started before, but for me that night marked the beginning. Sam never bothered with a homecoming dance. She skipped both her junior and senior proms. But from that night until the day she moved across the country to go to school, there was a constant flow of mostly older boys who found their way to our doorstep whenever our mother was going to be out, most leaving an hour or so later the way Gino did—like scolded pets. She was surprisingly smart about her promiscuity. She never got pregnant, never came close to getting caught, and it took me a long time to admit that she wasn't really the one being used.

When my mother came home she seemed genuinely happy for the first time in a long while. Mr. Garabedian had closed the office and invited everyone to his place for the game and dinner, which he cooked himself. "You should see his house," she told us. "Big and spacious. And you'd never guess a bachelor lived there. It's clean and decorated so tastefully, and the kitchen is like something you'd see in a restaurant."

"Does he have a pool?" Ruthie asked.

"No. No pool that I saw."

"If I was rich, I'd have a pool."

We all went upstairs and talked about the game together. Ruthie got out of bed and did her impression of Nellie Briles flopping to the dirt after every pitch, and we laughed, so she did it three more times.

"Henry," my mother said. "Mark told me he's been watching Clemente ever since you two talked about him. He wanted me to tell you he makes everyone else out there look like a minor leaguer."

"Pfff," said Ruthie, getting back into bed.

"Excuse me, young lady?"

"He doesn't even like baseball."

"Ruthie, why don't you like Mr. Garabedian? What exactly has he done to offend you so acutely?"

Ruthie shrugged.

"You were rude to him when he was here for dinner the other night. And you're rude any time there's talk about him at all."

Ruthie shrugged again.

"You like Jeanine, right?"

"She's okay."

"So why is Daddy allowed to have a friend but I'm not?"

Ruthie shrugged.

"You can keep shrugging your shoulders all night if you really don't know the answer, but if you do, I want you to tell me. You and Henry are the most important people in the world to me, and I care what you think. Do you understand that?"

Ruthie nodded.

"So can you tell me?"

Ruthie's mouth started to twitch and I thought she was going to cry. She blinked hard a couple of times and pressed her lips with the fingers of one hand.

"Jeanine's never going to try to be our mom," she said. "She's never going to move in with us. That's why I like her."

My mother put her hand on Ruthie's chest and slid it down one arm. "Ruthie," she said. "Is that what you've been worried about this whole time?"

Ruthie nodded.

"Sweetie, this might not be something you can understand right now, but your father and I are very different people that way. I can't just go right from the end of a marriage into another relationship. It's a little sad to say, but I still think of myself as *being* married most of the time because I thought I always would be. Mark is my friend. He's nice to me, and we have a nice time together. And right now I need that very badly. Nothing is for sure, but me marrying Mr. Garabedian, or anyone else for that matter, isn't something you should be worrying yourself about right now."

"Did you tell him that?" Ruthie asked. It was such a wise and unexpected question that my mother paused, her face momentarily going blank.

"I'll be honest with you, sweetie. I thought it was too soon to even talk about something like that. But I will. I promise you that I will."

She kissed us both goodnight and we talked about how hard it was going to be to wait for Game 6 on Saturday. She promised to make our favorite foods and said we could each invite a friend over to watch, assuming, I'm sure, that we'd invite friends from school.

"Ooh, can Henry's friend John come over?" Ruthie asked. "He can make spaghetti."

"Not in our kitchen," I said.

"Oh yeah. But can he?"

"Sure. Whoever you two want."

"And I'm inviting Daddy," she said.

My mother closed her eyes, lowered her head and seemed to gather herself.

"Ruthie, I'm really not anxious to sit and watch a baseball game with your father and his girlfriend."

"I'm not inviting Jeanine," Ruthie said. "I like her, but I'm not inviting her this time."

"But he's going to want to bring her."

"But I'm not *inviting* her."

"Ruthie Graham, you are the most *stubborn* child God ever put... Fine. Call him. See what he says. I'll watch in the kitchen."

"Daddy and I will come keep you company sometimes."

"Perfect."

Maggie, Unfinished

Upstairs in her third floor studio, Maggie is vaguely, viscerally displeased with the images before her. All seven of them. Subtractive charcoal is analogous to sculpture, a black space that is rubbed away to reveal the subject, and for the last six months Maggie has been at work on a series of life-size self-portraits in which she gradually emerges from the black and then disappears into the white. What she can't understand is why it is easier to convey what *is* than what *isn't*. Her fingers black and smudged, she moves down the line from one panel to the next, rubbing at the charcoal cloud that would be the right side of her chest on each. What she is still seeing, to her frustration, is simply blank space. What she envisions is absence, something that isn't just missing but missed. Phantom pain made evident.

The rest of the project has proceeded with assembly line precision. At one time, all seven panels looked exactly like the first does now, only the gray cloud of Maggie's missing breast emerging from the surrounding black. Then, later, all but the first looked exactly like the second, where her full image begins to appear out of a dark haze. By the fourth and middle panel, the self-portrait is the one you'd expect to see hanging in the living room, mounted and track-lit: Maggie's eyes downcast, the horizontal scar line sharp and defining. There were four such perfect likenesses for a time, panels four through seven, Maggie working with dogged precision to make sure that each panel would depend on the one before it and lead inevitably to the one that followed. Now in the final panel there is only a puff of smoke in a field of white, an exact negative of the first, every trace of the original black rubbed away over this half-year by Maggie's fingers pressed into lump after lump of pliable kneaded eraser and thrown away.

She has lost track of time. A frayed wool sweater that used to be Henry's lies bunched on the wide-planked floor and Maggie stands, staring, braless in a gauzy white t-shirt and jeans. The light, usually even and white-blue up here, is starting to slant in from the far bank of windows yellow and warm when Allie calls from the bottom of the stairs.

"*Mom?*"

Maggie rubs her hands together and looks up to a corner of the ceiling as if that is where the voice is coming from. "Allie, is that you already?"

Allie's footsteps start up the steep, uncarpeted stairs. Maggie hears Franny's nails on the bottom step, stopping there, afraid of the tractionless climb. Allie is talking as she comes.

"It's like four-thirty, Mom. I've been home for— *Whoa.*"

When she is most of the way up, her face appears in the doorway and she stops. Although the late afternoon light has made Maggie's work more difficult, the effect on the panels is dramatic, turning all of the whites and grays gold. "Are they finished?" Allie asks, rising the rest of the way into the room.

"I'm not sure."

"They're incredible." Allie approaches the last panel and her hand instinctively moves toward the cloud floating just left of center, but she doesn't touch.

"You think?" Maggie asks.

"Mom."

The back of Maggie's right hand goes to her forehead and stays there as she surveys the line of panels. She is still unsure but doesn't want to dismiss Allie's compliment. She has no energy left, mental or physical, to fix whatever it is that isn't working anyway. Her left arm hangs limp-tired at her side, and her remaining breast aches in a way she doesn't trust.

"Thanks," she says finally, her right arm dropping to her side as well. She walks into the small bathroom to wash her hands and face, and Allie moves down the line, stopping to look at each panel from close in.

"Where's your brother?" Maggie calls over the running water.

"He and Alex got off the bus together and asked if they could play at Alex's. I figured that would give you more time so I said fine."

"Thanks."

The water runs quietly into Maggie's cupped hands, then loudly into the drain as she splashes her face once, twice, three times.

"Is this how you feel?" Allie is standing in front of the last panel.

"What do you mean?"

Allie's hand rises again toward the gray cloud. "Like there's nothing there."

Maggie comes out pulling a hand towel down over her face, her eyes showing red where she stretches the lower lids.

"No. That's the problem. Sometimes I feel the opposite of that. Like my whole self is in there, in that one spot. But I don't know how to draw that."

"Oh."

This feels like the beginning of a conversation, but neither of them speaks, and Maggie wonders if Allie has noticed the uncomfortable silences that have crept into the way they communicate: Maggie unsure of how much to share with her adolescent daughter, and Allie equally unsure of how much she wants to know.

After a beat, Maggie says, "Have you seen your father yet?"

"No."

"I guess I'll go start dinner." She walks down the line of panels and releases the roll of wax paper above each, smoothing them as she goes. When she is finished, she bends and reaches for her sweater, but Allie has already done the same and is handing it to her as they almost knock heads.

"Oops."

"Here."

"Oh. Thanks, sweetie."

"Sure." Allie's hands are both in the single pocket at the front of her sweatshirt, and she pushes them down and away, stretching and shrugging, as if she has just woken up, and the action lends a falseness to what she says next.

"Mom? Can I go to the Emery's for dinner? All four of us are going to run lines there."

"Are his parents going to be home?"

"Yeah. I mean I assume. He invited us over for dinner. *Someone's* cooking it."

"Can you find out?"

"Mom. It's not a party. It's a rehearsal."

Maggie holds the sweater up by its shoulders, folds them in, tosses it up lightly and catches it in the middle to fold again. "Ten o'clock," she says. "Nine if his parents leave."

"Okay." Although Allie doesn't say this grudgingly, there is something hesitant about her demeanor that makes Maggie uneasy for her. She isn't lying—Allie is a terrible liar—but she is nervous.

"Are you okay, honey?"

"Yeah. Fine."

"Not worried about something?"

"No. Well. Two weeks. The show's in two weeks. We're not even close."

"I remember. You never feel like you are. It always comes together right at the end."

"That's what Mr. Berger says."

"Just remember the audience doesn't know what you know. Even if you make mistakes, you're the only one who'll notice. It will look perfect to everyone else."

"Okay."

Allie walks back through the doorway to the narrow landing and Maggie follows, pulling the studio door closed behind them. Franny's front paws are still perched on the bottom step and, upon seeing Allie, she has begun to tap one, then the other, walking in place.

"We're coming, girl, we're coming."

"Can you take her for a short walk before you go? I've been neglecting her all day."

"Would you like that, girl? You wanna go for a walk?"

The pace of Franny's tapping increases as Allie and Maggie descend, and then she pushes off and heads down the carpeted stairs to the first floor, crosses the hall and rings the string of sleigh bells hung by the front door with a swipe of her nose.

"Guess that answers your question," Maggie says.

Allie grabs a jacket and Franny's leash from the wooden coat tree in the hall, and Maggie turns toward the kitchen. She hears the front door open and close, and when she pulls the refrigerator and freezer open simultaneously, she stands and stares into both with the same look of exhausted indecision she had offered her self-portraits a moment ago.

"Christ," she says to no one.

Tuesdays and Fridays are her "free" days, with no classes and nothing to do but work and make dinner. And no matter how hard she works upstairs, she almost always finds new energy in the kitchen.

But her fatigue has followed her down today and, after standing for a full minute letting the icy steam cool her face, she pulls a frozen pizza out of the freezer and lets it thud onto the countertop.

"Dinner is served," she says.

When the phone rings Maggie believes for an instant that Henry has somehow heard her, that he is calling to suggest dinner out. But the caller-ID reads "Loren Strummer," and Maggie almost doesn't answer. She doesn't have the energy for Elvira, and she doubts her ability to be civil to Loren. The slim chance that it's Walt, or someone calling to tell her that Walt has severed a limb while Elvira was touching up her makeup, is the only reason she lifts the receiver out of its cradle.

"Hello."

"Maggie?"

"Yes."

"This is Elvira. Elvira Strummer?"

"Oh, *that* Elvira." Maggie pauses but isn't surprised that the joke has missed its mark. "Is everything all right?"

"No, Maggie. Everything is *not* all right. Your Walter has beaten our Alex nearly bloody with his lightsaber."

"He *what*?"

"And now he is refusing to leave unless you come and get him."

"I'm sure it was an accident, Elvira. You know how the boys swing those things."

"It wasn't an accident that he kept swinging at Alex when he was crumpled in a ball on the floor."

"Oh," Maggie says. "I'll be right over."

"That would be advisable."

The cold air is returning, the warmth of the past few days a brief tease, and without thinking to put her sweater back on, Maggie runs out the back door, cuts behind the carriage house and slips through the hedge onto the cobblestone. The houses on Emerson share an alley with the ones on the next block and, once across it, Maggie has to push through another row of hedges and jog between two houses to the sidewalk on Virginia. Whatever really happened at the Strummers', Maggie is certain that Alex precipitated it. She is equally certain that Elvira, who thinks her only child's crap could be dried and used as potpourri, will find a way to pin it on Walt.

When she turns up the walkway below the Strummers' porch, Elvira is already holding the screen door open for her.

"I don't know *what* got into your Walter. They were playing so *nicely*."

"Boys aren't very mysterious, Elvira. I'm sure there's a simple explanation." As Maggie passes through the open door, Elvira's gaze moves quickly from Maggie's face to her chest.

"My goodness, Maggie. I can just about see your bare boob right *through* that skimpy thing. And on a cold day like today, your... well, you know."

Maggie looks down at herself. "Oh," she says, and might have been embarrassed if she weren't already in full defense mode. "Well, at least we know Loren won't look twice."

"It's not Loren I'm concerned about," Elvira says, the implication of Maggie's remark missing her by a wide margin. "It's the boys."

"*My* boy sees it all the time," Maggie assures her. "And isn't Alex still breastfeeding?"

"Well. There's no call for rudeness, especially when your Walter has—"

"I'm sorry, Elvira. But can we please avoid prejudging this until we've at least talked to them?"

"You can talk to them all you want. I *saw* it."

"The entire incident?"

"I was upstairs taking care of a few things and I heard Alex screaming. I came running and your Walter was—"

"Where are they?"

"In the den."

Maggie follows Elvira through her spotless, unused kitchen, through the formal dining room where, earlier in the week, Walt no doubt sat staring at his anchovy pizza, a cloth napkin on his lap. When they round the corner into the den it occurs to Maggie that a stage director couldn't have blocked the scene she sees any better. The two boys both sit on the floor back-to-back, their plastic light sabers—one red, one blue—unsheathed and crossed between them. Predictably, there is no blood, although Alex is rubbing what looks like the beginning of a nice welt on one forearm, and Walt's own arms are crossed in defiance. He looks briefly at Maggie, then back at the empty space in front of him.

"Walt?"

He tightens his grip on himself and Maggie kneels beside him.

"Can you tell me what happened here?"

"I hit Alex."

"I know that, buddy, but why?"

Walt hesitates then looks at Maggie. "He said it again, Mom."

"What?"

Maggie sees her son's eyes begin to fill and is amazed when he manages not to cry.

"He said that we are moving."

Maggie glances sharply at Elvira who simultaneously rolls her eyes and shrugs her shoulders. It looks like a confused attempt to make a statement about both the meagerness of Walt's excuse and her own innocence.

"He said that we are moving even though I told him that my Dad said that we are not." Walt's low, contractionless monotone clambers through this sentence as though being read from a cue card by a bad actor.

"So you hit him?"

"Yes."

"Buddy, you know better than that."

"But he would not stop. He just kept saying it over and over even after I told him I was going to crack him one and I got really really angry."

"I understand you were frustrated, Walt, but you shouldn't have hit Alex. You know that, don't you?"

"Yes."

"Have you apologized to him?"

"No."

"Why not?"

"I am waiting for him to apologize first."

"Ah. An old-fashioned standoff then."

"Yes."

Maggie raises her eyes to Elvira, hoping she might mediate the other side of this rift, but Elvira's look of impatience now encompasses all three of them. Maggie walks on her knees to where Alex is sitting.

"Alex?" He rubs his arm but doesn't answer. "Alex, honey, why did you keep saying what you said even after Walt asked you to stop?"

"That's no excuse for hitting," Elvira contributes. "You said that yourself."

Maggie continues as if she hasn't heard her.

"Who told you Walt was moving, Alex?"

Before Alex has time to respond, Elvira is speaking again. "I told him you *might* be moving. There's nothing wrong with telling a child the truth, is there?"

"Alex," Maggie says, ignoring Elvira again. "Do you want Walt to move?"

Alex looks directly at Maggie for the first time. "No," he says.

"Are you a little bit upset about it?"

Alex nods.

"Do you understand that if you're upset about it, how much

more upset Walt must be?"

Alex nods again. Maggie knee-walks back to Walt and then sits on her heels.

"Did you think Alex wanted you to move, Walt?"

"Yes."

"Mystery solved," Maggie says, looking up at Elvira, then back to Walt. "Do you understand now that he was teasing you because he really *doesn't* want to lose you as a friend?"

"No, Mom. That does not make any sense."

"I know it doesn't seem to, but will you trust me on this one?"

"Yes, Mom. I will trust you."

"And I would like you to apologize first, because I will not tolerate hitting to hurt for any reason. Is that clear?"

"Sorry."

"To Alex."

Walt turns his head to the side and speaks over his shoulder. "Sorry, Alex."

"What about you, Alex?"

"Sorry, Walt."

"There, now," Elvira says, as if she has brokered this truce. "Was that so hard? Why don't you boys shake on it."

Elvira holds the door for them and places a hand on Maggie's shoulder as they pass. "I'm pulling for Henry, dear," she says in an exaggerated confidential tone. "Loren and I both are."

"Yeah."

"And I know Atlee's working very hard on his behalf, so that has to help, doesn't it?"

"What are you doing talking to Atlee about my husband's job?"

"Oh, no. I just know through Loren is all."

"Ah. Henry's other cheerleader. At least he'd look good in the skirt."

As usual, Elvira's face registers nothing. "Incidentally, I just spoke with Loren and you might expect Henry a little late this evening."

"Why's that?"

"Loren said he was giving some individual attention to one of his students. I just didn't want you to worry."

"Elvira, if anyone other than *you* were telling me that, I just might be."

"You said it yourself, Maggie. Boys aren't that mysterious." Elvira smiles without showing her teeth. "Bye now, Walter. You come back soon, all right?"

"Bye."

Maggie and Walt take the long way back home, up Virginia, left on Fourth past where it crosses the alley, then down Emerson. Walt pulls his lightsaber behind him at first with the sound of a muffler being dragged by a slow-moving car, but when Maggie doesn't tell him to stop he puts it over his shoulder like a rifle.

Maggie wraps her arms across her chest against the chill. "Walt, do you know who Alex's dad is?"

"Daddy's boss?"

"That's right. Sort of. The important thing to remember is—and, believe me, I'm telling myself this as much as I'm telling you—the important thing is that until this thing with Daddy's job is settled, we have to try not to do anything that might affect that decision."

"You mean be nice to them?"

"Yes, exactly."

"Mom, I like Alex. I am almost always nice to him."

"I know you are, buddy. Like I said, I'm reminding myself that I need to be nice to his mommy too."

"She is an idiot."

"Walt—"

"Mom, you are the one who said that about the little fish on my pizza."

"I didn't say '*idiot*.' I don't like that word. I said she was *clueless*. And if you want to be treated like the big guy you're getting to be, you have to understand that certain things your father and I say around you are said in confidence. Do you know what that means?"

"That means it is a secret."

"Yes."

"Mom, I think everyone already knows Alex's mom is clueless." He laughs at his own joke and Maggie bumps her hip into his shoulder, sending him tipping into an adjacent lawn.

They are almost home before Maggie notices Allie sitting on the porch steps, stroking Franny's head. When they turn up the walkway, Allie stands.

"Mom, where *were* you?"

"Your brother went Jango Fett on Alex Strummer and then refused to leave the Death Star."

"She wouldn't move." Allie is close to tears, or has been crying, Maggie can't tell which.

"What do you mean?"

"Franny. She sat on the sidewalk to let some little boy pet her and then she wouldn't get back up."

"Couldn't or wouldn't?"

"I don't know. When I started walking again she just stayed put. She didn't look upset or anything. She just sat there with her tongue hanging out. When I tried to lift her backside, her legs just stayed folded up like they were stuck."

"How did you get her back here?"

"All of a sudden she just stood up like nothing had happened and looked at me like, *Are we going or what?*"

Maggie steps back a few paces. "Come here, girl," she calls, patting her thighs. Franny stands and walks gingerly—though no more gingerly than usual—over to Maggie and nuzzles her nose between Maggie's legs. "Atta girl. Good as new."

"I swear, Mom. She couldn't get up."

"Maybe it was a sit-down strike. Maybe she and Walt are subliminally linked and she was joining him in protest."

"Mom, don't joke about this."

"I'm sorry, sweetie, but whatever it was, she's fine now. Either your dad or I will take her back out after dinner and see how she does." At the sound of the word *dinner*, Franny turns and almost bounds up the porch steps.

"Where is Dad?"

"I don't know," Maggie answers. "What time is it?"

11

Ruthie and I were up and out of bed by seven a.m. Saturday morning. With the Pirates up three games to two, I didn't know how I was going to get through the hours until game time, but Ruthie already had the day planned: we had to get ready for the party. John and my father were both to arrive before the first pitch, and Ruthie physically pulled my mother out of bed and badgered her until she agreed that, yes, they could make a list of all the things to be done before then.

Parties had themes, in Ruthie's mind, and every decoration and food item had to relate. We would buy black and gold napkins, streamers and balloons. There would be pretzel rods (bats) and marshmallows (balls) on a plate together as snacks. That theme had to carry through to dinner afterwards, which would consist of chicken legs and little potatoes. When my mother insisted on a vegetable, Ruthie allowed that peas were the color of grass and therefore tolerable. Coke was almost black; John liked beer, and that was gold; orange soda was an Oriole color and unacceptable. For dessert there would be a round cake decorated to look like a baseball with Clemente's number 21 in the center. She wasn't entirely inflexible. Although cheese and crackers was not a suitable appetizer (crackers weren't enough like bases to overcome the complete irrelevance of cheese squares), cheese *balls* were okay, as long as they were yellow (close enough to gold) and not orange (Orioles again) and you stuck them with black toothpicks.

John arrived first and it would have been easy to forget that my mother had never met him before. She seemed unfazed by his handicap and she was welcoming and kind when he came to the door with a bouquet of flowers in his harness pocket that nearly blocked his vision. Ruthie didn't say anything about the flowers not being color-appropriate, and John was properly impressed by all of her preparations.

"You've outdone yourself, Miss Bambino," he said.

We all claimed our seats in the living room, and my mother turned deftly away when she realized that John didn't need any help getting into the armchair. She offered him a beer, and he said she'd never have to ask twice.

We passed around the pretzels and marshmallows and cheese balls.

We settled in to watch the Pirates win the World Series.

In the middle of the first inning, my father called and said that he and Jeanine were committed to making an appearance at a party Jeanine's father was throwing for the executives in his company, but that he'd sneak out as early as he could.

In the third inning, he called to say they'd just arrived at the party and couldn't get away just yet.

By the seventh, Ruthie was upstairs listening to the game in her room with the door closed. When my father called again, my mother answered.

"Don't bother," was all she said before hanging up. She excused herself and went upstairs to talk to Ruthie, and John said maybe he ought to get going, mindful, I think, of the fact that his presence probably wouldn't help matters if my father did eventually appear.

He called up the stairs to thank my mother and reminded me that, whatever happened today, we had Blass going again tomorrow.

Unable to get Ruthie to come out of her room, my mother came back down to the living room and sat next to me on the couch. We watched the rest of what should have been the most exciting baseball game of my life in complete silence. The Pirates lost Game 6 in ten innings, but Clemente almost won it by himself. He legged out a triple in the first and homered in the third. In the bottom of the ninth he cut off a ball deep in the right field corner, wheeled and threw 330 feet into the air to home plate to keep the winning run from scoring. Sanguillen didn't even have to move his glove. Had it been a pitch, the umpire would have called it a strike. The Orioles finally gave up trying to get him out and walked him intentionally in the top of the tenth, but the Pirates left the bases loaded. The Orioles won what felt like the longest game I had ever sat through on a very shallow sacrifice fly to Vic Davalillo, brought in late in the game as a defensive replacement for Al Oliver in center. Had the same ball been hit to Clemente, Frank Robinson wouldn't even have bothered tagging up.

Fifteen minutes later, the doorbell rang. It was my father. He had something in his hand.

"Don't say anything, please, Beth. We got held up." Jeanine was with him as well.

"Yeah. I'd say so."

"Look, it couldn't be helped, okay?"

"You've been drinking."

"It was a party."

"So was this."

"I didn't know. Ruthie just asked if I could come over for the game."

My mother turned to Jeanine. "And *you* weren't invited."

"Beth, there's no call for—"

"You have seen your children exactly *twice* since the day you left this house, and your daughter is locked in her room because *her* invitation," my mother said pointing to Jeanine, "was more important to you."

"Look, Jeanine's father was the reason the kids got to go to the game the other night in the first place. It would have been rude for us not to go."

"Since when are you concerned with decorum? Does *she* know I was your student once too? Does *she* know how many students there have been between me and her that I ignored?"

I had never seen my mother truly angry, never heard her raise her voice. The day my father left she had stood silent in the doorway while Ruthie clutched at his legs and Sam pounded on the hood of his car. Something had been swelling inside of her since that day, and this had finally ripped it open.

"Beth, can we please not do this in front of Henry?"

"Oh no. God forbid he should know his father is a fucking fraud. Emphasis on the *fuck*."

"Beth—"

"*Shut up!*" By now my mother was screaming, tears coursing down her face. It was like she was shouting the life right out of herself. "You don't get to say anything anymore! *Nothing!* I have made this *so* easy for you, Ned Graham, and I'm *done*. I've known this was coming for years, but *they* didn't. They lost you like *that*," she snapped her fingers, "and you don't even have the decency to let them down slowly. Your new life has started; your old life is over. That's how you think of it. Well fine. Stay away. Stay the *fuck* away! Anything else just gives them hope, and like everything else about you, Ned, it's false hope. So just don't bother. Don't fucking bother."

She left the three of us standing there, and I could hear dishes clattering in the kitchen. I don't know why she didn't take me with her. She had delivered her exit lines, but she was leaving me to make my own decision.

My father stood silent. Jeanine had turned away and was covering her mouth.

"Hey, sport, I brought you those player photos." He handed them to me. Hebner, Alley and Sanguillen. I had them all. He'd been with me when I got them.

"These are old ones, Dad."

"Really?"

"Hebner was June. Alley and Sanguillen were July."

"Huh. They were in Jeanine's car so I assumed they were the newer ones."

I looked more closely. One had been faded by sunlight; another had a stain on one corner that could have been coffee or maybe Coke.

"No."

"Well, sorry. I'll keep an eye out."

"Sure. Thanks."

"Maybe I should go talk to your sister for a minute."

"Yeah."

He went upstairs.

When he was out of sight, Jeanine put her hand tentatively on my shoulder. "I'm sorry," she said. "He never told me. We would have been here."

"That's okay."

"Here, give me those. I'm sure we can find the right pictures."

"Thanks."

My father wasn't gone long. He came down the stairs slowly, his demeanor as close to exhibiting shame as I would ever see. The fact that nothing changed after that day led me to the conclusion, many years and many disappointments later, that shame didn't affect my father the way it affected other people. He made decisions and suffered the consequences but never actually learned from them. It seemed a strange trait in a teacher.

He looked at the photos in Jeanine's hand.

"Where did she get all of that candy?" he asked me.

"What?"

"Your sister. There are candy wrappers scattered all over the floor, and she just..." He trailed off, shaking his head. "Where does she get all of that?"

"I don't know. She collects it."

"I told her it isn't good for her. Maybe she'll listen to you."

"I doubt it."

"Yeah. She's a stubborn one."

He was quiet for a while.

"You going to watch the game tomorrow?" he finally asked.

"I guess."

"You guess?"

"Yeah, I'm going to watch."

"Blass, right?"

"Yeah."

"Think he can do it again?"

"I don't know."

"Come on. You've got to have more faith than that."

"I guess."

He put his hand on Jeanine's shoulder and she looked away from him.

"Well. I guess we'll see you soon," he said.

"When?"

"I don't know. I think maybe I'd better give your mother a chance to cool down a little first, don't you think?"

"Maybe."

"Soon, though. I promise."

The hand that wasn't touching Jeanine reached out and took me by the side of the face and pulled me toward him.

Another Invitation

When Henry arrives home after class, Maggie is already taking the pizza out of the oven.

"No comments about the meal, please," she says. "I've had a day. You're later than usual."

"I stayed after to talk to a student. Then Loren stopped in. Then I had a strange chat with Atlee. Smells great."

"Anything new? With Atlee I mean."

"He's in love."

"I said anything *new*."

"No, I mean for real."

"Come on."

"He won't tell me who. It might even be you."

"Atlee being in love with me isn't new either."

"No, I mean for real. He seemed desperate, even a little sad, like he's considering some major life change."

"Then it's not me."

"I suppose not."

Maggie goes to the refrigerator and takes some Romaine, carrots, green and red peppers and avocado from the hydrator. She takes a large salad bowl down from the cabinet, breaks the Romaine and drops it in. Henry gets out two small cutting boards and two knives. Maggie hands him the carrots and green peppers. She keeps the red and the avocado for herself. They cut.

"Where's Allie?" Henry asks.

"At Nathan Emery's house, running lines."

"Really?"

"Don't say it like that. And don't embarrass her when she comes home. It's not just Allie and Nathan anyway. There are four of them. All the leads."

"What about Walt?"

"In the den saving the universe. He was part of my day."

"So I gathered. Loren gave me a preview. Apparently, Elvira couldn't wait until he got home to share."

"He goes home?"

"Sometimes. What happened?"

"Can we not? I'm exhausted."

"Sure."

They finish preparing the salad and Maggie sets two places at the small kitchen table.

"What about Walt?"

"I was going to let him be for a while. He likes it better cold anyway. You can try him if you like."

"*Walt*," Henry calls. "*Your pizza's ready*."

There is no answer.

"He can eat in there if he wants," Maggie says. "He's had a tough day too."

"*Walt, buddy, do you want to eat in the den?*"

Nothing.

"He can't hear when he's playing that thing. Just go drop it in front of him and he'll smell it eventually."

Henry separates a slice from the pie, puts it on a plate and walks out of the kitchen. When he returns, he is shaking his head.

"Incredible. I even stood in front of him when I put the plate down. I think he was looking right through me and still shooting down attackers. Are we bad parents for letting him play that thing?"

"No, but I'm a bad parent for thinking that at least when he's playing Nintendo he can't be quizzing me from his dog-eared Pokedexes on which Pokemon has which powers; whether Bulbasaur evolves into Ivysuar or Venusaur. Ugh. Besides, there are professionals now."

"Therapy?"

Maggie dishes salad onto Henry's plate next to his pizza as he sits.

"No. Professional video game players. Walt made me watch this special. People pay to watch other people play video games."

"How many seats can you sell to people looking over your shoulder?"

"They project it. The players are looking at their regular screens but the game is being projected onto really *huge* screens to people in an auditorium."

"Oh, by all means then. Let's encourage him."

"I'm just saying. It gave me a new appreciation. Who thought skateboarding could be a profession?"

Henry stands. "Do you want water?"

"Oh, sorry. My green tea, please."

Henry pours her drink, gets ice and water from the tap for himself and sits. Franny shambles in from the den.

"Isn't he paying attention to you either, old girl?" Henry asks. He puts his hand out to greet her once she arrives.

"She was another one today."

"What?"

"Allie took her for a walk and on the way home she sat down on the sidewalk and wouldn't get up."

"Wouldn't or couldn't?"

"My question exactly. Allie says couldn't."

"I'll take her again later and watch her."

"Could you? I promised Allie one of us would and I just don't have the energy."

"Sure. I'll see if Ruthie wants to go."

"Shit."

"What?"

"I didn't even think about her. I forgot she doesn't eat pizza anymore."

"She'll be fine with the salad."

"I can't believe I forgot her."

"We'll cover for you, won't we?" Henry's hand strokes Franny's head. When he stops to take a bite of pizza a large, mostly gray paw comes up and rests heavily on his thigh. "Okay, okay," he says, scratching her ears. "I see you. Time to lie down."

They eat quietly for a while, Franny on the floor between them, until Henry breaks the silence.

"Are we doing anything tomorrow night?" He has asked this rather loudly and in a sweetly cheerful voice that brings a quizzical look from Maggie.

"I don't think. Why?"

"Natalie Currant asked me if I'd stop by her sorority house to talk more about her novel."

Maggie raises an eyebrow. "Did she?"

"You're invited too. It's a small party."

"Why didn't you say that the first time."

"What?"

"That I was invited."

"I did. I asked if *we* were doing anything tomorrow night."

"And then you said that Natalie asked *you* to stop by."

"She did. And then she invited you too."

"Before or after you hesitated accepting?"

"Mag."

"She doesn't want me to come, Henry. Neither do you, really."
Maggie says this matter-of-factly, without any visible jealousy.

"Don't be ridiculous."

"I'm not. I'm being practical. You're going because she says she
wants to talk about her work, right? What am I supposed to do while
the two of you are off chatting? Make nice with the sisters? I never
went to one of those things in college, and I'm not starting now just
so you can feel safe."

"What's that supposed to mean?"

"Just what I said."

"I'm perfectly capable of handling myself in any kind of situation
that might arise."

"*I* know that, but you don't."

"Don't you mean that the other way around?"

"No." Maggie rips a bite of pizza with her front teeth, a piece
of pepperoni falling to the floor near Franny. "Just go," she says, her
mouth half full. "You can bring me back some finger sandwiches."

Franny stretches her neck and reaches the pepperoni without
getting up. She chews with her eyes closed.

Allie's jealousies aside, Pamela Metz really is a perfect Laura
Wingfield: a nice, pretty girl who no one much cares for without
knowing precisely why. And Allie notices for the first time that
Nathan Emery feels the same way, that the charged moments between
them onstage are just that: staged. Here in the Emery's basement,
outside of school with him for the first time, all of Nathan's attention
is focused on Allie, and she is feeling as if she is being followed by a
bright, warm spotlight.

"Come on, try again," Nathan says. "It tastes just like

peppermint." He puts the clear bottle to her mouth and tips it. Allie squeezes her eyes and lips closed and lets the smallest bit of the thick, warm liquid seep through to her tongue. It doesn't taste quite as bad the second time, and Allie nods to let Nathan know she has gotten some. "There you go," he says.

"Hey guys, are we going to run Scene 6 again or what?" Pamela is rifling through her script.

"It doesn't make much sense to run it without Max. Tom's got half the lines." Nathan sips the beer in front of him and holds the other bottle out to Allie. She laughs and shakes her head but lets Nathan wet her lips with it again. Eighth grade boys fall into two broad categories in Allie's mind: those who look like they could be in fifth grade, and those who look like they could be juniors in high school. Nathan clearly fits into the latter. He isn't tall, but he's broad-shouldered with thick black hair that is always falling across his deep-set eyes. Nathan Emery flipping his hair back is a much discussed phenomenon among the girls of Panama Middle School.

"What's the deal?" Pamela says. "I thought Max was coming back."

"Parents must have busted him," Nathan says. "He was supposed to be grounded. Want some schnapps, Spamela?"

"No thanks. That stuff is disgusting."

"You sort of get used to it," Allie says. Nathan holds up a fist for Allie to bump with her own.

"What if your parents come down here?" Pamela asks.

"Not a chance. They respect my right to privacy. Plus they're both on about their third martini by now."

"But won't they notice stuff's missing?"

"My sister got this for me. My own private stash."

"So what are we going to do?"

"Face it, Spamela. You can't do *Glass Menagerie* without your Tom. Dude's in every scene."

"Stop calling me that, please. Why don't we run some of the two-person sections again. Laura and Amanda, Laura and Jim."

"Laura, Laura, Laura. How about some Jim and Amanda?" Nathan says, looking at Allie. Allie smiles and takes a small sip of the schnapps on her own.

"There *is* no Jim and Amanda," Pamela answers. "No long bits anyway."

Nathan jumps up and runs over to the light switch. "Let's do the beginning of Scene 7. When the lights go out."

"Come on, Nathan. Quit goofing around. Can we get back to work before you're too drunk to concentrate?"

"I'm not goofing around. That moment's totally pivotal."

"But Tom's in that scene too."

"Not the first part. I mean he's there at the dinner table, but he doesn't say anything. And Laura's pouting on the couch in the living room, as I recall, so why don't you go lie down in the office back there?"

"This is stupid," Pamela says, but she stands and walks into the other room and sits.

"Start right at the light cue, Allie, okay?" Nathan says.

"Okay."

"Ready?"

"I guess."

"Action!" Nathan flips the switch and the basement goes coal black. "Line, Allie!"

"Oh. Uh... *I guess the fuse is burnt out. Mr. O'Connor, can you tell a burnt-out fuse?*" Allie hears his footsteps moving further away and she feels momentarily lost, floating. *"Oh, be careful you don't bump into something. We wouldn't want our gentleman caller to break his neck. Now wouldn't that be a fine how-do-you-do?"*

"Ha-ha! Where's the fuse box?"

"Right next to the stove. Can you see anything?"

"*Just a minute.*"

"*Isn't electricity a mysterious thing?* Uh... *We live in such a mysterious universe, don't we?* Shit, I forgot the part about Ben Franklin."

"I can't find the fuse box, Mrs. Wingfield!" Nathan calls from the laundry room. "Would you be so kind as to come in here and help me?"

Pamela yells from the office. "That's not your line, Nathan, and you know it!"

"I'm not talking to you, Laura! It's your lovely mother I need!"

Allie's face is on fire but she stands and begins feeling her way tentatively toward the laundry room. She's only had a thimbleful of the schnapps, so that can't be what has her off balance. It's her sense that everything is changing, or is about to. In this darkened basement, Nathan Emery is about to make her visible.

As her eyes adjust, she is able to make out the doorway to the laundry. When she is through it, she stops.

"Right here," Nathan whispers. He is just inside the door to her right, and he takes her forearm in his hand. He misjudges her height and kisses her on the chin. Allie leans down and finds his mouth. Their teeth clack together and Nathan pulls away.

"Have you ever made out before?" he whispers again.

"Not really. Have you? I mean, I'm sure—"

"Lots."

"Oh."

"No. That's cool. I can teach you. Here. Make your lips do this." He takes her hand and brings it to his mouth. She touches his lips all over, her heart thundering in her ears, and bends to kiss him again. Then the lights flash on and Pamela is in the doorway.

"I'm leaving. You guys have your own little rehearsal."

Allie spins and looks at her feet, tucking her long hair behind both ears. "What time is it?" she blurts.

"Almost ten."

"I have to go too."

"Come on. Stay a little while."

"Yeah, stay. He needs the practice." Pamela starts up the stairs. "I'll see you guys Monday. Let's try and focus then, huh?"

Allie goes to the table and gathers her script.

"You're not really going now, are you?" Nathan asks.

"I have to. I promised my mom I'd be home by ten."

"Can you come back tomorrow night?"

"I don't know. Maybe."

"Come on. We'll rehearse some more."

"I'll try."

"Cool. I'll see you then," Nathan says. He flips the hair out of his eyes.

When my father walked off our front porch and opened the passenger side door of Jeanine's car for her, I had no way of knowing that they would be married less than a year later. I didn't yet know that Jeanine would be the only one of the four women my father would marry that I would think of as my stepmother, that the designation would eventually become meaningless for his subsequent wives, even ridiculous, as I got older and his taste in women didn't. I didn't know that Ruthie would one day become unrecognizable in her own body, that Sam would take out her inability to hurt my father on as many other men as she could until she simply ran out of energy, that my mother would never marry again. I didn't know that I would, in a sense, be the lone survivor of that night, or that I would risk my status as such many years later in a dark, unoccupied house on a college campus I didn't even know existed. The only thing I knew was that my father was gone. And I knew it in a way I hadn't before.

Ruthie knew it too. She never came out of her room after the game, and it was the only night for at least a year after my father left that she didn't sleep in my other bed. My mother spent a long time in her room with her before coming in to kiss me goodnight. She sat on my bed.

"Hey," she said.

"Hey."

"Tough game."

"Yeah."

"There's still tomorrow."

"Yeah. Is she okay?"

"I think so. She wouldn't talk much except to say she's got a stomachache. She's working on one of her designs. With all the colored shapes? She was concentrating very hard."

"She's good at those."

My mother put her hand on my face and glanced around the room at all of the bumper stickers, the player photos, the signed World Series program propped up by my mitt on the shelf. Then she looked back down at me.

"I'm sorry," she said, and I was surprised to see that she was smiling.

"For what?"

"Oh, for a lot of things, I guess. Mostly for my little outburst. Maybe it was for the best, you know? You would have figured things out for yourself eventually, but maybe it's okay to learn it all at once. Like pulling a Band-Aid off real fast, right?"

"I guess."

"I know you miss your father. You may not believe it after tonight, but I do too. The problem is we're both mostly missing what we think he could be if he really tried. We miss the guy who buys the tickets to the ballgame, and what we get is the one who doesn't show up. People are who they are, Henry. Do yourself a favor and learn that sooner than I did."

She kissed me again.

HENRY AND RUTHIE

They both wear their winter coats tonight. The weather has turned, or, more accurately, has turned back, and there is a chance of a late March snow over the weekend. Franny huffs between them, stiff but seemingly spry. It is much later than they usually walk, after nine-thirty. Henry spent the earlier part of the evening re-reading Natalie's pages in preparation for their meeting tomorrow, making a few notes this time, mostly about the mother character who, for someone newly imprisoned, comes across as already hardened. The rest is uniformly strong, its effect on him undiminished upon a second reading.

Ruthie has said something that Henry hasn't heard, and he looks over at her.

"Sorry, what?"

"I said, you seem distracted."

"No. It's just." He nods down at Franny. "Does she seem okay to you?"

"She's walking better than I am, if that's any comfort."

Ruthie moves more gingerly than she did the other night with Allie, dropping heavily into her right side.

"How *is* the foot?" Henry asks.

"Good days and bad. Today's a bad one. Not pain-wise, mind you. Less pain, more numbness lately. Sometimes I look down and I'm almost surprised to see it there."

"Should we be having it looked at?"

"What for? I'm doing all the things I'm supposed to. Unfortunately, my foot knows what it's supposed to be doing too. This is what happens, Henry."

"Still, it couldn't hurt."

"Maybe when I get back. I'm not having some doctor tell me I can't go to Spring Training."

"More likely, he'd tell you to move down there, instead of someplace where winter hangs on like this."

"Are you trying to get rid of me?"

"Not a chance." Henry drives his hands—including the one holding Franny's leash—deep into his coat pockets. "But if we have to leave this place, I'm limiting my applications to nice little Southern Baptist schools."

Ruthie is quiet, catching her breath, but the timing of her silence doesn't escape Henry. If he doesn't get tenure, Ruthie stands to lose as much as anyone. But she has never asked him about his review, and she won't.

"Did you get your flight changed?" he asks, changing the subject for her.

"I did. I'm flying straight to Mom's from Pittsburgh after the memorial. Do you mind driving home alone?"

"We're flying. You don't need to be sitting in a car for eight hours. Maggie will take us to the airport if she decides not to come."

"Well, thank you, big brother. Just a one-way for me."

"Got it."

Walking down Fourth Street, the audible beginnings of Friday night on fraternity row three blocks further on make their way to

Henry and Ruthie, competing fragments of music carried on the cold breeze from doors and windows left wide open no matter what the temperature outside. Henry looks toward the sounds.

"Where's Allie?" Ruthie asks.

"Hm?"

"Allie. She didn't want to join us?"

"Oh, sorry. She's rehearsing. At some boy's house, apparently."

"Nathan's?"

"Yeah. How did you know?"

"Oh, my. *Major* crush."

"Allie?"

"Look around, Henry. Your dog's not the only one getting older."

They have reached Fourth and Virginia, halfway around the block, and Ruthie needs to stop and rest. The corner lot there is ringed by a low, cement retaining wall, and she sits next to the keystone endcap that marks the exact corner.

"Hoo. Sorry."

"We're in no hurry, are we, old girl?" Henry ruffles Franny's head and she sits, her tongue hanging out of one side of her mouth. "There's something I wanted to ask you about anyway."

"Oh?"

"Something about Dad."

Ruthie laughs at her brother.

"What?" he asks.

"You always get this very *weighty* look on your face when you talk about him that's so out of proportion. Sort of a world hunger, Middle East peace-talks kind of look."

"Forget it."

She laughs again. "No! I'm sorry. Start again. I promise to be good."

"It's just that I've been thinking about him a lot. It's weird, but I think I've thought about Dad more since John died than when *he* died."

"You had a few other things on your mind then."

"Do you remember the day Dad didn't show up for your World Series party? John was there and you'd made all of these—"

"Of course I remember. He and I even talked about it once."

"When?"

"Toward the end. I've often wished you'd had that chance."

"What did he say to you when he came up to your room?"

"Why?"

"He was back downstairs so quickly. He looked like a dog that had been hit with a newspaper. What happened?"

Ruthie shakes her head slowly. "When he came up I had my candy out, spread all around me like I used to do. He said he was sorry about missing the party, and he looked like he really meant it. He had this hang-dog expression I'd never seen on him. Anyway, the very next thing he said—mostly because he didn't know what else to say, I think—was that I should be careful how much candy I ate."

"What did you say?"

"I didn't say anything. I just grabbed about six candy bars and ripped them open and started stuffing them all in my mouth at once. He reached out and tried to stop me, but I ran and crawled under my corner desk." Ruthie laughs. "God. I was crying again by then, and snot was running over my lips and into that big wad of chocolate in my mouth, but I was determined to get them down. I was *not* going to throw up in front of him and give him the satisfaction of being right."

"Did you? Get them down, I mean."

"I did. But he never saw it. When we talked about it, he said he just didn't know what to do. And that was his way of dealing with things he didn't understand. He left. But even after he was gone, I kept on chewing. My eyes were watering, and I could hardly breathe, but I put my hands over my mouth and kept pushing them in and chewing and swallowing, pushing and chewing. Down it all went. Every last morsel. My hands and my face were covered with melted chocolate, so I licked my fingers, and then I wiped the chocolate off my face with my hands, and I licked my fingers again. And do you know what I remember most about all of it? Do you know what memory is most vivid for me? How *good* it tasted. Not Dad leaving, not the things Mom screamed at him, none of that. It tasted so *good* to me, Henry. The sweetness of all that chocolate stuffed in my mouth, touching everywhere at once—my cheeks, my tongue, my lips—all that sweetness driving straight up through the roof of my mouth and right into my brain. I will *never* forget how good that felt. Never."

Henry looks at his sister. "What are you saying to me?"

"I'm saying you can blame Dad for whatever you want, but I was *this* person, the one you're looking at, before that day, and I would have found a way to be this person one way or another."

"You wouldn't have started eating the way you did if he hadn't left."

"It's the way I'm wired, Henry. It's my coping mechanism *and* I love it. You think I wouldn't have found something else to cope with?"

Henry lets a small smile pass his lips. "What kind of therapist are you? Isn't it always the parents' fault?"

"Finding who's at fault, even if it's true, isn't very productive. Better to find out who you are and either accept it or change it. I'm trying to change. You tried to be a lawyer, but you weren't wired that way. Dad was wired to love women and he never saw anything wrong with that."

"Love?"

"He understood the kind of man he was, and I have a certain amount of respect for that. And what if he'd stayed? Do you think he would have hurt us less? He loved a lot of women, but he *loved* all of them."

"You really believe that?"

"I do. Henry, I saw the look on his face when he talked about them. Even Mom. Thirty years later."

They pass the rest of the walk mostly in silence, Ruthie working hard. Once in a while Henry has to give Franny a gentle tug to slow her down, so that his sister doesn't feel rushed. When they make the last turn, there is no moon to lead them up Emerson toward home, the clouds low and heavy and damp with cold. As they approach the main walkway to the house, Allie appears around the far corner. Ruthie waves, and Allie jogs to meet them.

"How was Franny, Dad?"

"Fine."

"She really scared me today."

Ruthie reaches out to touch Allie. "She's just muddling through like the rest of us, sweetie. How was rehearsal?"

Allie smiles broadly. "Great."

"Great?"

"Yeah. Great."

"Hm." Henry sees Ruthie wink quickly at his daughter. "Do you want to come in and warm up with me and tell me about it?" she asks.

"Sure."

Franny is looking longingly at the front door, and Henry strokes her head. "Why do I sense I'm not invited?" he says.

"You're not," Ruthie says. "Girl talk."

"Did you tell him your news, Aunt Ruthie?"

"I didn't have the chance."

"News?" Henry says.

"Aunt Ruthie's thinking about seeing patients. At the carriage house."

"Just a few, at first," Ruthie assures. "See if I've still got it."

Henry smirks. "Why do I feel like I was just your first?"

"Oh, I'd have to work up to you. So, what do you think?"

"I think it's great. Really. We'll have to see about the zoning, but I'm sure something can be worked out."

"I already called the township office. They're putting it on the agenda for next month."

"Come on, Franny," Henry says, giving a tug. "Apparently, we know nothin about nothin."

Allie takes the leash from him. "She's coming with the girls, Dad."

I woke the next morning with the feeling that I had lost something other than my father. I felt as if I had lost baseball. It was Sunday morning of the day of Game 7 of the World Series, and I didn't care. I smelled the pancakes and bacon that were my mother's attempt to put the previous night behind us, and I wasn't hungry. I thought of all the games Ruthie and I had listened to in bed at night, or watched on television on beautiful weekend afternoons, and I wondered why we had wasted all of that time. It was almost nine o'clock when Ruthie finally looked in.

"Are you going down for breakfast?" she asked.

"I don't know. You?"

Ruthie shrugged.

My mother called from downstairs. *"Come on down, sleepyheads. Breakfast."*

Unlike us, my mother seemed energized. She scurried from one side of the kitchen to the other, taking down plates, glasses, getting orange juice from the refrigerator, syrup from the cupboard, all while humming the Pirates' fight song.

"I thought you guys would be up at the crack of dawn again."

She set steaming plates down in front of both of us without asking. "So what's the plan for the day?"

"I don't know," I said.

"I don't know," said Ruthie.

"Mark, Mr. Garabedian called. He's having another party but I told him we'd probably do our own thing. We're all invited, though."

"No thanks," I said.

"No thanks," said Ruthie.

My mother got herself a plate and sat down. I waited for some sign that her good mood was artificial, but there was none. "We still have a lot of the stuff from yesterday. We didn't touch the cake. Did you want to see if John is interested in coming over again? There's plenty of Iron City left."

"I think he's busy," I said.

"He's busy, Mom," said Ruthie.

"Oh," she said. "Okay." She reached over and cut Ruthie's pancakes before cutting her own. Then she poured syrup on all three plates and started to eat. I bit the end off a piece of bacon and crunched slowly. Ruthie sat with her hands in her lap.

"The two of you can mope all the way through this historic day if you want to, but I'm done with all of the self-pity. One thing you have to give your father credit for is knowing how to make a clean break. He's started a new life for himself. And I, for one, am going to join him." She laughed at herself. "Well, not *join* him, of course, but you know what I mean."

When she was finished, she cleared our dishes, not commenting on the amount of food left on each. "Please take your long faces into the living room," was all she said. Ruthie and I sat on the couch in silence and watched *George of the Jungle* and *Penelope Pitstop* without laughing. At a little after ten, the phone rang, and we could hear my mother in the kitchen.

"Of course, you're so nice to ask. We'd love to. What can we bring?" Ruthie and I looked at each other. "What time would you like us? Fine. We'll see you then." She hung up the phone and came into the living room. "You were right. John is busy. He's having a party."

I clung stubbornly to my gloominess all the way up until game time, but Ruthie brightened on the walk to John's, carrying the untouched Roberto Clemente baseball cake from the day before carefully in front of her on the sidewalk like a ring bearer. I had brought my autographed game program, but only because Ruthie had insisted that it might be good luck.

"You should see his house, Mom," Ruthie said.

"It's not a house," I said.

"But you should see it."

"She's *going* to see it in about five minutes."

"Henry, that's enough."

"It's hard for him to go down stairs," Ruthie said. "So his steps only go up, and he has poles like a fireman to get down."

"Really?"

"And he has this big long shelf you can walk on, and that's where I'm going to watch the game because it was good luck last time."

"A shelf you can sit on? That sounds very cool."

"And *walk* on."

"It's scaffolding," I said.

"But don't go in his bedroom, Mom. It's private. You have to be careful because there's no door."

"I'll be careful."

When we arrived, there were huge blue letters over the old double kitchen doors that said: "Gate C," and there was laughter coming from inside. My mother knocked, but when no one answered she pushed one of the doors open and put her head inside. "Hello!" she called.

John's voice answered from far back in the room. "Come on in, folks. Mitch will take your tickets."

Standing just inside the door was one of the two young amputees who had come to talk to John after my chorus concert. He wore a stadium usher's uniform and stood balanced on one crutch, the other held out like a parking gate, blocking our way in.

"But we don't have any tickets," Ruthie said.

Mitch slipped three old Pirate stubs to my mother. "Shh," he said. "Don't tell the management."

My mother passed stubs to us and we all, in turn, handed them to Mitch, who raised his crutch, first for my mother, then for Ruthie, then for me.

"Oh my goodness," my mother said, seeing John's room for the first time.

"Whoa!" said Ruthie, seeing how it had been transformed for the party.

Two of John's poles, one by the light switch on the far right side of the room, and one at the far end of the countertop on the left, had been painted yellow, like foul poles. Red, white and blue bunting hung all along the scaffolding, and a blackboard sat on the counter done up to look like the stadium scoreboard. An American flag hung from the most central pole in the room, and John stood beneath it, dressed in abbreviated concessionaire's garb and Pirates' cap, a six pack of Iron City hanging around his neck on a makeshift strap, a bottle opener dangling on a string from the neck of one of the bottles.

"Welcome to Three Rivers Stadium," he said. "Home of the soon-to-be World Champion Pittsburgh Pirates."

"This is incredible!" My mother walked over and rubbed the bunting between her fingers. "Where did you get this?"

"That's the real stuff. A couple of sections were ripped during the NLCS, so they replaced it. My friend who gets me the tickets got a few feet for me. A little needle and thread, and it was good as new."

"When did you do all of this?"

"Last night and this morning. I had lots of help," he said, nodding to the others in the room. "We figured they won every game at home, lost every one on the road, so they need a little home cookin today. Which reminds me. Those are genuine Three Rivers Stadium hot dogs boilin on the stove. They're awful, but it's all about the karma. Smother them in the fixins and they go down without too much trouble. They'll talk to you from down below later, though, scuse my French."

John introduced us to Ed, the man who had pushed Miss Donovan's wheelchair out to the bus the night she cartwheeled over John and off the stage, and to Emma, the nurse who had taken care of her ankle, and to the two young soldiers, Mitch, the ticket-taker, whose right leg had been taken from the knee down, and Tony, the quiet one who had lost his from the hip. The television was already on with the sound turned down, and Prince was doing his pre-game on the radio. A few extra folding chairs had been brought in from the auditorium, and I noticed that seat numbers had been taped to the backrests, as well as to John's cut-off couch and chairs.

"Check your tickets and find your seats," John announced. "You can move down front later in the game if there are any no-shows. I know the usher."

"I'm moving *back*," Ruthie said, walking up the stairs by the refrigerator to the scaffolding.

"Right you are, little missy. I almost forgot. Once everyone's in their seats, I've got a few announcements to make."

"There's a shocker," said Ed.

"Okay, first: we don't have an organ, but I do have this kazoo, so when I blow the usual trumpet intro, I expect a hearty 'CHARGE' out of everyone. Ed's in charge of the foot stompin that begins the 'Let's Go Bucs' cheer. Those of us hampered in one way or another south of the equator will yell louder to make up for the missing feet. We want them to hear us in Baltimore. The aisles and sightlines are to remain clear during play. You may leave your seat for concessions or the restrooms only between innings or during a pitching change, and if you're late comin back, stay at the top of the aisle until the next pause in the action. Contrary to standard practice, beer *will* be sold after the seventh inning stretch, and the lovely cake brought in by the lovely short person sitting up in peanut heaven back there is off-limits until the post-game celebration. Oh, and Hank, shorten up that long face you brought in here, or I'll slap an Orioles cap on your head. Any questions? Miss Bambino."

"Should I sit or stand? I think I did both last time."

"Someone toss her a pillow. Start off sitting and we'll re-evaluate if necessary. Anyone else? Okay. I think The Gunner is just about ready for the starting lineups."

We all settled in. My mother looked young and beautiful seated between Mitch and Tony, and they both seemed shyly pleased to be next to her. Ed sat in the cut-off armchair, Ruthie on her perch, and John was at the center of everything, on the couch between Emma and me. Curt Gowdy's mouth moved on the television screen, but the sound was coming from the radio sitting on top. As the Baltimore crowd worked itself into a roar in the background, Bob Prince recounted everything that had been working against the Pirates from the beginning: that the Orioles were the defending champs who had won a hundred or more games three years running; that before the Pirates' come-from-behind victory in Game 4 the Orioles had won fifteen in a row, including an easy sweep of the Oakland A's in the ALCS; that three of their four twenty-game winners would get two starts each in the Series, while the Pirates had trotted out six different starters, "*seven, if you count young Bruce Kison's masterwork taking over for a struggling Walker in Game 4.*" Prince let his own voice build with the Baltimore crowd: "*Some would say they've got no right to be in this thing at all,*" he said, "*but here they are, folks. Your Buccos are twenty-seven outs away. Here we go.*"

Everything I had built up against my own hope since the night
before, everything that had felt like disinterest but was in fact a way
of protecting myself from disappointment fell away at once, and
suddenly I didn't just want them to win; I needed them to win. It was
physical, like hunger, and I sat shaking as they went down quietly
in order in the first. When Blass walked the first batter he faced on
four wild, off-balance deliveries, I knew that whatever I was feeling,
he was experiencing the same emotions a hundredfold. The Orioles
manager, Earle Weaver, saw it too, and he tried to shake Blass further,
complaining to the umpires that Blass was pitching from the side of
the rubber. "Rule 801!" Weaver yelled. "He's got to pitch from the
center or in front of the rubber!" Sanguillen went out to settle Blass
down with a smile and his broken English, but Weaver's ploy had
backfired: he'd gotten Blass angry, and that had quelled his nerves.
He found his rhythm instantly, erasing the only other two base
runners of the first three innings by inducing a double-play ball in
the second, and picking Buford off first base himself in the third.
But the rest of the Pirates seemed frozen at the plate by the pressure.
They went down in order again in the second, again in the third and
recorded two quick outs in the top of the fourth. Mike Cuellar was
threatening to throw a World Series no-hitter, and with every Pirate
that walked back to the dugout, my hands gripped each other harder.
Ruthie stood and paced the scaffolding. My mother hid her face in
Mitch's shoulder, and then Tony's, unable to watch. John's thick right
hand found my shoulder.

"Relax, Hank," he said, his own voice calm. "Here comes your
man."

Here's how Prince called it:

*"Two outs in the fourth, and here's Bobby Clemente. Bounced to short
his first time up. Here's the first pitch from Cuellar... Bobby hits a screwball
a mile into left center field! It's going, it's going, it is... gone! Kiss it goodbye! A
homerun for Clemente!"*

The communal noise that went up in that room would probably
have been enough to bring the police had the rest of the city not been
doing the same thing at the same time. In my memory, I can almost
hear the occupants of the houses around us, and the houses beyond
them, and so on out fifty miles in every direction of Pittsburgh,
and it *is* like a home game, only with a million people in attendance
surrounding our little section inside Gate C at Three Rivers Stadium.

Blass was virtually unhittable after that, his head snapping back
with each sling of his rubber arm, like Game 3 on rewind. But Cuellar
was just as good. After Clemente's homerun, he went right back to
work, striking out five of the next ten batters he faced and giving up
nothing in that stretch but a wasted leadoff single to Sanguillen in
the fifth. When the Pirates came to bat in the eighth, they had just
two hits and still clung to a one-nothing lead. I'm not sure any of
us had made a sound for an hour. Ruthie had tried sitting, standing,
and lying down with her head hanging off the scaffolding, watching
the game upside down, as both Pirate and Oriole batters went down
one after another. The rest of us sat silent and immobile, clenched
like fists in our seats. When Willie Stargell strode to the plate to
lead off the eighth, he was an incomprehensible two for thirty-six
in the post-season. The man who would go on to become one of the
greatest sluggers of all time and the hero of the 1979 World Series
against these same Orioles had struck out in almost half of his at-
bats, screwing himself into the ground with one wild swing after
another. Since his unlikely, rally-starting double in the night game,
he had just one meaningless single. There was an audible groan from
nearly everyone in the room.

"Hank, you still got that program?"

"Yeah."

"Hurry up and turn it to Dock Ellis."

"What?"

"Just *do* it!"

I flipped the pages until I came to the one that Shangelesa Ellis had spent Game 4 drawing on with John's "magic pen."

"Now what?" I asked.

"*I* don't know. It worked once before. You got any better ideas?"

I held the program facing the television screen. "How about this?"

"Perfect."

Unbelievably, Stargell bounced a single through the left side of the infield.

We stomped our feet, the kazoo blew, and I shook my program at the television. Jose Pagan, a thirty-six-year-old utility infielder who was platooning with Hebner at third against lefties, stepped in and promptly drilled a double over the center fielder's head, driving Stargell home.

"That'll do it!" John assured us. "Blass'll shut em down from here!"

But it wasn't that easy. Blass gave up two quick singles to lead off the bottom of the eighth, and the Orioles scored their first run with a sacrifice bunt and a fielder's choice grounder to third. The tying run was on third, two outs, future Mets manager Davey Johnson at the plate. My mother jumped up from her place next to Mitch and Tony, hurdled Emma's legs and wedged herself between John and me on the couch, grabbing my arm and squeezing until I felt my hand go cold.

"I can't take this," she said.

John leaned forward to talk to me around her. "Think that program works on defense?"

"I don't know."

"Give it to me!" Ruthie shouted from behind us.

"Toss it to the Bambino!" John agreed. "A good luck charm holding a good luck charm. You can't beat that."

Ruthie caught the program, barely keeping her balance on the scaffolding. Johnson looked at ball one.

"Hold it up like Henry did!" my mother yelled.

"It closed up when he threw it! I'm trying to find the right page!"

"Hurry up!" everyone in the room seemed to shriek at the same time. It didn't matter to us that all over Pittsburgh, in every house and in every bar, thousands of others were undoubtedly carrying out their own rituals, performing their own superstitions. Hats were turned backward and inside out, incantations spoken and sung, talismans rubbed and chewed and prayed to. People who had the bad fortune of arriving at their gathering shortly before the Orioles' first run were treated like kryptonite and banished willingly to the silence of media-less dining rooms and bathrooms, forced to follow the game through the reactions of their friends and family. And every one of those people believed what we believed: that ours was the only one that mattered, the only one that worked.

Ruthie fumbled through the pages.

Johnson fouled one off.

"Got it!" Ruthie called. She stood and held Dock Ellis's picture high over her head, Shangelesa's scribbled hearts like hundreds of clear bubbles through which her father could watch the fate of his teammates. "He's no batter, he's no batter!" Ruthie sang.

Johnson grounded the next pitch to shortstop Jackie Hernandez, who threw to Bob Robertson at first, and the threat was over.

We yelled until we were hoarse. We were raucous and ridiculous and unashamed, and I have no better childhood memory than the rest of that afternoon. Blass came back out for the ninth, heroically shrugging off his wobbly eighth and, with Ruthie still standing behind us, holding the program shakily aloft for the entirety of the inning, he induced a weak grounder from Boog Powell, an infield pop-up from Frank Robinson, and a Series-ending grounder to short from Rettenmund. For the second inning in a row, Hernandez threw to Robertson for the final out, and all of us (or those who were able) jumped from our seats just as Blass leaped into Robertson's arms, straddling his teammate's chest like a frightened acrobat. Any other year, Blass would have been named the Most Valuable Player, and his performance remains one of the most dominant by a pitcher in Series history: eighteen innings, two earned runs, thirteen strikeouts, just four walks, and two complete game victories. But this Series belonged to Clemente. To put what he did in perspective, no Oriole player had more than seven hits. Clemente had twelve, including two doubles, a triple and two homeruns. He was relentless and graceful and indomitable. He had, in fact, made everyone else look like minor leaguers.

The rush of players from the field and from the dugout that had formed a bobbing mass around Blass and Robertson broke reluctantly apart and headed for the locker room. Prince was already there, the post-game television interviews the one crumb he had been thrown by NBC, and John sent me to turn up the volume on the TV. The criticism most often leveled at Prince was that he was a "homer," shamelessly rooting for the Pirates as opposed to calling a neutral game, and as the players poured in, clapping Prince on the shoulder as if he were one of them, it was clear that he both deserved and welcomed that moniker. When Prince interviewed Clemente, Blass poured champagne on both of them, whooping like a schoolboy, and Clemente flashed that rare and beautiful smile.

"You must be proud of him," John said, shaking my hand.

"Yeah."

"Wish you'd gotten his autograph now?"

"No."

"No. This is better." He still had a hold of my hand, and he pulled me in. It was a strange sensation, hugging a man whose head rested on my chest, but he wrapped his heavily muscled arms around me and clapped me on the back until I relaxed and returned his embrace. "That's my boy," he said.

I had known him for eleven days.

A Basement

Allie had never spent a day the way she had spent this one. Locked in her room, she practiced holding her lips the way Nathan had showed her, pressing them against the underside of her own arm, testing the way different pressures made her feel, letting the tip of her tongue play along the tendons leading to her slim wrist. She had looked at herself in the mirror and ignored her boyish body. It was only her mouth that would matter, and her fingertips on his face, and the way she would lift her chin to expose the length of her neck to him. She knew that much of what she was picturing, anticipating, was pure fantasy, perfectly scripted scenes that had no chance of playing out in the life of Allie Graham. But until yesterday, isn't that what Nathan Emery had been? Anything seemed possible now.

Except this.

She could hear the music from a block away and told herself that it wasn't coming from his house. But now she is standing directly in front of it and every window is dimly lit, one of them in deep red, silhouettes passing back and forth. Cars fill the driveway and both sides of the street, and the volume of the music surges and fades, not with any discernible rhythm, but as if a door is being opened and closed somewhere.

Allie stands, looking at his house, watching her breath in the cold.

Everything is so at odds with the intimate imaginings that had filled her day that the only choice seems to be to turn and go, but she doesn't. She had been so certain that this was the night her life would change that she can't let go of the possibility. It would be like rehearsing for months and then being told that opening night has been canceled. So she hesitates, hoping for some excuse to do anything but go home.

When Nathan appears in the light of the front stoop and waves to her, it is more than enough. She rewrites everything in an instant. He had been waiting, watching for her. Maybe he mentioned the party and she hadn't heard him. Maybe he had been looking forward all day to showing her off to his friends, and maybe they would become her friends too. She wouldn't have to do all the things they do to fit in. She was Nathan's new girl, and that would be sufficient.

She waves back and starts up the walk.

"Hey, I'm glad you came," he says over the music behind him. "I almost called you."

"Yeah?"

"Yeah. Sorry about this."

"No problem."

"My parents decided to drive up to Athens to check on my grandmother, and that's a no-brainer for my sister. This has been going all day."

"So these are all your sister's friends?"

"Mostly. But I know a lot of them. This isn't exactly their first visit. Do you want a beer?"

"No thanks."

"Schnapps?" Nathan smiles. "I've had it on ice for you."

"Maybe just a taste."

"Cool."

He takes her hand and they make their way through the crowd and into the kitchen. When they pass by someone who is lighting a cigarette, Nathan taps him on the shoulder.

"Hey. Smokers on the back porch only."

"Sorry."

Nathan leads them out onto the porch where the keg sits in a tub, the schnapps bottle sunk in the border of ice around it. A group of kids are leaning against the railing, smoking. Two boys are passing a joint back and forth. It has started to snow, and both boys, in short sleeves, lean out over the railing and stick their tongues out. They settle back, and the one closest to Allie holds the joint out to her as she watches Nathan pump the keg and fill his cup.

"No thanks," she says.

The boy shrugs, puts the joint to his lips and makes it crackle.

"Is a beer cup okay?" Nathan asks. He has taken the bottle of schnapps from the ice and is holding it up next to a red plastic cup. "I'll pour you just a little so it stays cold."

"Sure."

He pours, hands the cup to Allie and takes a long sip of his beer. Allie lets the schnapps wet her lips.

They stand, shoulder to shoulder, looking toward the backyard. The snow disappears when it touches the grass. Allie puts the cup to her lips again and, like last night, the second sip is easier, the cold liquid spreading warm in her chest.

"Can I ask you something?" she says.

"Sure."

"How come it took you until last night to notice me?"

"Man, you're not much for small talk, are you?"

Allie shrugs.

"Of course I noticed you," Nathan says. "We've been rehearsing together since January."

"How come it took you so long to be nice to me, then?"

"I wasn't nice to you?"

"I'm sorry. I'm not saying this right at all. It's just that you sort of come in to rehearsal and do your thing and leave. And you're so good you can get away with it. Max and I were talking the other day, saying you're just like Jim O'Conner. Everyone gets all worked up about this 'gentleman caller,' and then he finally arrives and he's all superior and pointing out their flaws, and then he leaves for something better."

"You really think of me like that?"

"Not as bad as that sounded. Just, I don't know, everybody admires you so much, but you don't seem like you belong there."

"Thanks."

"I didn't mean—"

"No, really, thanks. I don't want to belong there. There's so much drama. I'm just trying to get through the next few months."

"Are you going to the High School?"

"Naw. My parents are sending me to this boarding school in Connecticut where my dad went."

"Oh." Allie looks away. "Great."

"Yeah. Hey. You'll have to come visit me sometime."

Allie looks into her cup and takes another sip. "You still haven't answered my question."

"What?"

"Why me?"

"I don't know. You don't seem like you belong there either."

"You mean because I tower over everyone?"

Nathan laughs. "No. Like last night, tonight even. You seem like you're up for stuff, but you don't make a big deal out of it."

"I guess."

"Or right now, for instance. You up for some dancing?"

"Sure."

"Let me grab another beer and pour you a little more of that, then we'll go."

On their way back through the kitchen, a tall boy with a goatee claps Nathan on the shoulder, points to Allie and gives the thumbs up sign. They bump into a girl with sleepy eyes and a tattoo of the Chinese Yin and Yang on her shoulder whose breasts are spilling out of her tank top.

"Little brother!" she exclaims, throwing her arms around Nathan, kissing him full on the mouth. She looks Allie up and down. "Is she being nice to you?"

"Hey, Sasha."

"If she's not nice to you, come see me, okay?"

"You wish."

Sasha cackles and Nathan pushes past her.

"Please tell me that *wasn't* your sister." Allie has to shout as they get closer to the living room.

Nathan laughs. "No. A lot of her friends call me little brother."

"Oh."

Nathan leads her back through the crush of the hall and into the living room. The bulbs in the wall sconces have been replaced with red Christmas lights, and the room vibrates with bass. The music is so loud it's a physical presence, surging from the speakers, bouncing off walls and bodies. They dance with their faces almost touching in the packed room. It is unbearably hot and pretty soon Allie is drinking just to keep her throat moist.

"*That's my girl*," Nathan shouts in her ear. Allie smiles, they touch their cups together and Nathan leans in to say something else. "*When do you have to be home?*"

Allie puts her mouth to his ear and shouts, "*Ten again.*"

"*We better start rehearsing soon then.*"

"*What?*"

"*Our scene, remember? The one we started last night.*"

"*Oh.*"

"You want to go someplace quieter?"

"I guess."

He pulls her through the crowd, and they make their way back to the kitchen and the basement door.

"Hey, little brother," someone calls. "Isn't that one too young to take down there?" Nathan laughs, opens the door and pulls it closed behind them.

Everything goes dark. And, although the music still vibrates around them, the abrupt change in volume makes it seem suddenly quiet.

"Looks like Tom forgot to pay the light bill again, Mrs. Wingfield," Nathan says.

Allie forces a laugh.

"Come on, let's find our spot."

Allie's hand is on his shoulder as they descend. "Can't we turn a light on?"

"Shh. That would freak everyone else out."

"Everyone else?"

When they reach the bottom of the stairs, Allie's eyes have started to adjust. The glass block windows in the main room to her left, the one they all rehearsed in last night, glow dimly with the streetlights from outside, and Allie can just barely discern what must be couples in various places throughout the room. She follows Nathan into the laundry room and he pulls her against the wall with him just inside the door.

Nathan whispers, "This is where we were, isn't it?"

"I guess. I don't know."

"Did you practice what I showed you?"

Allie's face flushes, thinking of kissing her arm in her room.

"No."

"Come here."

He reaches up and takes her face in his hands. The first kiss is clumsy, though Allie manages to keep her teeth from touching his. Then she relaxes, and the warmth from his mouth and from the alcohol spreads all the way to her feet and she finds that she is clenching her toes. She matches the gentle pressure of his mouth, and the softer he kisses her, the harder her heart beats. He takes first her upper, then her lower lip between his, and then his tongue finds hers and she flicks at it gently, just like she had done to her own wrist. When he puts a hand under her chin, lifts it and kisses down her neck, she is sure that she was right after all: everything is changing.

He is breathing heavily now, and she can feel the heat on her neck. His hands slide over her shoulders, down her back, and when they reach the base of her spine, he pulls her in to him, and she can feel him hard between her legs.

"Hey!" Allie pulls away.

"Shh. What?"

"Slow down."

"That's what happens. It's a compliment." He takes her hand, rubs it gently, and guides it to his crotch. Allie pulls away again.

"I said *no*," she whispers loudly.

"Come on. Haven't you liked everything I've introduced you to so far?"

"Not that."

"I'm not talking about all the way. Just a little fun."

"Nathan, please."

"Here, look how easy."

He takes her shoulders and turns her around, and for the first time Allie realizes that they are not alone in the laundry room. She sees a figure in the corner. She hears kissing noises but doesn't immediately see anyone else. Then her eyes see movement down low. The other figure is kneeling. Allie hears Nathan opening his pants behind her.

"Is that what you think I'm going to do?"

"If you don't, someone else will."

"What? Oh, *fuck* you, Nathan."

"No, no, I'm sorry, don't go." He grabs her arm hard. "Here, just try it like this first. Just with your hand." He guides her hand with both of his, making her grasp his erection, then moving it for her. "That's it," he whispers. "Just like that." Allie closes her eyes, tries not to cry, and uses her hand as a point of reference.

When she brings her knee up, with all of her strength, there is no sound at first, and she wonders if she did it right. Then the air creeps out of Nathan in short, choked gasps as he folds to the floor. No one notices. The sounds he makes are not out of place down here. She draws her foot back to kick again, then lets it fall and feels her way around the doorway and up the stairs. A boy is leaning against the door and she has to push her way out. A girl sees her and calls, "Hey darlin, where's little brother?"

Allie fights her way through the crowd, out the front door and runs through the silence of the late spring snow.

My father took my mother at her word that night on our porch. For most of the next year he didn't bother with us. When he did, it seemed to be at Jeanine's insistence. It became a pattern with him to disappear from our lives during the first year or so of a new relationship, and then, as if he'd never left, resurface, wondering why Ruthie and I didn't rush to greet him.

John and I went to at least a dozen baseball games together in 1972, always sitting behind home plate in the seats Dave Ricketts got for him. Sometimes there was an extra ticket for Ruthie as well. The players had family tickets for every game, but there were often spares and we benefited from a rocky relationship or two. Ballplayers were notoriously wayward, and if one of the wives wasn't speaking to her husband, those tickets invariably ended up in John's hands.

The games we attended in September of 1972 were rare bright spots in my first month as a Middle School student, as we seventh-grade boys were being taught our place throughout that desultory fall. We were shoulder-checked daily into the rattling metal lockers; notebooks filled with loose papers were batted out of our hands from behind to tumble down stairwells; and in the gymnasium showers, we faced our hairless bodies to the wall, washed quickly and hoped not to attract the attention of one of the brazenly naked, muscled boys wielding a wet, snapping towel. There is no more miserable age for a boy than twelve.

Fortunately, the Pirates looked like a team headed for another World Series. Blass was even more dominant than the year before, winning eighteen games, going to the All-Star Game for the first time and finishing second in the Cy Young voting. Clemente won his twelfth Gold Glove, appeared in his twelfth All-Star game, and in the last game of the season, before a sell-out crowd that included John and me, he collected the 3,000[th] hit of his career, guaranteeing his eventual entry into the Hall of Fame. As John and I watched the bizarre ending to that season—the Reds beating the Pirates in the last inning of the National League Championship Series on a wild pitch—it certainly never occurred to either of us that we would never see Roberto Clemente play again.

On New Year's Eve, 1972, I was sitting in our living room with Ruthie, who had just fallen asleep while waiting for the ball to drop in New York. My mother, who had been seeing Mr. Garabedian at least one night a week all year, was at his house for a party, having promised to be home in time to bring in the New Year with us. Sam, who was ostensibly babysitting, had just sent a tall, stooped boy home and was upstairs in her room. I was therefore very much alone when Times Square disappeared from the television screen, replaced by the words "News Bulletin," a voice telling me this:

"A plane carrying baseball great Roberto Clemente and four other men crashed into the waters off Isle Verde, Puerto Rico shortly after takeoff from Luis Munoz Marin Airport. The plane was carrying relief supplies to earthquake-torn Nicaragua. There are not believed to be any survivors."

As if understanding that I wouldn't believe what I had heard, the voice repeated the bulletin again, suggesting I stay tuned for further details. Then Times Square and its revelers reappeared. Impossibly, nothing there had changed.

There was a loud rush of blood to my face and I thought I was going to be sick. I don't think I said anything out loud, but Ruthie woke next to me and must have been alarmed by what she saw.

"What's the matter?"

"Roberto Clemente is dead."

"What?"

"In a plane crash. He's dead."

Ruthie looked at the television. Dick Clark introduced The Beach Boys. She started to cry. "What are you talking about?"

"I have to go. Tell Mom I went to John's."

"No! Don't leave me alone!"

I was already in the hall and Ruthie was following. "Mom will be home any minute," I told her, "and Sam's upstairs."

"But she won't care! Don't go!"

My bike had been put away for the winter so I ran, the air like a cold cinch around my lungs at first, and then burning my throat. A train whistle blew, and its distant rumbling urged me on faster still. I didn't realize I was crying until the tears started to blur my vision, and, when my hands went to my face, it was already wet. There were lights on at the VFW. The front door was open. I heard music from the auditorium, but I knew John would be in his room. He had refused an invitation to our house the previous December 31st, saying curtly, almost impolitely, that he never celebrated the New Year.

The hallway was dark once I turned the first corner, and I had to pull my hand along the wall, still running, until I reached the second turn and saw the dim light glowing between his double doors. There were sounds coming from behind them that stopped as soon as I started pounding.

John's voice came first, but different, angry. "What the *hell!*"

Then another voice, quieter.

Then John again, yelling from far back in the room. "*Who is it?*"

"It's me, Henry!"

"*Who?*"

"Hank! Hammerin Hank!"

"*Go home.*"

I was crying harder now, confused by the unfamiliarity of his voice which was hard and devoid of kindness. The only reason I could put to it was that he knew what had happened and had reacted in some unexpected way. Had I been in any other frame of mind I would have walked away, hurt but obedient. Instead, I pounded on the door again.

"Let me in! Please!"

"*Jesus H. Christ.*" There was movement behind the doors and then his voice was closer but no less angry. "What are you doing here?" he asked, his words running together, slurring.

"The crash," was all I could get out.

There was a long silence.

"How do you know about that?" he asked. It seemed a strange question.

"The news. It's on the news. He's dead."

"Who's dead?"

"Clemente."

"Jesus," he said. Then he opened the door.

I had never seen him out of his harness. Even the tuxedo he had worn the first night I visited his room had fit over the top of it. Now he stood before me in nothing but a dirty undershirt that fell to the ground around him. He was disheveled and bleary eyed, and I could smell the alcohol on his breath. Behind him in the lamplight, having just come out of the bedroom, stood a mostly naked woman, who was just then folding a short, silk robe over her sagging breasts and loose stomach. Her legs were long and white and skinny. She wore high-heeled shoes.

"Come on in, then," he said to me. He turned, and as he pulled himself slowly back toward the woman, the short, thick stumps of his legs appeared and disappeared, calloused and red.

"You might as well get dressed and go, Lena," he told the woman. "The envelope's on the table in the bedroom."

"You sure? You got plenty of time left."

"No. You go on. Maybe you can still find a party before midnight."

"Not me, honey. I'm going to soak in a tub. I'll just get dressed."

She disappeared into the bedroom and John went to the couch, saying nothing to me. When she emerged again a minute or two later, she walked over to him, bent and took his face in her hands and kissed it. "Maybe you'll call me next year?" she said.

"Yeah. Maybe."

Lena touched me on the shoulder on her way to the door, and then the echo of her heels in the hallway slowly receded and John and I were alone.

"He's really dead?" John asked.

"Yeah."

"How?"

"A plane crash. He was going to help in that place that had the earthquake."

"Nicaragua."

"Yeah."

"Come sit."

I sat next to him and he pulled his palms down over his rough face. "Sorry about this," he said, turning his hands loosely in the air to include both Lena and his own condition.

"That's okay," I said.

"No, it isn't. But it's what I do. Sometimes."

"Oh."

He folded me in with his heavy arm and I started to cry again. I thought about the day I had first visited John here: how I had gone home and found my father sitting at our kitchen table; how I had resisted going to him, afraid that his touch would bring tears that would shame me by revealing the rawness of his absence. Why was I able to cry with this man but not my own father?

"Hey," he said, patting my arm with his thick fingers. "That's enough, now. This is someone else's tragedy. He wasn't ours to lose."

He stiffened when he said this and took his arm from around my shoulder. He shifted on the couch until he was facing me.

"Why are you here, Hank?" he asked.

"What?"

"Why did you come here to see me tonight?"

"I don't know." I rubbed at my eyes with a sleeve. "When I heard what happened, it felt, I don't know. Like the world was coming to an end or something. And I just ran."

"But why me? I mean, I know we're friends, but..." He trailed off and seemed unsure of himself, which was unsettling to me. His eyes appeared to grow heavy. "I'm not really who you think I am."

"What are you talking about?"

He didn't say anything for a long time and I could tell that he was gathering himself.

"There are things you don't know about me. Not just you. Most are things hardly anyone knows, so it's not like I singled you out. I just feel worse keepin it from you is all, knowin how you think of me." He slid off the low couch and swung over to the refrigerator where he took a beer from the inside of the door. "I suppose I've had too many of these already, but I'm gonna need another one to keep goin, if you don't mind."

I shook my head. It could have meant that I didn't mind. Or it could have meant that I didn't want him to continue. I wasn't even sure myself which I was trying to convey, but he pried his beer open on the underside of the counter and kept talking from there.

"I'm no war hero, for one. No hero of any kind."

"You weren't in the war?"

"Oh, I was there. Better part of two years. But I was lucky. Luckier than most." He saw me looking at him, uncomprehending. "You know that picture of me and Kathy? The one on the wall in my room that Ruthie found?"

"Yeah."

"When do you think that picture was taken?"

"I don't know."

"I don't mean exactly. But I bet you think it was taken just before I went off to the war, don't you?"

"Yeah, I guess."

"Everyone does. Why wouldn't you, right?"

I started to nod, but the expression on his face stopped me.

"That picture was taken the day I came home," he said.

I looked at him, bewildered.

"Listen to me, Hank. If you don't remember anything else I ever tell you, I want you to remember this."

"Okay."

"One of these days you'll wake up and you won't recognize yourself. And not the way you think I mean. More than likely, it won't be because you're a victim but because you've been careless with somethin precious. And you'll think, just like tonight, that it's the end of the world. But it ain't. It's just the beginning of somethin else. That's the great and terrible thing about this life. There's no batter up behind you. It's just you, takin a swing at one beginning after another. Now come with me a minute." He started pulling himself toward his bedroom. "I should be lookin at her when I tell you the rest."

ANOTHER BASEMENT

Henry is on the sidewalk outside Theta House. He isn't surprised by the lack of cars. Because of the local ordinance, no one can actually live here, and the campus is small enough that most students walk everywhere. What is unsettling is the lack of any signs of activity whatsoever. It is still early, just after eight o'clock, and the parties on Fraternity Row two blocks east of here won't be in full voice for hours. But these sorority socials typically start early, polite prologues to the late-night debauchery devised by the boys, and Henry had expected to be part of at least a small stream of nicely dressed students heading for Theta House. In the distance he can hear the muddle of open-windowed music that always accompanies kegs being rolled into place and furniture being pushed to the walls. But here, on this block, he is alone and the houses are quiet.

His steps slow as he arrives at the flagstone walk that leads to the front door, and he stops and turns to face the house, blinking behind his glasses. There is no wind, and the snow begins to fall around him, light and gray as ash. The flowerbeds have been cleared and edged but won't be planted for weeks. The shutters and window trim are being given a fresh coat of deep green paint, and an extension ladder

lies on its side against the clapboard. There is light behind one of the
windows, just to the right of the front door, but all of the others are
dark.

It occurs to Henry that this is the point at which he can turn
back. He tries to stop the thought from coming because, until this
very moment, he has never admitted to himself that there might be
something to turn back from. But there it is, a decision to be made.
He could go home now and tell Maggie that there had been some
kind of mix-up. Or that the gathering had been too noisy to talk
productively about Natalie's writing so they had agreed to meet again
after class one day. But even as he thinks of the things to be done he
is taking his first steps up the flagstone path, his body tingling and
light and unfamiliar to him, snow melting the instant it touches his
shoe-tops.

He had always assumed that men who were unfaithful to their
wives were driven to it—by an unsatisfying marriage, a tragedy that
demanded newness as a cure, even love. In his own novels he had
created characters who faced similar choices, and even if he hadn't
known exactly what would happen from the beginning, how the
stories would unfold, the choices his characters eventually made were
inescapable, following inevitably from the attributes and weaknesses
he had given them like genetic code. He would never have thought
to create a happily married man who would walk toward the front
door of this house, a woman—a girl, really—waiting on the other
side. Of course, he doesn't know himself as well as he knows his own
characters. He doesn't know, or won't acknowledge, that these past
two years have changed him as a husband, changed the way he looks
at his wife. And he doesn't know, or won't acknowledge, that not
sitting down to write—not engaging in the kind of self-reflection
necessary to create truth out of fiction—is his way of not finding this
out.

The porch is solid and level, the mosaic of penny tile having been meticulously restored after a generous alumni gift, but Henry still feels uneven and outside of himself as he reaches toward the doorbell that is glowing like a small full moon. Before he has touched it, there is the sound of a latch being turned from the other side, and the door opens.

"Hi, Professor," Natalie says.

"Hello."

"I'm glad you could make it."

"Where is everyone?"

"Everyone?"

"You said there was a social."

"I said there was a *small* social."

"Ah. I missed that."

"Sorry. I didn't think you'd come otherwise."

"Probably right."

"Do you want to leave?"

"No. Not yet."

"Good. Come in and get warm."

Their footsteps echo together in the large foyer. A staircase that looks like it was borrowed from a southern plantation arcs away and then over their heads as they pass underneath.

"I'll give you the full tour a little later," she says. "But we'll start down in my office."

She leads him through a narrow hallway, past a dim sitting room at the back of the house, and opens what Henry would have taken to be a closet door until he sees the stairway.

"They won't let me keep my computer upstairs," she says over her shoulder. "Antiques only."

The basement is one large, low-ceilinged room finished in dark oak paneling. A couch and a few chairs are arranged around a small television set on one side of the room. The only light comes from a laptop screen and the green hooded lamp that sits next to it.

Although the basement seems to run the entire length and width of the house, there is no other furniture. An old exercise bike occupies the center of the room with at least twenty feet of space on either side of it.

Henry points at the laptop screen. "Is that your manuscript?"

"Yeah. I come here to work a lot. Something about all the emptiness works for me. Like I'm supposed to fill it up."

"I must admit it crossed my mind a few minutes ago that you hadn't actually written what you showed to me."

"No. It's mine. I did give you a very carefully selected section, but it's all mine."

Henry pictures the scene, and not for the first time. Natalie with a stranger. Her hands gripping her ankles, a submission both violent and tender.

"It's very good," he says.

"Yes, so you said."

"When you can make another writer jealous you're doing something right."

"You were jealous?"

"Yes."

"Of what I wrote?"

"Yes, I was."

"Why?"

"I have too much compassion for my own characters. It's a fault I recognize but can't seem to remedy. At first I thought it was a matter of experience, something I would grow out of as a writer, but I haven't. You're so merciless already."

"That doesn't sound like a compliment."

"I'm not talking about cruelty. I'm talking about honesty. You're brutally honest. That's what made me jealous. Makes me jealous."

"Thank you."

"Where does it come from?"

"What do you mean?"

"I mean you claim to have come from an abnormally normal family, but there's anger in this piece."

"I told you. It's the sex."

"I'm not sure I follow."

"I gave my first blowjob when I was thirteen. He was my science lab partner and he was a total geek but I was crazy in love with him. I'm not sure he'd ever even been kissed before, but I went down on him in the back of the bus one night on the way home from a ski club trip. After he came he found a seat by himself in the middle of the bus and he asked for a new lab partner the next week. When I was fourteen I lost my virginity to my older brother's best friend. We only had one computer in the house and sometimes an IM from Josh would come up while I was sitting there and we'd just start chatting. I wanted to have sex so badly, and he was a nice enough guy. He hardly said a word to me when he was around the house, but he was crystal clear during our little chat sessions about exactly what he would do to me if I'd let him."

"So you decided to let him?"

"Yeah. I've probably had sex with thirty guys since then, and it's been my idea most of the time. So I guess I'm sort of wired like a man in terms of my sex drive, but the weird part is that I'm still wired like a woman emotionally."

"Meaning?"

"Meaning there are a *lot* of one-night stands in that total, and I felt like shit after every one of them. Intellectually, I hate double-standards, but there must just be something physiologically different about a man putting something inside someone he doesn't love and a woman having someone who doesn't love her putting something inside of her. It's like that old joke, only his brain really *is* in his cock and you can feel what he's thinking. I've fallen for more sincere lines and puppy-dog eyes than I can count, but as soon as a guy is inside of me I can tell *exactly* how he feels. But by then it's too late. You wake up feeling like shit about yourself enough times and the anger part just starts to come naturally."

"You're angry at the men?"

"God, no. Women who play the victim really piss me off. Other than rape, the woman is *always* the one who decides that sex is going to happen. We have a standing fucking invitation. Literally."

"So you think that's why I'm here?"

"Of course."

"And all you have to do is say 'yes' and we're off."

"No. That's what makes you so interesting. I said yes by asking you here. But I don't think you've decided yet."

"But you said I came here for sex."

"You came here to *decide* about sex. One way or the other. One thing I know you didn't come here for was to help me with my novel."

"But that contradicts everything you've just said. You said it's always up to the woman, but now you're waiting for *me* to decide."

"No. I know what you'll decide. I'm just waiting."

"For another one-night stand you'll regret tomorrow?"

"If you were that type, you would have done this a long time ago. With someone much prettier. Admit it, Professor. You're here because I make you feel something you've never felt before. I don't think once will be nearly enough."

They are silent, still standing through this entire exchange, and Henry looks away, then down at his shoes.

"Have you ever tried it?" Natalie finally asks.

Henry looks up. "What?"

"That kind of sex. From my book. With your wife."

"No."

"You should. Men love it. Women too, with the right kind of man. Which you are."

"Okay."

"Okay? You're funny."

"Why is that?"

"You're so easy to embarrass."

"Sorry. I'm a little out of my element here."

"Should I keep asking you if you want to leave?"

"I'm afraid you'll keep getting different answers."

"Is it yes or no right now?" She touches him for the first time as she says this—just the back of a fingernail that starts gently at his sternum and falls absentmindedly down the front of him on its way back to her side. A current surges through Henry and he has to close his eyes to regain his balance.

"Can I ask you something?" he says.

"Sure."

"You told me to bring Maggie."

"Yes, I did."

"How did you know I wouldn't?"

"I wasn't sure you wouldn't ask her. I was only sure she wouldn't come. She hates me and she trusts you."

"Oh."

"Are you okay?"

"No." Henry removes his glasses and squeezes at the bridge of his nose, his eyes clenched closed again. "I have no idea why I'm here."

"You haven't been listening, have you?"

When Henry opens his eyes he can barely make out that her hands are at her throat. By the time he slides his glasses back into place she has undone the top two buttons of her shirt. She looks at him as she continues, unhurried. When she has finished, she lets the shirt hang open by its own weight, and the two perfect inside half-moons of her breasts appear in the shadowed pillar that runs from the nape of her neck to the top of her jeans. She takes his hand and slides it inside, over her stomach and slowly up.

"See," she says. "Not so bad."

"Natalie—"

"Shh. Relax," she whispers. She leans into him and her smell is comforting, almost familiar, though he can't think why. She slides down the front of him, drops to one knee and then the other, and lays one hand on the crotch of his pants. She moves it slowly, up and down, not pressing but waiting for him to rise to meet her. When he does, she looks up at him and smiles. "Seems you've decided," she says. Then she stands and takes his hand again, guiding his fingers back inside her shirt and up, lightly over one breast and then the other, making his hand push her shirt aside. "Nice?"

"Yes."

"Do you want to kiss them?"

"Yes. I do."

She puts a hand behind his head and pulls him to her, arching. Her other hand moves down between his legs where he is now fully hard. His breath is coming in short bursts through his nose as he pushes her breasts together, taking one nipple into his mouth and then the other.

"Oh God," Henry whispers.

"You miss these, don't you?" she murmurs, stroking his hair.

The turn his stomach makes is violent and sudden. Everything stops.

"What?"

"You must—" she begins, less sure.

He has to pull his hands away from her abruptly to cover his mouth, but the smell of her skin is there, on his fingertips, and he suddenly places it. It is Allie's smell, after a shower, and the image that he can't stop is of his daughter and his wife sitting in their living room, Maggie thin and weak from fighting the drugs that are supposed to be fighting for her, Allie brushing her hair, over and over, in case it might be needed.

"Please button your shirt," he says into the back of his hand.

"Oh God. I can't believe I said that. I'm so sorry."

"No. This is my fault. Just please. Button your shirt."

"I wasn't thinking... I didn't mean—" Natalie turns away as she works, quickly this time, to cover herself. "I didn't mean it that way," she says to the dark wall behind her.

"I know. And I'm sorry. I just have to go." He starts to leave, then stops again. "I need you to bring a drop-add form to my office next week. I'll sign it."

"You're kicking me out of class?"

"No. I'm asking. Please."

"Professor."

"Please."

He finds his way back upstairs, past the sitting room to the foyer and out the door. The snow is heavier now, thick and wet. Once on the flagstone path he starts to run but stops, thinking how strange it would look to anyone who happened to be passing by. Moving slow is harder somehow, and he slips once in the new snow. Fighting to find his equilibrium, he rocks to the outsides of his feet, forcing his right arm forward with his left foot, then the reverse. He finds himself wondering what his father would have done in his place tonight. And although he has no doubt that his father would still be inside, he believes that if Natalie had said anything else—anything other than the pitiful truth she had chosen to reveal—he would still be in there too. Which means he is not at all the man he thought he was.

15

On December 31, 1953, nearly six months after the end of the Korean War, John Kostka was still celebrating. No one called him on it. Not his mother and father, who were too thankful to have him home to care. Not his brother—4-F and going to law school while John was being shot at—whose own guilt was salved by John's safe return. Certainly not Kathy, sitting just an arm's length away in the passenger's seat of his father's car, hands folded primly in her lap, trying not to grasp the dashboard as John took the dark corners.

No one called him on it because it was John's that seemed the most natural reaction to having come home whole. It was easy to sympathize with the ones who weren't as lucky. Like John's cousin, his mom's sister's kid. Everyone understood why he sat and did crosswords all day, his right forearm that ended just before what had been his wrist holding the paper steady as he marked the letters carefully with his still unreliable left hand. It was the malaise that had settled upon so many of the others, so many of John's friends, the ones who came home unharmed like him, that no one could quite comprehend. It was true that John wasn't accomplishing much more than they were, but that didn't seem significant in light of the circumstances. He'd been stingy with his combat pay so there was still some of that, and the mustering-out pay would buy him at least another month, so why not just let the boy have his fun? The Army would pay for school if he decided not to take the job with his father at the mill, but what use was school anyway, his mother asked her friends, when the boy couldn't sit still for a minute? Up and out of the house at dawn, down to Ritter's for breakfast, dissecting the Sports section all morning with regulars three times his age, then over to the South Side to shoot pool at Dee's, drinking just enough Iron City to keep him loose, but never so much that the angles stopped making sense. Picking up Kathy after class, maybe catching a night game at Forbes Field, then up to The Hill for jazz, Little Harlem, maybe the Crawford or the Hurricane until God knows when.

Kathy was willing to be patient. She was in her last year at Chatham, studying to be a teacher. She'd be working soon. Maybe they'd get married right away and get a small apartment, or maybe she'd save her money, wait for John to start working again too, both keep living at home until they had enough for a down payment on a little house. Her patience was partly in her nature, but it was also true that she hadn't yet gotten over the simple fact of him, still skinny inside his old clothes, the new way he made love to her, slow and frantic all at once. When they were out together, his fingers never stopped moving—on the tabletop, on the steering wheel, on her knee—so she finally bought him a book on sleight of hand to give him something to do with them, and he started making things appear: coins for the bartender, pencils at the ballgame, a ring with a small diamond that made her cry. For some reason, he never made anything disappear.

On that New Year's Eve, she went through the windshield at the same instant the steering column cut him in half. In his brief remaining flash of consciousness after the impact, John saw her arcing out over the hood of the car, the hem of her dress fluttering, as if she was flying directly from the seat next to his into whatever afterlife there might be.

WINDOWS

Ruthie spends more time at her bay window looking out at the main house, especially at night, than she would ever admit to her brother. Sometimes she even sits in the high-backed chair in the window's alcove, her own lights turned off, so that those of her brother's house illuminate glimpses of the lives on whose fringe she has dwelt for the past two years: Maggie framed in the side window, at the kitchen counter, chopping; the top of Walt's head followed by his arm reaching up to feed his fish; Henry in his study at the far end of the front of the house, reading or writing; Allie up in her room, picking out tomorrow's outfit. Taken separately, none of these images would seem likely to arouse profound sentiment, and yet watching them play out simultaneously always makes Ruthie keenly aware both of how blessed she is to be with them, and of how she will always be something of a bystander here. The latter provokes something else too: a yearning that is almost a physical ache for what has been lost. To Ruthie, this bank of lighted windows, and what she can see in them, recall the very symbiosis that existed in her own childhood home before her father left, before the four of them retreated from the unit that remained, each to seek his or her own kind of solace. She is aware that this recollection is more likely a product of desire than of memory—that, like a long, well-traveled bridge that suddenly shimmies and collapses into the river, there must have been fundamental, invisible faults underlying her family's happiness long before the actual crack appeared. She is even aware that some of those same imperfections might exist here, in her brother's house. But the visual power of these four people living their various lives both separately and together is always more than enough to overcome whatever skepticism logic might try to impose. They are a family.

Although she will sometimes choose to sit and watch her brother's house to pass the time, more often she is simply drawn to her window by a sense that something is happening. Whether certain important events generate a palpable energy, or she simply catches movement in her peripheral vision as she passes, she can't say. But she has stopped being surprised by the fact that whenever she is drawn to look, there is almost always something to see. Like tonight, for instance. Ruthie is otherwise occupied, moving about the carriage house in her slow, deliberate way, putting away dishes in the kitchen before limping into the living room to set out her glass and cutters and oil to begin a new mosaic she's been considering, this time for Walt. Just as she is about to switch on the tall reading lamp by her chair, she looks up to see Allie running out of the darkness through the snow, fast enough that when she makes the turn up the walk to the front door, her hair is trailing behind like the tail of a comet. She isn't dressed for running or for the weather, in a skirt and flat shoes, and she collides with the door as if she didn't see it coming. For a moment she stands there, leaning heavily and breathing hard, before she pushes inside and closes the door quickly behind her. Within seconds, the light in her room comes on, and she is at her window, pulling the shade. Ruthie watches for a few minutes longer to see whether Allie will appear elsewhere, and that is when she notices the side of Maggie's face, alone at the kitchen table.

Other than at mealtime, Maggie never sits, and Ruthie thinks perhaps that is why she didn't register her presence there at first. Moreover, the kitchen lights have been dimmed, and Maggie is so still that she might be sitting for a portrait. She is too far away to discern her expression, but when her face drops slowly into her hands, Ruthie knows that she has been crying. It is such a private moment that Ruthie can't help but feel some shame at having witnessed it, and she is about to turn away from the window when another figure catches her attention.

At first, she doesn't recognize her own brother in the furtive posture of the man who approaches the side door. He seems not to be coming home but to be lurking, or, at the very least, unsure of whether or not to enter, snow gathering on his slumping shoulders. Maggie doesn't know what Ruthie knows, doesn't know that her husband is less than ten feet away on the other side of the door, and for a few moments each appears, despite their proximity to one another, to be utterly alone. Ruthie sees her brother in profile now, his left shoulder bearing his weight against the doorframe, his face set at a downward angle that mirrors that of his wife's. Henry pauses there long enough that Ruthie almost believes that it is possible that her brother will decide to turn and leave. And then he straightens, kicks his shoes one at a time against the doorframe, and enters his home.

16

He didn't get out of bed for a year.

His arms withered. His shoulders protruded like a clothes hanger draped with his own skin, and his chest shrank into itself until it was nothing but a cage for his heart. He refused most food and all physical therapy, and they let him have his way because there were so many others. He told his brother and his parents to stop coming to see him and, once he stopped talking altogether during their visits, they obliged. He endured obligatory sessions with the staff psychiatrist only because the doctor came to him and he couldn't leave the room. On December 31st, 1954, exactly one year after the accident, the doctor asked him if he could try to name just one thing for which he was thankful as the New Year approached.

"Yeah," John said. "I'm thankful that she'll never see me like this." Then he turned away and the doctor left without saying when or whether he'd be back.

The following week, his roommate, who had lost most of the right side of his face to a grenade, moved back home and, in his place, two nurses wheeled in a limbless black man. "Nothing but a sack of flour with a head," John said on the night he finally told me all of this. "Or a body that had nothing to do but keep the head alive, I guess, depending on how you look at it." For a month John watched them feed, change, prop and roll the man all day, then lay him down at night. The man almost never spoke—except to say that his catheter had to be changed, that he needed to be scratched and where, that he wanted pain medication, that he didn't like part of his meal and wanted no more—but he talked incessantly in his sleep, mostly nonsensical outbursts or snippets of conversation in which he seemed to be speaking both parts: *Don'choo touch my cigarettes nigger, relax I ain't but seein how many you got, because I'll beat yo black ass bloody you as much as lip one a them smokes, you have to catch me first heh-heh, oh I'll catch you mothafucka I'll catch you.*

A white woman came to visit once a week. She looked like she had once been pretty, but exhaustion had curled her posture and dappled her skin. She kissed the man's forehead when she arrived and again when she left. In between, they spoke a few hushed phrases while she fed him his lunch, dabbing dutifully, without affection, at his mouth with a napkin after each bite. John's lunch sat in front of him as well, and without fully realizing what he was doing, he took a small bite each time the man did.

After a month, without explanation, the man was moved again. The next week, the psychiatrist doctor returned, apologizing for his absence, and John started to talk. Having gained a few pounds, he allowed himself to be wheeled down to Physical Therapy and showed some interest in the small hand-weights cradled in a rack by the wall. Officially, he was a Traumatic Bi-lateral AKA—above knee amputation—his stumps too short for prosthetics. Even if they could be secured in place, the energy required to swing their dead weight would be too much for the few inches of leg he had left. He was told that he needed to rebuild the shrunken muscles in his arms and upper body so that, eventually, he could move the wheelchair on his own.

Over the next few months, as some of his strength started to return, he discovered, mostly by accident, that his arms were long enough to raise the rest of his body off the ground a few inches. At first, he could hold himself like that for only a second or two, but then he made it part of his daily regimen—hold, release, hold, release—and eventually he could lock his elbows for a full minute or more. One morning, a dumbbell he was working with slipped from his hand and rolled a few feet away. The physical therapist who had been working with him was helping another patient, and in much the same way that an infant first learns to crawl by wanting to reach a toy, he realized that if he set his hands in front of his body he could scoot it forward a few inches at a time that way. He reached the dumbbell in seven or eight tiny steps and resumed his work.

The stronger he got, the further out in front of himself he could reach and still create enough leverage to pull even with his hands. Seeing the value in what he was doing, his therapist encouraged John to begin working on his abdominal muscles, and by the fall of 1955 he was piking forward and setting himself down well in front of his hands, nearly doubling the length of his stride. By then, his room was nothing but a base camp of sorts, and he spent his days swinging up and down the long hallways visiting other soldiers, flirting with the nurses and doing magic tricks for some of the kids who came as visitors.

He never saw the limbless man again, and although the psychiatrist professed ignorance, he did ask if John would be willing to visit with a few of the soldiers he was having trouble reaching: just stop in, show himself, make conversation. By late 1956 John was on the hospital payroll. Lacking the credentials to be an official member of the medical staff, he was listed as a "Senior Custodian." His paycheck was signed in Washington and no one ever asked. Every time he entered a soldier's room for the first time, he thought he might see the limbless man again but he never did. "That man saved my life," he told me. "Try feelin sorry for yourself after you've seen that."

In 1958, a hospital nurse made him the heavy leather harness he has been wearing ever since, though Otto's Shoes in Riverside had replaced the bottom numerous times. He added the work gloves himself and started venturing off the hospital grounds.

In 1960, he rediscovered his love for the Pirates and took the streetcar, and later the PAT bus, down to Forbes Field at least once a week. He broke his nose three times getting off the streetcar that first season.

In 1962, he started playing catcher for the VA staff team. The first time he got on base, he stole second. The game was delayed ten minutes because the opposing catcher started laughing and couldn't stop as soon as John took off.

In 1965, just as the hospital population had begun to dwindle to the long-term residents and the routine flow of outpatients, the wounded from what John called "a whole new kind of war" started to appear, and his days got busier and busier.

In 1968, a young soldier he'd been counseling, newly home from that war, hung himself from an overhead pipe in a supply closet with an extension cord. There was a one-word note pinned to his gown and addressed to John. It just said: "Sorry."

In 1970, he was offered the chance to leave the hospital: a free room in the back section of the VFW in exchange for an open-door policy for ambulatory patients from the VA Hospital. He spent most of that year planning what the room would look like, and then building it with the help of a few patients with two good legs and at least one good hand.

And in 1971, he rescued an eleven-year-old boy on a city bus.

CONFESSIONS

When Henry comes through the door, Maggie is sitting at the kitchen table with her head in her hands, and he is certain that, somehow, she already knows. But when she sees him, she wipes quickly at her eyes with all of her fingers, as if she is the one with something to hide, and shakes a wan smile into her face.

"Hey there," she says. "Mentoring session over?"

"Yeah."

"What's the matter?"

"Nothing. I was going to ask *you*."

"Oh, this?" she says, wiping her face again, outward this time, with her palms. "This can wait. Or, rather, I need it to wait. Yours?"

"My what?"

"Your little whatever it is that's making you look like something out of a George Romero movie."

"Hm?"

"Henry. What's the *matter*? Did you see Atlee? Did you hear something?"

"No. Still nothing. As far as I know. Where's Allie?"

"I heard her come in just a few minutes ago, but she went

straight upstairs. I'm guessing that means her visit to Nathan's either went too well or too poorly to share with me, and I haven't got the energy to press her on either one."

"Nathan?"

"The boy who's in the play with her." She waves her hand in front of his face. "Where *are* you?"

He says it before he has even heard it inside his head, looking past her. He says it despite having spent his entire walk home trying to compose an unremarkable recounting of his evening. Just a moment ago he stood outside the kitchen door and resolved to lie to his wife for the first time in their marriage, and yet he knows that what he is about to do has nothing to do with altruism or honesty and everything to do with self-preservation, with salving his own guilt. He simply doesn't have the strength not to tell her.

"Something just happened, Mag," he begins.

"What do you mean?"

"I think..."

"Henry?"

"I think I was just about to be unfaithful to you."

Maggie looks up at him, an exasperated look on her face. "*What?*"

"With Natalie."

"Christ, I know the *who*, but what am I supposed to do with that... whatever it was. Was that a confession? '*I think I was about to...*'"

"I left before it could happen."

"Henry. Believe me when I say that I'm in no mood—"

This is not at all the reaction Henry had expected, and he is left sputtering. "There was no one there. There was no social tonight. It was just Natalie and me. When I realized that, I thought about what you'd been saying. And Atlee. And then I thought maybe I'd known it all along too."

"And?"

"And I went in anyway."

"Why?"

"I don't know. It felt like it wasn't even me. Like I was watching myself do it."

"But you said nothing happened," Maggie says carefully. "Should I ask what you watched yourself do?"

"No."

"All right." Maggie drops her head into her hands. "God. Not today."

"I'm sorry."

"For what? Jesus Christ, you're not *telling* me anything."

"I'm telling you that I think I had every intention of being unfaithful to you tonight."

Maggie is shaking her head, still in her hands. "No you didn't."

"And then something stopped me."

When Maggie turns her face up to him, Henry thinks he has never seen her look this tired, even when the chemo was taking all of the disease and all of the life from her at once. She looks besieged. And when she speaks, there is none of the anger he expected, but a quiet aggravation she usually reserves for Walt. "Henry," she says. "You wouldn't have had sex with that girl in a million years."

"How do you know?"

"Because I know *you*."

"You weren't there. That wasn't me."

"Why are you telling me this?

"What do you mean?"

"Are you in love with her?"

"No. Of course not."

"Given the opportunity, right now, would you have sex with her if I'd never find out?"

"No."

"Then for God's sake, why didn't you just keep this to yourself?"

"You're angry at me for telling you the truth?"

"No, I'm angry at you for *hurting* me just to make yourself feel better!"

"I don't feel any better."

"Even worse."

"So you think I should have lied to you?"

"No. I think you should have *protected* me! Like you promised: *'to love, honor and protect.'*"

"You left out *'forsaking all others.'*"

"Christ. That's a fuzzier one and you know it."

"Mag, don't make this a joke."

"Your *confession's* the joke! How can you be so goddamn *selfish?*"

"Mag—"

"Okay." Maggie shakes her head slowly and her voice goes quiet. "Maybe if this had happened any other day I'd be raging through the house, breaking my mother's china. But with a healthy dose of perspective as a backdrop, I can see how insignificant this is going to be very shortly. Crushes are unavoidable, Henry. You just happened to avoid yours longer than most."

Henry sits down heavily across from his wife. He feels silly, an emotion last on the list of what he might have expected. How can one woman, he wonders, be so consistently generous and perplexing?

"Does that mean I've held out longer than you?" he asks warily.

Maggie hesitates. "Yes. It does."

This jolts Henry. He looks at Maggie and a surge of jealousy so strong it feels like fear rises hot into his face.

"Who?"

"*I'm* compassionate. *I'm* not telling."

"You can't do that. You can't tell me you've been unfaithful to me and not tell me with whom."

"I didn't say I'd been unfaithful."

Henry takes one long, slow breath, trying to settle his racing heart.

"Okay." Maggie pauses, and Henry knows it's for effect, so he braces himself. "Andrew."

"*What?*"

"I warned you."

"*My Andrew?*"

"Yeah."

"Best man Andrew? When?"

"God." Maggie looks genuinely bored at the prospect of retelling the past, but resigned as well. "Do you remember when we were first married and we'd just fixed up Andrew and Sarah and we all went to the Jersey shore together?"

"Yes. That awful house."

"Remember that night we'd had a few drinks and I suggested that you take a walk on the beach with my best friend and I'd take a walk with yours?"

"Yes."

"I kissed Andrew."

"Just like that? On the beach with me walking the other direction?"

"I was drunk and twenty-seven."

"And married."

"Newly, and not very good at it yet."

"Then what happened?"

"It was just to see, you know? The kiss. I mean, Andrew and I had our history, short as it was, and I guess I just wanted to see how it would make me feel."

"What did he do?"

"He kissed me back. Really hard."

"Jesus Christ, I'm going to kill him."

"And then I threw up, of course."

"Mag, don't patronize me."

"I'm serious."

"One of my students just got skewered for a similar trick."

"But that's what happened."

"That's what he said."

"Andrew's pawing at me and I suddenly realize what I've done, and the combination of that and all the wine and his usual cloud of aftershave spun my head around, and I tried to push him away and when he wouldn't budge I chundered all over the front of him. That's why he was drenched when we got back."

"He didn't trip?"

"Dove. I think that's what finally woke him up. Though it could have been the scampi on his chest. He apologized the entire way back and begged me not to tell you."

"So all these years, all time we spent with those two before we came up here, you just kept that in?"

"I never *think* about it. I got to keep you. You got to keep Andrew. All the risk was in *telling*, so we didn't. Henry. Look at me. I'm not trying to trivialize. It was a big deal for about forty-eight hours, and then it went away. It felt like something, and then it was nothing, just like tonight. You want me to be angry with you. I *am*. I'm angry. Even more than that, I'm mortified for you. But this is going to go away. I wish I could say the same for everything."

She stands, hesitantly.

"Maggie?"

"Come here." When Henry is close, she takes his hand and slides it up underneath her shirt. She guides it, presses for him. "Here," she says. And he can't help but think of his youth, the years spent dreaming of being invited to touch a girl's breast, and Natalie, too, guiding his hand just like Maggie is now, and how that has all led, somehow, to this—touching without wanting to feel. "You really have to press," she says. "This one's trying to hide."

And then, there it is. Small, hard, self-contained, deep in the tissue but unavoidably there.

"Aw, Mag."

"Yeah."

"A cyst again. Maybe."

"Maybe." She lets her head drop to his chest. He holds her and touches her hair.

"I love you, Maggie."

"I know."

"No. I mean, I *really*—"

"We're not going to tell Walt yet. Until we know everything. I have to tell Allie. Tonight. Because you know her; she'll *know*. But I can't tell Walt. I can't." She is shaking her head into his chest.

"No. Okay. I'll tell him for you. Once we know."

"You have to promise again," she says, crying softly now.

"I'll think of something. I'll tell him for you. I promise."

"No. Not that."

"What?"

"You have to promise you'll protect me."

17

My mother didn't make it home before midnight as she had promised. When I got back from John's it was after one a.m. and Ruthie was asleep on the couch alone. My mother arrived home shortly after I did, her face ashen. She sat down heavily. Ruthie stirred but didn't waken.

"What a night," she said.

I assumed she was talking about Clemente. "Yeah," I said.

"I'm sorry I'm late."

"That's okay."

She leaned over and kissed me, half on the cheek, half on the ear. "Happy New Year, little man."

"Happy New Year."

"How did you guys do here?"

"Fine."

"Where's Sam?"

"Upstairs, I guess."

"In bed before you?"

"Maybe. I don't know. How was your party?"

"There was no party."

"What do you mean?"

"It was just the two of us. Mark and me. He asked me to marry him."

Neither of us said anything for a long time. My mother looked at her hands, spreading her fingers wide, and then making two fists, over and over.

"What did you say, Mom?"

"I said no."

"Oh."

"Do you know why?"

"No."

"I don't either."

I looked over at my sister, who was still sleeping. "Because of Ruthie?" I asked.

My mother looked at her then too and put a hand on Ruthie's leg. "Maybe a little bit. Mostly, I guess, because I just don't feel about him the way I felt about your father. Still feel about him sometimes, Lord help me." She took the hand that wasn't touching Ruthie and dragged it backward through her hair, closing her eyes.

"What did he say?"

"Not very much. I told him a year ago I couldn't see myself getting married again, but I guess he hoped my seeing him all this time meant maybe I'd changed my mind. I think I've hurt him badly, Henry."

I didn't know what to say to that. I thought about changing the subject, telling her about the plane crash, but that didn't seem right either, so I didn't say anything.

"I don't think I can work there anymore," she said. My mother had gotten the house in the divorce, along with the mortgage that my father's nonexistent alimony and child support payments were supposed to cover. I learned years later that he stopped paying for anything the day he left, subsequent court orders notwithstanding. "I don't know what we'll do." She rubbed Ruthie's leg. Ruthie opened her eyes slowly, and then, seeing our mother, woke quickly and sat up.

"Hey, sweetie. Happy New Year."

"Happy New Year, Mommy."

"Did you see the ball drop?"

"No. I fell asleep."

I waited for Ruthie to continue, for her to say that I had left her alone, but she didn't.

"Maybe next year," my mother said. "I promise I'll stay home and we'll play games until midnight."

"Just us?"

"Yes. Next year I'm sure it will be just us."

Upstairs, after my mother had left my room, Ruthie rolled to her side and faced the wall. I realized that she hadn't said a word to me since I'd returned from John's.

"So you didn't stay awake for the ball?" I asked. She pulled the covers up over her shoulder but didn't answer. "I missed it too. John didn't even have the television on."

"John's my friend too," Ruthie said to the wall.

"I know that." I thought about Lena and about how glad I was that Ruthie hadn't been with me. I thought of everything John had told me, and I wondered whether he would have protected Ruthie from that knowledge. Part of me couldn't help but think that I would have been better off without it too.

"I had to watch the news alone," Ruthie said after a while.

"The news?"

"They came back on. There were people on the beach where he lived holding candles."

"Really?"

Ruthie turned to face me.

"Everyone was crying. A man said they were waiting for him to walk out of the water."

"That can't happen."

"*I* know that. I'm not a baby."

"Sorry."

Ruthie rolled to her back and wiped at her eyes with the backs of her hands. "I watched him as much as you did."

"I know."

"I never knew anyone that died and you left me alone."

I thought about what John had said, about the loss not being ours.

"We didn't even know him, Ruthie," I told her.

"*Yes* we did," she said. "We *loved* him."

RESTLESS

In the middle of the night, thinking that she is the only one awake, Maggie rolls away from Henry and swings her feet quietly to the floor. Strangely, her restlessness has nothing to do with her earlier discovery, nothing to do with having to tell Henry, and then telling Allie, nothing to do with Natalie Currant, but comes instead from a sudden and unexpected need to work. She never works at night, seldom stirring between the time Henry settles next to her to read and Walt wakes her the next morning. But her characteristic energy, missing these past few days, has returned in the aftermath of this strange evening, along with a sense of clarity that demands her attention. Henry, who has been pretending to sleep next to the woman who has been pretending to sleep next to him, says nothing as she stands and leaves the room to cross the hall and pad quickly up the uncarpeted steps to the third floor.

The snow has stopped, the sky cleared, and the light new coating of white glows under a full moon. In the six months that she has been working on them, Maggie has never seen her panels in artificial light. And although she isn't conscious of the choice, registering only that she is in a hurry, she passes the switch on the wall without flipping it on and begins rolling back the wax paper covers in the reflected moonlight that spreads upward from the floor, where it first strikes white in stretched, mullioned squares. She sets her tackle box down in one of the diamonds of light and opens it. In the large bottom section, there are five or six boxes of new black charcoal and several packaged blocks of kneaded eraser. But Maggie is sifting through the small square compartments on top that contain mostly used pieces until she finds a small, brick-colored scrap. She rises and goes to the first panel, the one that is completely black but for the gray mist of her missing breast, and she begins gently brushing a hint of color into the vague oval of haze.

Hearing what she knows to be her mother's footsteps above, Allie abandons her own indifferent attempts at sleep. She turns on the small nightstand lamp, gets out of bed and stands in front of the mirror that hangs above her dresser. She is wearing her favorite nightshirt, the one with the comedy and tragedy masks that Aunt Ruthie gave to her after the sixth grade play. Then, it had hung below her knees; now it barely covers her underwear, and small holes have appeared around the collar and shoulder seams. Allie fingers the largest one just below the nape of her neck and then traces upward, raising her chin, touching the spots that Nathan Emery had kissed a few hours earlier. Allie's hair hangs almost to the hem of her shirt, and she picks up her brush and begins brushing it in long, slow strokes.

Walt knows nothing about what happened to Allie tonight, nothing about his father and Natalie Currant, nothing about his mother's growing secret, but is awake only because everyone else is. He gets out of bed and crosses the hall to his parents' room. He speaks in his normal voice, as if approaching his father in the kitchen at lunchtime.

"Dad, I would like to check on Freddie."

"We did that before bed," Henry answers in a whisper. "Remember, buddy?"

"Yes. But I would like to check on him again. He did not look good, Dad."

"No, he didn't, did he?"

"No."

"All right. Come on."

When Henry flips the upstairs switch for the foyer light, Franny's tail thumps on the floor below them. He takes Walt's hand, and as they make the turn at the landing, Franny struggles to her feet and stretches as much as she is able, giving the appearance of a disinterested shrug. When Henry and Walt pass, Walt pats her head and she follows them into the kitchen.

Henry, who has been preparing for this moment for weeks, is rendered silent by the other events of the evening. He and Walt don't say anything for a minute or more as they look at Freddie floating belly up in the small tank. Henry puts a hand on Walt's shoulder. Franny sits.

"I told you, Dad."

"You were right, buddy. What should we do?"

"I think we should flush him."

"You don't want to say a prayer or something?"

"We will say one while he swirls around. And we will salute."

"Okay. That sounds good."

Henry lifts the tank from the counter and they leave the kitchen together. Neither of them notices that Franny has remained seated, not following.

Above them, Allie has finished brushing her hair. She drops to her knees, lifts the spread on the extra twin bed, reaches her arm underneath and pulls out a folded red gift bag that opens to about the size of a shoebox. She stands, unfolds the bag and sets it on the dresser in front of her. Then she takes a pair of scissors from a mug filled with markers and pencils, grasps a section of hair in her fist and cuts it just below her right ear. She lifts the hair high until the bottom hovers over the red bag, and then she lowers it in slowly, letting it collapse over itself, back and forth. She takes hold of another section and does the same thing, then another, and another. When she has finished laying in the last panel, she pushes her hands deep into the pile and squeezes, crying silently. Then she picks up the scissors again and tries to even out the ragged edges.

Above Allie, Maggie is working on the last portrait. In the moonlight it is difficult to tell what she is doing. But the color, nothing more than a faint presence in the first panel, seems to be coalescing into something. By the center portrait, there are sharply distinguished strands of brick-tinted smoke that weave through the gray of her absent breast. In the fifth, where Maggie herself begins to disappear, the strands start to move toward the center, like pairs of DNA lining up to divide. By the sixth, it's hard to say whether the letters are actually discernible, or whether they only become so in retrospect when they appear in the seventh and final portrait, dim but unmistakable in the center of the cloud that floats in the white background. Maggie steps away and the moonlight sets the letters aglow: *HELP*

Without looking away from her panels, Maggie tosses the charcoal toward her tackle box and misses. The fingers of her right hand, stained with the earthy red, slide under her tee shirt to scratch at her scar, trailing color there as well. She turns, leaving the wax paper up, and heads down the stairs without washing her hands.

Ruthie knows nothing about the events of the evening, but she has seen the lights go on and off: in Allie's room, in Walt's, in the kitchen.

She is both a part of this family and not. And since she has been alone for most of her life, she doesn't equate her solitude with loneliness, except during those rare times, like this one, when the lives next door seem to thrum with so much pain or joy or merely change that her exclusion from them is like being in the eye of a storm, a silence in the midst of a great noise. The sensation is so convincing tonight, her isolation so complete, that she initially dismisses the soft knocking at her door as nothing more than a part of the hum next door, until it comes again, more insistently, emerging as both distinct and beckoning.

At first she sees only the hair, bobbed at the chin line, and not the face it frames, and so there is an instant during which Ruthie knows neither that this is her niece, nor that she is crying. Then the face emerges from the shadow, Ruthie's heavy arms open, and the tall child falls into them.

Back up in Walt's room, the brief bathroom ceremony completed, Henry is tucking his son into bed. There were no tears during Freddie's farewell, and Henry wonders whether Walt can perhaps sense that there are events of greater magnitude transpiring in the house, secrets that are being kept from him. Henry has no idea how to begin telling Walt about his mother: what may or may not be growing inside of her; what may or may not happen as a result. There is too much they don't know.

"Do we have time for a story, Dad?"

"No, it's late, buddy."

"Just a quick one. A new Swinger one maybe."

"I don't have any new ones, but I'll think about that, okay? I'll try to think up a new one."

"Okay."

Henry looks around the room: Star Wars action figures,

Pokemon posters, Bionicles, Nintendo DS and game cards scattered on his desk.

"Walt, what would you think about going to a baseball game sometime?" he asks his son.

The look he receives in return is a quizzical one.

"Dad, we do not have a baseball team."

"There's a minor league team over in Binghamton. We could go on some nice day, maybe sit in the sun, and I could teach you how to keep score."

"Dad, it is not hard to keep score in baseball."

"Not just counting the runs. There are all these symbols and things for everything that happens, so you can look at it later and replay it in your mind. It's sort of like a video game."

"Dad, you do not have to lie to me. I will go to the game with you."

"Okay," Henry says, surprised at how excited he is by the prospect. "Good. They start in a couple of weeks, I think. We'll go on the first nice day. Maybe even skip school."

"Yes, I think we should skip school. And Dad?"

"Yeah, buddy?"

"Can I bring my DS?"

When Henry returns to his room, Maggie is under the covers, facing away from him. He slips into his side of the bed. He is certain that she isn't sleeping, but she remains still as he settles in.

"Did I hear you go upstairs?" he asks.

"Yeah."

"Working?"

"Mm hm."

"At night? That's new."

"Yes."

Henry waits for more, but she is quiet. He lies on his back, looking at the ceiling.

"How did it go?" he finally asks.

"It's finished."

"The whole project?"

"Yes."

"That's great, Mag." He turns his head toward her on the pillow. "That's incredible. Can I see?"

"I'm tired, Henry."

"Oh. Okay. Maybe tomorrow then."

Maggie doesn't say anything, nor does she turn to him.

He thinks of putting a hand on her hip but doesn't.

18

Ruthie and I were sitting on the couch watching the Rose Bowl Parade when Mr. Garabedian rang the doorbell the next morning. There was bacon popping in a frying pan in the kitchen.

"Could one of you please get that?" our mother called.

I looked at Ruthie who was pretending not to have heard. I couldn't tell whether she was worried about missing the next float or the next news bulletin about Clemente, but she was acting as if she was engrossed in an interview with parade Grand Marshall, John Wayne. When I opened the door Mr. Garabedian wasn't holding wine or flowers, but he didn't look any more sure of what to do with his hands than he had the first time he'd stood in that spot.

"Morning, Henry."

"Hi."

"Is your mother here?"

"She's making breakfast."

"Smells good." He said this matter-of-factly, making no attempt at false pleasantries. He looked haggard, his thick helmet of hair swooped in every direction like a jumble of untamed cowlicks. "Can you tell her I'm here?"

I turned to go to the kitchen but she was already coming quickly around the corner into the hall, wiping her hands on the apron tied at her waist. Seeing Mr. Garabedian, she stopped momentarily before continuing more slowly toward the door.

"Mark."

"I'm sorry. I know I shouldn't be here."

"Don't be silly. You're welcome anytime."

"I'm not here about us, what we talked about last night. I respect your decision. I can't make you feel something you don't."

"Mark, don't make it sound like... Henry, could you go sit with your sister, please?"

By the time I took my seat on the couch next to Ruthie, she had already turned the volume all the way down on the television, and we sat and listened together.

"Beth, I want you to stay on at the office."

"You only think you want that, Mark."

"No, I've thought about it all night. I want you to stay."

"I wouldn't do that to you."

"I don't care what anyone thinks. You can't afford to be without a job and you're the best employee I've ever had."

"That's very kind of you."

They were quiet for a while. When Mr. Garabedian spoke again his voice sounded small, as if he might be fighting to keep himself composed, and the sudden realization of the power my mother held over him was a revelation that this was the kind of power my father held over her.

"Beth, I can't just *not* see you. I thought I was going to see you every day for the rest of my life."

"You can't have thought that, Mark. Not if you've been listening."

"What if I hadn't asked you to marry me? When would this have ended?"

"I don't know."

"But not last night."

"No."

"Maybe not for a long time. We were comfortable together, weren't we?"

"Yes."

"Then I wouldn't have asked. I didn't ask."

"I can't just pretend that."

"Why not?"

"Don't make me say it again. It's not fair to make me keep hurting you."

"Beth, love isn't the most important thing. Not now. There are other things you need more, and I want to give them to you, whether you feel precisely the same way I do or not."

"Can't you see the unfairness in that, Mark?"

"What do you mean?"

"You love me. You have what I don't."

Mr. Garabedian didn't say anything for a long time after that. Then he said, "What will you do?"

"I'm not sure. I have a sister in York. She's wanted me to get out of here ever since Ned left."

"I see."

"Mark."

"No, I understand. You're right, of course. Okay then."

I didn't hear his footsteps across the porch, just the sound of the front door closing softly. There was only quiet from the hall as well. I don't know if my mother leaned against the door, if she stared at the floor, or if she watched him go. I never asked her, that day or any other, whether she regretted her decision. I never asked her why loving a man who had left you prevented you from living with a man who loved you. I never asked because, even though I wasn't as forthright as Ruthie, I was no less selfish: I didn't want a new father. Finally, my mother crossed the hall into the kitchen. I heard the scrape of a pan, and then the flame caught and the bacon started to sputter again.

"How far away is York?" Ruthie asked.

"I don't know."

"Can you hear the Pirate games from there?"

"I don't know that either."

We both watched the floats go by for a while.

"Will they still play?" Ruthie finally asked. "Without him?"

"Yeah. They always play."

"That's good, I guess."

NEWS

It is Tuesday afternoon, exactly one week after Henry first came home with the invitation to John's memorial and Natalie Currant's chapters tucked under his arm. Maggie has spent the morning in her oncologist's office getting a needle biopsy. She was relaxed, familiar with the procedure this time, more prepared for the eerie similarity of the ultra-sound's jellied search to the search for a fetal heartbeat. And now she is doing precisely what she was doing when Henry walked in through the back door a week ago: she is cooking, though for a distinctly different reason.

When the doorbell rings, she stops cutting the red pepper but doesn't move from where she is standing; there is no one she can think of who would come to the front door that she would care to see right now. Over the past few days, the enormity of her discovery has receded into the practicalities of diagnosis and treatment, making room, finally, for her husband's indiscretion to sting like it should. It had seemed so silly then, so insignificant in the face of what she had been waiting all that evening to tell him—until she had to lie next to him in bed that night and felt the unfamiliarity of the space between them. She knows better than Henry himself that he is not his father;

his well-intentioned if selfish confession was proof of that. But it is equally true that she doesn't see him quite the same way as she did before, and she is afraid that she never will. *Why now?* she wonders. *After all these years?* The answer to that question—as she contemplates the likelihood of losing her other breast—is the true source of her hurt. Henry and Ruthie are leaving for Pittsburgh in a few days to attend the memorial service, and Maggie is looking forward to the time alone, time to try to make sense of what has happened without having to look at his face.

She waits to find out how persistent her visitor will be, and when the bell rings a second time, she sets down the knife and goes to answer it. On her way through the living room she leans toward the front picture window to catch a glimpse of the back side of a very white head of hair that could only belong to Atlee Sproul. Maggie can't remember Atlee ever showing up uninvited. She never even considered him as a possibility when deciding whether or not to come out of the kitchen. And when she opens the door, it is with the realization that he is both the one person outside of her family that she wants to see and the one person least likely to be bringing good news.

"Atlee," she says. "You've finally come to take me away."

The weekend snow is already gone, the temperature pushing sixty, and Atlee stands on the stoop in his tweed, no sweater underneath.

"Hello, love. Is your husband about the house?"

"No, I just sent him to the grocery store. He's been my errand boy the last few days. Would you like to come in and wait for him?"

"Can you just tell him I stopped?"

"Sure. Any message?"

"No."

"Atlee?"

"Yes."

"Aren't you going to flirt with me?"

"Sorry?"

"Maybe pretend you're glad he's not home, and then make some poorly disguised reference to your superior skills as a lover—*something* to hide what it is you've come to tell us?"

Atlee looks at his Italian leather shoes and back up at Maggie.

"Am I really that obvious?"

"Contrary to campus myth and your own woefully inaccurate self-image, you are one of the least mysterious men I know."

"So you must know that I have been desperately in love with you since the moment your husband had the poor judgment to introduce us."

"Nice try, but too late."

"It's the truth."

"That doesn't change your timing issue."

"No. I suppose not."

"It's Natalie Currant, isn't it?"

Atlee does a serviceable job of hiding his shock at her guess. "Fraid so."

"She's told someone."

"Not quite as diabolical as all that." Atlee hesitates. "Maybe I will come in for a minute. Seeing as you already know more than I would have surmised, you might as well know the rest. I'd rather let you tell him anyway."

"Only if you promise to bend me over the kitchen counter when he's coming in the back door. I should rephrase that. The last part anyway."

"No need. Done."

"Come on then."

Atlee follows Maggie into the kitchen where there are pots boiling on all four burners, a knife and vegetables of every color on the cutting board and a deep, meaty smell coming from the oven.

Maggie has spent the day filling freezer bags with main courses for Henry and the kids. It is an activity that has served dual purposes, keeping her mind occupied and easing it at the same time.

"A party I've not been invited to?" Atlee asks.

"No. Not exactly." Maggie checks two of the pots, stirs one and then gestures to a chair. Atlee sits and Maggie remains standing, steam rising behind her. "What did she say?"

"To her credit, nothing really."

"Then what happened?"

"She submitted a drop form yesterday."

"So?"

"So it's after midterm. She can't get credit for Henry's class and it's too late to pick up another. All late drops go to the Department Head. Loren called her and asked why she was dropping the class, and she'd only tell him it was for personal reasons."

"That could mean anything."

"Except that he'd just seen them being chummy together after class this week. He can't force Natalie to tell him anything, but he's going to ask Henry what happened. I take it you already know what that might be."

"Mostly."

"He's a terrible liar, you know."

"He doesn't practice much."

"No, he doesn't. So are you two...?" Atlee allows his pause to ask the rest of his question.

Maggie waves a hand. "We'll be fine. Eventually. I was quick to absolve, and now I'm being pissy as hell. The insecurity has taken me by surprise."

"You've no reason to be."

"No?"

"No."

"Tell me that when they start lopping off your man-parts.

Speaking of which, I understand that someone has had the audacity to see past your man-parts to your heart."

"Hm?"

"My husband claims you're in love."

"Well..." Atlee looks down, but only briefly. "Actually, I'm here to make a confession."

"Christ, not you too. I'm going to have to install a wooden booth."

"I think some of this might be my fault. Loren's little vendetta, I mean."

Maggie has lifted the lid from a sauce pan, and her wooden spoon pauses in midair. "What are you talking about, Atlee?"

"For quite some time now—more than a year, actually—I've been sleeping with his wife."

Maggie drops the lid onto the pan loudly and askew, and she fumbles to get it to fit. "Elvira?"

"Yes."

"That's who you're in love with? Elvira Strummer?"

"Yes."

"Ha!" Maggie starts to laugh and puts a hand to her mouth. "I'm sorry. It's just that... Well, it's official, I guess: I know absolutely nothing about either of my favorite men. Elvira?"

"Might you stop saying her name as if you've just learned the moon is made of Swiss?"

"I said I'm *sorry*. But you have to give me a minute. You know, Henry was sure it was me?"

"You're taken."

"So is Elvira."

"No, not really. It won't shock you to know that Loren hasn't had much interest in fulfilling his marital duties since Alex was conceived. But what might come as a surprise is that Elvira is a sad and beautiful woman."

"You got me there."

"Everything you think passes over her head? Nothing but Southern decorum. She registers every insult. Of course, she's already got it in for you because of our chumminess. I don't think I've ever met anyone so unsure of herself."

"But what's this got to do with Henry and Loren?"

"Loren's not stupid. He's known about us almost from the beginning. Just because he's a counterfeit husband doesn't mean he's willing to play the cuckold. He can't get rid of me, so my best friend will have to do. The fact that Henry is also the one who has taken all of his students is just a capper."

Maggie sits heavily in a kitchen chair, still holding a wooden spoon. "Fuck."

"Sorry."

"Come on, Atlee. Did Loren really have a chance of swaying the committee his way before Natalie?"

"Not likely, no. Still. I thought you should know."

"Thank you." Maggie stares at the various bubblings on the stove and, after a moment, looks at the timer on the oven. She watches it count down for several seconds before turning back to Atlee. "I've always wondered something."

"What's that?"

"Why didn't you ever get married?"

"Only fell in love once. Before, that is. Real love. But she was smart enough to know I was trouble, long-run wise."

"And Elvira?"

"Well, 'long-run' is no longer applicable to me, is it?"

Maggie gives Atlee a rueful smile. "Excuse me a minute, will you?" She rises and blows a long breath before moving back to the stove. Taking one pot off its burner and replacing it with a frying pan, she makes a generous pour of olive oil, gathers the red, green and orange peppers, broccoli flowerets, onion and garlic, and drops them in.

"What is all of this anyway?" Atlee asks.

Maggie uses the spoon to move the vegetables briskly. "Right now, veggie lasagna, spaghetti sauce, and stuffed pork chops. That's what's in the oven. Speaking of which." She crosses to the oven, opens the door, peers in and smells. She turns the heat off, takes oven mitts from a drawer below and removes the Pyrex pan.

"Come live with me and just cook, will you? You don't even have to do the other."

"Your sad Southern belle takes care of the more unseemly acts?"

"Something like that, yes."

"Bet I'm better at those too."

"There's no doubt in my mind. The question wouldn't be *my* satisfaction."

"Was that modesty I just heard coming from you?"

"No. Just a touch of realism. And a compliment."

"Thank you."

"You didn't answer my question."

"Sorry?"

"What is all of this?"

"I can't even smell food cooking when I'm going through chemo. Sends me over the edge." She has said it without thinking to blunt its effect in any way, and she sees Atlee's face go limp, aging him. "Sorry. Yeah. I might be back at it again."

"Maggie."

"It's all right. I've done it before. And nothing's for sure yet."

"Bugger all."

"Yeah."

Atlee is still stunned, and Maggie turns back to the stove to allow him a moment to recover. It takes him longer than she expects, but he doesn't disappoint.

"You know you once promised to show it to me if you were ever going to lose it."

Maggie laughs, still facing away. "God, you're awful! And I don't know anything yet. *And* I was drunk when I promised."

"Still."

"Christ." Maggie is smiling as she turns, wiping her hands on her tee shirt. "Why the hell not? Everyone else is acting like an idiot."

Atlee's arms both go up and he looks away. "Hold on, love—"

"All talk. I knew it. I deserve a little admiration, so you'll look, and you'll like it. Open your eyes, Atlee Sproul, or never loft another double entendre my way again for as long as you live."

Maggie presses her tee shirt flat to her missing breast with one hand, holding it there, and lifts the shirt quickly over the other. At first, Atlee's face is still turned, but he opens his eyes and looks sidelong. Then he pivots fully to face her as she drops her shirt again.

"My Lord." He appears ready to say something else but can't quite get it out. "My Lord," Atlee says again, looking at the floor.

"Thank you."

The back door opens and Henry pushes through with an armful of grocery bags.

"Ha. I've finally caught you two."

"Actually, you're late," Maggie says, taking one of the bags from him.

"Oh?"

"I just showed Atlee my boob."

"Spectacular, isn't it?"

Atlee is still looking at the floor, so Maggie answers for him. "He's been able to speak only in religious terms since."

"Perfectly understandable. So to what do we owe this unexpected visit?" Henry looks at Maggie, who turns to check something on the stove. Then he looks at Atlee, who smiles with just half of his face.

Roberto Clemente's body was never recovered. Major League baseball waived its five-year waiting period for the first and only time in its history, and Clemente was inducted into the Hall of Fame on August 5, 1973. His tragedy may not have belonged to me, but it belonged, in a very real way, to Steve Blass. The season after Clemente died, Blass, who had been famous for his clubhouse pranks and had always seemed the carefree antithesis to Clemente, was utterly lost without him. He didn't just perform poorly in 1973; he literally lost the ability to pitch. He had trouble letting go of the ball and often bounced it to the catcher. He pitched only 88 innings in 1973 but still managed to lead the league in hit batsmen. He had three times as many walks as strikeouts and averaged giving up a run for every inning he pitched. The strange thing was he could suddenly hit. In the twenty-four games in which he appeared that season, he batted .417, almost the precise average that had made Clemente the MVP of the World Series. He came back to try again in 1974 but lasted just one game, walking seven batters and giving up eight runs in five innings. He woke up the next day, his thirty-second birthday, and knew that he was done with baseball.

For the most part, so was I. I never cared about a team again the way I had cared about the 1971 Pirates. Six months after my mother quit her job at Mr. Garabedian's insurance company, we did indeed move to York, PA, a small town in the middle of the state, equally divided among Pirates, Phillies and, worst of all, Baltimore Orioles fans. The Pirates were seldom on television and, much to Ruthie's disappointment, KDKA radio only came in clearly on certain nights. Then, after the 1975 season, Westinghouse Broadcasting, which owned KDKA, unceremoniously fired Bob Prince after twenty-eight years. I haven't listened to a game since.

A few days before we moved, John came by to help pack up my room. He stationed himself at the center of the floor, surrounded by boxes that he marked and filled as I handed him my childhood, piece by piece. He took extra care with the baseball memorabilia, sliding each game program and player photo into a clear plastic bag of its own. The signed World Series program got two. Ruthie sat on the bed and watched.

"I'll go get the ball," she said, sliding off the mattress.

"That's yours, Miss Bambino."

"I know, but I don't have any other Pirate stuff. I want it to ride with the rest."

John and I continued to work in silence, and when Ruthie returned she tossed the ball to me underhand across the room.

"Here, catch," she said.

When it was in my hands, hard and smooth, I looked at it for what seemed like a long time. And I can say with some conviction that I trace my beginnings as a writer back to the instant I caught that ball. It's the first memory I have of being able to see the interconnectedness of things. I didn't just see the ball in my hands. I saw it in my mitt at the bus stop, John Kostka seeming to grow out of the sidewalk next to me; I saw it sitting in front of Ruthie on the floor of her room, surrounded by magic markers and candy bars; I saw it being passed from one pair of large, mostly black hands to another in the celebratory dampness of the locker room, its surface gradually covered with every signature but one, passing then to Ruthie, waiting with my father in the stands, then back to me, there, in my room, then from me to John, who slipped it into a plastic bag that he spun closed and tucked inside my mitt in the corner of a box headed for a place I'd never seen. An ending, and a new beginning.

Fifteen years later, the ball would find its way into the hands of a tall, sharp-angled girl waiting nervously in my first apartment in Washington, D.C. before a date with my roommate, feigning interest in the signatures.

"You a baseball fan?" I would say to her, entering the room, just making small-talk until Andrew would emerge from the bathroom, no doubt slapped with enough after-shave to create a visible halo.

"No. You?"

"Not really. Not anymore. I'm Henry. The roommate."

"Hi. Maggie. Nice to meet you."

John wrote to me often, but I didn't see him again until I came back to Pittsburgh to go to law school. We went to opening day together each of those three years and, I think, watched the Pirates lose badly every time. They were awful, and I went only to be with him. He looked exactly the same, his hair still thick and wiry, though a little more gray. His shoulders and wrists were already starting to break down, though, and he moved much more slowly. He still knew everyone at the stadium, and he showed me off to them in his own way. "Law school," he'd say, hooking a thumb at me. "Like we need another one of those."

After graduation, I moved to D.C. and never saw him again. He continued to write, though less and less frequently as my own life kept me from much more than a few lines in response. By the time Allie was born I hadn't heard from him in years, and he had become less real to me. It was impossible that someone like him existed, wasn't it? So I turned him into something else, and that is how Allie and Walt have come to know him.

The only time I have heard from him in the last ten years was after my first novel was released. I received a short e-mail from someone whose return address was "71Buccos." John Kostka had discovered the internet:

> *You're writing quite a story for yourself, Hank.*
> *I always knew you would.*
>
>   *Love, John*

LAST STOP

Driving into the city of Pittsburgh from the airport is like bearing witness to a momentous magic trick. Even for someone like Henry Graham, who, despite his long absence, already knows what is coming, the miles of rolling hills and emptiness lull and divert his attention like good sleight-of-hand. When he and Ruthie finally enter the tunnel, it is no longer the sights but the sounds that distract him, the drone of engines and the high-pitched whine of spinning tires on concrete echoing like one long trumpet note off the glossy white tile walls. When the city bursts into the sudden silence at the far end, it is as if it is coming into existence in that very instant, and it seems impossible that every car coming behind will get to experience the same miracle: the shock of the first sight of the city, dense and looming, squeezed to a point by water and displayed in shifting views through the latticework of yellow iron all around on the bridge deck. The fountain at the confluence spouts high and white, and the rivers shimmer in a way that is new to Henry, no longer slow and brown, but slate-green and vital. Still, the view is familiar—it is *home*—which makes the odd, empty space down and to the left of the fountain all the more peculiar, until Henry realizes that he is looking at the spot where Three Rivers Stadium used to stand. He is about to say something to Ruthie, but she is already pointing off to the right, at the new ballpark, its blue-steel light standards rising from the limestone facade that glows gold in the mid-morning light.

As they head north along the Allegheny, Henry is struck by how much further along spring is here. There are irregular patches of deep green grass sprouting up out of the yellow hillsides that border the highway, and although the trees are still transparent, their unfurling buds create a hazy emerald veil over everything that lies beyond them. Henry cracks the window open and the air is moist and warm.

"Too bad today's not Opening Day," Ruthie says.

Henry shakes his head. "No. He'd never have scheduled this for Opening Day."

Ruthie laughs.

The VFW is only a few blocks off the Riverside exit, and down close to the river, the trees are fuller still and reach for one another overhead from both sides of the street. Three blocks short of their destination, there are no parking spots anywhere. Henry turns left and drives two blocks toward the river, and, when he realizes where he is, makes one more turn and parks at the corner in front of the house.

"Oh my God," Ruthie says.

Henry gets out of the car. He takes Ruthie's wheelchair out of the back seat, unfolds it and helps her in. Her foot has gotten worse all week, but she has stubbornly refused a doctor visit. Henry turns her toward the house and they both look at it in silence. It seems impossible that so little can have changed. The second-story windows could be new, Henry thinks, the color of the trim a shade lighter, but if he ignores the sleek, rounded lines of the cars parked nearby, it could still be 1971. Eventually, he finds himself staring at the heavy, leaded glass of the front door, the rest of the house receding out of focus, and he thinks, *This is how you look a house in the eye, in its soul even.* Windows reveal moments that might be remembered or not. But entrances and exits, events of permanence, require a door. His father had left through this one, and then the rest of them had done the same. Henry never met the family that moved in, didn't even remember anyone coming to look at the house. For all he knew, they were still here, their grown children gone and coming back for holidays with their own children. More likely, many had come and gone since then, some glad for the change, others as sorry to go as he had been; some families leaving together, others broken. As much of a fixture as John had been in this community, it was even possible that another man had already stood here today, or would stand here later, on his way to the service, with the same sense of nostalgia and pride and emptiness Henry feels now. Maybe that other man will even stand here for the same reason that Henry does: to try to recapture, or at least remember, what life was like when it was made up of nothing but possibilities, when the capacity to hurt seemed to lie with others, with adults, but without feeling like it was something he'd ever grow into.

The wide concrete steps leading up to the broad front porch are inviting. But both the heavy leaded glass door and its storm are shut tight. On a day like today, that can only mean that no one is home.

"It looks good," he says, finally.

"Yes, it does."

Henry hears something in his sister's voice.

"You okay?"

"Yeah, fine. It just makes me miss him."

"Mm."

"Dad, I mean."

"Oh."

"He loved this house. When he was dying—the last few days, when his memories were all mixed up—he talked about it as if he had grown up here."

Henry lets out a short, rueful laugh. "He didn't."

"Not today, okay?"

"Sorry."

"Do you need to stay longer? Look longer, I mean?"

"No. Do you?"

"No."

He tips his sister back and turns her toward the river, away from their destination. "Do you mind if we take the long way around?" he asks. "Since we're here."

"In this spring air, big brother, you can push me as far as you like."

As they approach the corner of Freeport Road, cars rush past in both directions, a train rumbles along the tracks that separate the far side of the road from the river, and Henry remembers his mother's old admonition not to stray this far down. The shoe store that was on the corner has been replaced by a law office but, again, bricks are bricks, and the sense that he is walking through another time is overpowering. Maybe if Maggie had chosen to come it would be different, as if he were visiting, instead of feeling as if he is back. But then the last of the train passes, and through a break in the trees lies a small marina, white and new, a few pleasure boats already docked there in the early spring, a long, narrow restaurant that hugs the shoreline. Riverside had discovered its river.

They turn right and Henry pushes his sister one more block before stopping beneath a PAT bus sign.

"This is where I met him," Henry says.

"It is?"

"The shelter wasn't here."

"I thought you met him on the bus?"

"I guess that's right. But I always think of it as being here." He looks down and half-expects to see blood. "Okay," he says.

"That's it?"

"Yeah."

As they move up and away from the river, back into the heart of the neighborhood, they begin to merge with other silent, well-dressed people. They nod to one another, acknowledging their common destination, polite eyes shifting quickly away from Ruthie. When they are within half a block of the VFW, their pace slows to match that of the approaching crowd. No one speaks.

When they make the turn up the walkway toward the entrance, there is laughter coming from inside, and the mood of the crowd begins to shift from silent obligation to a timid kind of anticipation. Henry notices for the first time that many of the men are carrying six-packs of bottled beer, which they now begin to lift to one another in greeting. Women carry small trays of food covered in foil or cellophane.

"We should have stopped," Ruthie says, noticing as well.

"It looks like there will be plenty."

At the base of the concrete stairs, Henry takes the switchback ramp with Ruthie, and the line stops when they are at the top to let them through. Once inside, the atmosphere is transformed entirely. The double doors outside the auditorium are flanked by two photographs, enlarged to poster-size. The one on the left is of John as a young boy with his mother, and in it he is wearing a mitt and a baseball cap pulled low over his eyes, and he is smiling broadly. The photograph on the right is a recent one—John in a wheelchair backed by a nice-looking woman about his age, her large, strong hands on his shoulders, his teeth capped and straight, his nose still a lumpy S-curve. Above and between the photographs, over the double-doors that the crowd is pushing through, a banner reads:

"You should always go to other people's funerals,
otherwise they won't come to yours."
-Yogi Berra

Just inside, positioned on either side of the entrance, are two large barrels filled with iced bottles of Iron City beer. Some of the men who have brought six-packs push their own bottles deep in and exchange them for cold ones. There is food everywhere. Hot plates sit edge to edge along black- and gold-covered tables that line the right-hand wall, using all of the available outlets, and a hodgepodge of card tables, also black and gold, are strewn around the open floor, crammed with plates of cold food, bowls of chips and cut vegetables and dip. The room is warm and smells of onion and bacon and stewed meats, and all around people are shaking hands and laughing. At the far end of the auditorium, above the stage, a large movie screen hangs from just behind the edge of the proscenium, and on it plays what appears to be a video loop of highlights from the '60, '71 and '79 World Series, starring first Mazeroski, and then Clemente and then Stargell.

At the base of the center of the stage, in the precise spot where Miss Donovan had come to rest after tumbling over his tuxedoed shoulder nearly thirty-five years ago, stands John's casket. It is open—the left half of it anyway, which surprises Henry for some reason. The right half is closed and has been cut completely away, pushed askew just as a magician would have placed it after sawing a man in half—a Big Trick to finish. There is a picture frame sitting on the closed half of the casket, and Henry assumes that it is some notice or other sight-gag that completes the joke. Near the open half stands a set of the stairs and one of the poles from John's old room. A boy, maybe ten or eleven years old, is on the top step, bending to peer into the casket, his blue blazer rising in back to reveal a partially un-tucked white shirt, and Henry notices for the first time that there are a number of children in the room. When the boy on the steps has finished visiting with John, he wraps his arms and legs around the pole and slides to the floor.

The line of people entering the room are moving to the left, and

Henry and Ruthie ride the flow to a bank of photographs displayed along the left wall. The photographs are a timeline of John's life, and it is obvious that great care has been taken to order and organize them accordingly. Most are small prints, three-by-five or four-by-six, mounted on large sections of posterboard that stand on the line of tables. The larger photos that Henry remembers from John's room at the VFW are there as well—the one of John and his buddies before shipping out to Korea; the one of him legless, suspended in front of the bar between two softball teammates; the one of him with Manny Sanguillen, Milt May and Dave Ricketts in full catcher's garb—still framed and standing in order along the tables. He and Ruthie are moving past all of them, slowly, pausing to lean in once in a while, approximating the pace of those in front of them. When they reach what is about the mid-point in the sequence—the time in John's life after which they never saw him again—there is a framed photo standing on the table before them that is both new and startlingly familiar. They both stop, and Ruthie picks it up.

"Oh my," she says, her eyes filling quickly.

It is a picture of John perched on a front-row seat along the third base side at Three Rivers Stadium, one arm around Henry, the other around Ruthie. Henry's Pirate cap is pushed up high on his forehead, his glove pinched under his outside arm, and he is clutching his autographed program tightly against his chest as if afraid that it will fly away of its own accord. Ruthie, so small under John's big arm, is showing off the baseball that Henry has just given to her, holding it to the side of her cheek and grinning. Jeanine is there too, looking up at their father, an open expression of devotion on her face, and he is smiling at her too, trying to show her the signed ball that John has just tossed to him. Ruthie, from her wheelchair, touches her small self under the glass and then touches her father's face, and as she does, Henry thinks that of all that is strange about seeing himself placed this way in John's life, the most startling is seeing that his father was happy that night. As he stands looking over Ruthie's shoulder, staring really, Henry is trying to find some measure of falseness in his father, but there is none. He looks as happy as a kid with that ball, no less so than Ruthie with hers. But it's not just the ball. It's Jeanine too. There is no mistaking his father's expression. He is in love. Henry stares for long enough that a wide gap opens in the line in front of them. Finally, Ruthie reaches behind her to touch his face.

"We can come back," she says.

The photographs become less faded, more vibrant as they go, even as the people pictured grow older. The one constant is John, whose face, old even as a young man, never changes. If anything, his rough, scarred skin and crooked nose fit him better in old age, and it is only the gradual advance of the gray throughout his pot-scrubber head of hair that marks any passage of time. On the last two boards John is in a wheelchair in some of the photos, and the same woman who is pictured in the large photograph out in the entryway is with him in many of these as well. There are no wedding photos, but seeing them together, seeing the obvious affection they have for each other, Henry suddenly realizes that there is a photograph missing: one from the first part of John's life; the one that Ruthie discovered that day in his bedroom. As they reach the end of the final table, Henry is wondering what could have happened to it—whether John grew tired of looking at it because of the story it told; or perhaps the woman pictured with him in these recent photographs didn't want it here with her own—when he notices that they are about to be greeted by that very woman. She is standing at the front of the room, at the base of the stage, halfway between the final table of photographs and the casket, shaking hands and smiling and nodding her thanks.

"I'm Henry," he says when they have reached her. "*Hank*, I suppose, to John. And this is my sister, Ruthie. We're the kids in the stadium picture over there."

"You're the writer," the woman says.

"Yes."

"He was very proud of you."

"Are you...?"

"No, just a friend. Martha."

"I was going to say, 'the one who did all of this.'" Henry gestures to the room around him.

"We did it together. Everything here was his idea. I'm sure you'll recall that he was very concerned with production value." She laughs. "The split casket was a last minute inspiration, a dying man's final request, if you will."

"I have to admit I was more surprised by the open casket than the fact that it had been sawed in half."

"You haven't looked yet have you?"

"No."

She smiles. "Please enjoy yourselves. There's plenty of food."

They move along and Martha continues greeting those who follow. The line of visitors in front of them, two or three deep, blocks their view of the casket, and all they can see are the images playing out above and behind: a young and skinny Bill Mazeroski windmilling his cap as he rounds third before disappearing into his teammates gathered around home plate, then shots of the crowd, the men in fedoras and the women in horn-rimmed sunglasses falling into one another in disbelief. And then it is 1971 and his old hero is sprinting to first, one long last stride to beat out an infield hit; wheeling after an over-the-shoulder catch in the right field corner to throw home; galloping around second for a pop-up slide into third, and always it is his legs that draw Henry's attention—gangly and churning—and he knows exactly what is waiting at the front of the line, so that when it is finally their turn, and he sees John's old boots reclining against the silk pillow, he laughs even as the tears begin to come. He knows something else now, too: he knows that John is under the closed lid to his right. And he knows before turning his head that the picture frame beneath which his friend lies doesn't contain a joke but the missing photograph. And when he finally turns to look at it, when he sees the girl again, Ruthie's hand reaches behind to find his, and Henry realizes that his friend has done the impossible: he has written his own ending.

More than that, it is one Henry himself can use. This last part comes to him more slowly, because there is so much about his own story that he doesn't know yet: whether or not he will get to keep the job that he loves, and, if he doesn't, whether even Maggie will be forced to admit that they can't stay; whether Maggie's forgiveness, already verbally given, will ever become evident in the way she looks at him; whether he might one day, too soon, be standing in a gathering like this for her. Better to begin, he thinks, with what he does know, little as that may be. He knows that they will spend far too much money to give Franny another good year or two because she's not a loss they can suffer right now. He knows that they will buy a new fish and that Walt has already decided to name it Freddie 2.0, and he knows that he and his son will sit together in the moist spring air and keep score for the Binghamton Mets. He knows that Allie will get her time in the spotlight, though she will probably have to take her bows first and then watch as the audience stands for a boy who seems, to everyone but Allie, to have something that sets him apart. He knows that on Monday, he and Maggie will go to see her doctor again and that they will listen to her. She will tell them things that are true, and those things will become part of their future, or at least its probabilities. For Maggie, there will be no real lessons or morals, only facts to be processed and reckoned, perhaps drawings in a third-floor studio to be changed again to reflect a new reality, a new absence.

So he will focus on each small task in turn, each new beginning, the first being to find a way to begin to tell Walt about his mother. And that is where his friend will come in. Henry isn't sure that a seven-year-old boy can understand the fact of death, let alone its possibility, so he's thinking that maybe he will begin their talk with a new story. Something that's mostly true; something that even the teller, in need of some comfort himself, might believe in. He's already decided—standing here, reaching out to touch the lid of John's coffin—to make it a story his colleagues would probably hate: something life-affirming and with perfect closure; something that doesn't just risk sentimentality but plows straight into it, unafraid. He'll make it an unabashed feel-good story about a half-man who gets to live a whole life, mixed with a story that's been told a million times about a stranger who helps a lost boy become a man, but without telling the parts about what that man grows up to lose. A story about someone who picks himself up from the sidewalk, bloodied for the last time, and passes from this world of uncertainty and loss and downward stairways to move gracefully into a world in which all of the stairs lead only upward. And at the top of those stairs are his boots, unlaced and waiting, lifted from where they stand by a young, barefooted girl in a white dress who holds them out to him in a posture of forgiveness.

*In memory of both the service and daily bravery
of Sgt. Kenneth Kocher*

An Unapologetic Plea for Help
from the Author

Dear Reader:

You may or may not have known it when you started reading, but what you hold in your hands is, essentially, a "self-published" novel. Not many years ago, I couldn't even have typed that phrase without feeling the urge to put my nose in the air. "Real" writers were discovered and nurtured by "real" publishers. "Real" readers (like you) knew this. And so when your quirky cousin cornered you at the family reunion to tell you that he was tired of being misunderstood by editors in New York while handing you a copy of his 800-page self-published fantasy novel, you congratulated him with what you hoped would pass for a sincere (rather than pitying) smile, and then you made a beeline for the potato salad.

Times have changed. Publishing may not be quite as far along the curve as music (mostly because it takes more effort to sample a self-published novel than it does to listen to a 3-minute indie song) but there are more and more writers like me out there. My first novel was a relative success; my second, not so much. That made novel #3 (the one you just finished) D.O.A. with "major" publishers. For the record, it collected something north of thirty rejection letters.

Fortunately, my brilliant agent, Jane Dystel, was already ahead of the curve. Shortly after the 2008-9 financial crisis rendered selling literary fiction in New York akin to selling beef in Mumbai, she started a little side-business: publishing novels she loved, but couldn't place, as ebooks. *Swing* was one of those novels. The relative success of that ebook led me to release this print version.

So what does all of this have to do with you?

First, unless you are a Facebook friend of mine, or you are named on my mother's extensive Christmas Card List, it is already a minor miracle that you hold my novel in your hands.

Second, whether or not anyone else reads it is entirely up to you. There is no advertising budget. No one will happen upon my book while strolling past the New Releases at Barnes & Noble. Neither Oprah nor Ellen will ever hear of it. The next reader will hear of it from you.

So I'm asking: If you finished *Swing* only because you never leave anything *un*finished, and you now find yourself in the camp of the thirty publishers who passed on it, keep quiet. Move on. Forget we've met. Back to the Barnes & Noble "Staff Recommendations" with you.

But if you found something to like—even love—tell someone. Better yet, tell a hundred someones. Email, post, review, tweet, gram, chat or (God forbid) call people who might feel the same way. I can't offer anything in return. But I do promise that if I ever find myself sitting across from Ellen, I'll thank you.

-PB, March 2015

PRAISE FOR

DEAR ZOE

(now in development as a feature film)

———

A *Book Sense* Pick

A Border's *Original Voices* Selection

One of *Booklist's* Ten Best First Novels of the Year

———

"Like *The Lovely Bones*, it is a piercing look at how a family recovers from a devastating loss. Everything about this moving, powerful debut rings true." —*Booklist* (starred review)

"*Dear Zoe* is an almost flawless novel of self-discovery and redemption. It is the sort of book that a generation can call 'theirs,' a book that captures the trials of adolescence and the aching numbness of America in the aftermath of 9/11."
—*The Press of Atlantic City*

"The whole novel . . . rings with truth. By the end of it, we're meditating on the ideas of loss and redemption, the ways in which personal tragedies get absorbed into larger ones, but never obliterated, never forgotten." –*The Buffalo News*

"Lovely . . . moving." —*Publisher's Weekly*

"Whatever comparisons are drawn, there is no doubt that this book is a gem all its own." —Bookreporter.com

CPSIA information can be obtained at www.ICGtesting.com
Printed in the USA
LVOW10s2139250716

497755LV00004B/229/P